SEE YOU AT THE SUNSET

SUSAN LEE

MIRA

MIRA™

ISBN-13: 978-1-335-01509-9

See You at the Sunset

For questions and comments about the quality of this book, please contact us at CustomerService@Harlequin.com.

MIRA
22 Adelaide St. West, 41st Floor
Toronto, Ontario M5H 4E3, Canada
MIRABooks.com

HarperCollins Publishers
Macken House, 39/40 Mayor Street Upper,
Dublin 1, D01 C9W8, Ireland
www.HarperCollins.com

Printed in U.S.A.
26 27 28 29 30 LBC 5 4 3 2 1

Praise for Susan Lee's *Julia Song Is Undateable*

"A spectacular adult debut! *Julia Song Is Undateable* is full of Susan Lee's trademark humor and vulnerability, but with swoonworthy spice! When I want utterly romantic novels full of hilarious hijinks, relatable characters, sizzling chemistry, and empowering storylines, Susan Lee is the author I go for!"

—Ali Hazelwood, *New York Times* bestselling author of *Problematic Summer Romance*

"Susan Lee's adult romance is everything readers are hoping it will be—and more! Introspective, funny, relatable, sexy—it's an absolutely perfect romance."

—Christina Lauren, *New York Times* bestselling author of *The Unhoneymooners*

"A must-read for those who enjoy a few laughs with their swoons. A moving slow-burn romance that explores the meaning of success, the importance of family, and learning to embrace what truly matters. I can't wait to see what she does next!"

—Adriana Herrera, *USA TODAY* bestselling author of *A Tropical Rebel Gets the Duke*

"A knockout! *Julia Song Is Undateable* is a delightful and engrossing rom-com that includes a funny and lovable cast of characters. Featuring Susan's signature wit, voice, and humor—now with more heat! I couldn't put it down!"

—Alexis Daria, bestselling author of *You Had Me at Hola*

"A swoonworthy rom-com about finding true love—and finding your true self along the way."

—Kirkus Reviews

Also by Susan Lee

Adult

Julia Song Is Undateable

Young Adult

Seoulmates

The Name Drop

The Romance Rivalry

To the people and places that have offered me a safe place to land . . .

SEE YOU AT THE SUNSET

PROLOGUE

Yesterday

9:00 a.m.

Henry Shin was having a very good day.

It was a gorgeous June morning in New York. Not too hot just yet, humidity at bay, and the greens at Bethpage Black, one of the most exclusive golf courses in the tri-state area, were, as expected, perfect. Henry was playing one of his best rounds of golf in a very long time. One thing was for certain, he always stepped up when the pressure was on.

And the pressure was heavy for him to impress today. He'd been invited by the CEO of Bakerson's Group, Eli Bakerson himself, to join their four-man along with the chief of staff, Edison Wainwright, and Henry's direct boss, general counsel of the company, Steven Sword. The message was clear: You're one of us now. Or, at least, you will be.

If Henry was the type to partake in office gossip, he might

have heard the rumors and worried that being invited as a fourth on this weekly golf game meant something shady was afoot and a fall guy was needed to be suckered into the mix. But Henry never interacted with his coworkers. And though he knew the lore, he wasn't worried. He was exactly where he wanted to be.

The entire vibe of the day screamed money and power and prestige beyond anything Henry could dream of. No, that was a lie. Henry dreamed of this very thing regularly. It's why he worked so hard. It's why he had no life outside of work and no other motivation than the ambition to succeed. The youngest senior counsel, the only person of color on the leadership team, and now playing golf on a Sunday with the bigwigs. He had done this. He was the one who'd gotten himself here.

Henry covered his mouth with his hand to not let the smile show through. *Play it cool, Shin.*

"I stand corrected, Henry. The 3-wood was absolutely the right choice for this one. I'm gonna be taking your advice both in the office and outside of it from now on, son." Eli Bakerson chuckled, patting Henry on the back. Henry smiled, trying not to stiffen at the use of the endearment.

It was not a word he was used to hearing.

But he allowed it to roll over him just for a moment. Because it signified he was in the inner circle now. He'd passed an unspoken test. And now he belonged.

And that was the only thing that mattered.

"Shin, a word," his boss said, nodding his head off to the right. Henry followed him the few yards away from gameplay.

"Yes, sir?"

"There's something we need you to take care of tomorrow morning. And we need it done—" Steven Sword lowered his voice "—discreetly, without any loose ends. We trust you can handle it."

"Of course I'll take care of it," Henry replied. And there it was: the ask. Whatever it was, he'd figure out how to do what needed to be done. That was his job. Find a way within the structure of the law, pushing its limits if necessary, to protect the company. And it's what Henry did best.

"We are more than confident that you will. Details in your secure inbox. Oh, and make sure you join us at ten for the executive meeting. You should definitely be involved in those from now on, son."

There was that word again. If Henry was going to keep climbing this ladder, he'd have to get used to the sound of it, he supposed.

Especially if he was going to get to the top and stay there.

2:00 p.m.

Jia Chung had always been a firm believer in work–life balance. She wasn't the type to be chained to her email on the weekends. Work ended at six on Friday evening and started back up again at nine on Monday morning—nine thirty if the weekend had been especially good. Life was too short to put work first.

But her new job was more demanding than her previous ones. The expectations a little harsher. A lot was riding on her keeping her job . . . for once. Thus, when she was sent a *gentle reminder* that she needed to be available on weekends for emergencies, she turned off Silent mode for her notifications and opened her email whenever her phone alerted.

She could not fuck up again.

Which meant, of course, her phone notified her of a message on a perfect Sunday afternoon. She begrudgingly, but without hesitation, opened it.

From: Genevieve Gordon
To: Jia Chung
Subject: Monday 10:00 a.m.

Hey Jia, just following up with an email. I sent you a calendar invite for a meeting tomorrow. Sorry about the short notice. Just need to discuss something that can't wait. Can you either accept the invite or reply to this email as confirmation you will be in attendance?

Thanks,
Gen

Oh, okay, that wasn't too bad. Jia liked Gen. She was nice for the most part. A last-minute meeting with HR would normally send most people into a panic. But Jia couldn't think of one thing that would be a cause for concern. And if there was something, Gen would say so in the email, right? Jia did her job as requested. And she made it her daily mission to do whatever she could to make it easier for everyone else. The people at her work were stressed and stretched thin enough; it showed all over their faces. In fact, she'd recently caught a costly error on an expense report and fixed it on her own without bothering anyone else. Jia was pretty sure a pat on the back was waiting for her.

She accepted the calendar invite and replied with a thank-you note back to Gen.

Now that that was taken care of, Jia had the whole evening ahead of her. Sunday nights were for self-care. An everything shower, full skincare routine, and her weekly hair mask.

Jia let out a deep breath. Life was finally starting to fall into place. She was starting to find her footing at her job. She lived with her best friend in her favorite city. Her parents weren't nagging her every single day. And all of this, she'd done on her own.

She felt pretty darn good about herself.

In fact, too good to be staying in.

Jia immediately knocked on Lizzy's bedroom door.

"What are you doing tonight?" she asked her.

"Uh, you know Sundays are for everything showers," Lizzy replied.

"Well, we're going out. We're celebrating." It was impulsive and possibly not the best idea. But it seemed like the right call in Jia's mind.

"We are? What are we celebrating? Wait, let me guess. The cute Irish bartender at McCoy's finally asked you out?"

"Nope."

"The boots you were eyeing online finally showed up at T.J. Maxx?"

"Wrong again."

"Your parents agreed to get off your back about moving to Florida?"

"Stop guessing, you're making me depressed. No, I think I'm getting some good news tomorrow at work," Jia said.

Lizzy jumped up from her bed.

"A raise? A promotion?"

"I don't know yet. I just have a meeting on the calendar and a very good feeling. So I'm claiming good news now, and we're celebrating before it happens." It was a trick Jia had used before. Claim the win and will it into existence.

"Well, okay then. I'm in. How about Willow?" Lizzy suggested.

Willow was Lizzy's favorite bar. Jia had only been a couple times. It was trendy and swank, not cramming a crowd in like animals. But more expensive than Jia's shoestring budget allowed. It was also three train stops away. Lizzy, with the stable job and a career with a future, loved it. But Friday was payday, and they were celebrating. She would be newly scrubbed and softened and smell divine. "Willow sounds perfect."

"Yay! I can't wait to precelebrate your pending good news." Lizzy truly was the best kind of friend.

6:00 p.m.

Henry didn't go out much. Sunday nights were usually reserved for planning out the week, not only reviewing his calendar and all the meetings he needed to be in but also what information he needed to have to give himself the advantage over anyone he'd be talking to. Always one step ahead, no surprises, being prepared for anything and everything.

It was the way Henry had survived, and eventually thrived, on his own his whole life.

But he'd felt on the precipice of something big all day. Yes, the acknowledgment by the executives of his company. Yes, the big responsibility they'd placed on him to handle business the following morning. But it was something else. He couldn't put his finger on it yet. He just knew something important was about to happen in his life. Henry always trusted his gut.

And it made him have the sudden and surprising urge to celebrate.

The bar on the ground floor of his building was the type of place where one could go alone and sit chest up for a glass of wine or a really good scotch. And Sunday nights were pretty chill.

A celebratory drink or two wouldn't hurt.

8:00 p.m.

Jia nursed her third glass of cava. It was the least expensive drink on the menu, and she held the glass casually like she belonged there.

She'd finally pulled out the butter-yellow Chloe silk minidress she'd picked up for a steal at Jenna Lyons's last closet clear-out sale. Considering Jenna Lyons had a good ten inches on Jia, she figured this was likely meant to be a top. But on her five-foot-two frame, it hit Jia a little above midthigh and made her legs look fantastic.

The vibes were just right at Willow. There was a decent crowd for a Sunday, she had a mellow buzz by now, and she wasn't ready to call it a night yet. But alas, her wallet and her bank account were not cooperating, and she really couldn't afford another eighteen-dollar glass. She downed the last of her cava and turned to Lizzy who was animatedly talking to the bartender.

"I should go," Jia said. It would be the responsible thing to do. She could get home early, sober up, get some rest, and be completely ready for her exciting morning tomorrow.

"Don't go, not yet. Let's have one more drink," Lizzy begged. "My treat. We were gonna try some scotch tonight."

Lizzy leaned over the bar and raised her eyes to all the bottles of brown liquor on the top shelves.

Neither of them were big connoisseurs of the good stuff, so Jia braced herself for what Lizzy would decide on.

"Jackson, can you get me two more glasses of the Oban 15 for the ladies here?" a man next to her called out.

"You got it." The bartender reached up to the top shelf and grabbed a long, slender bottle, pouring them each a glass.

Jia turned her body toward the generous man sitting next to her at the bar. She was such a sucker for a deep, sexy voice.

He was alone, both hands circling a short glass of amber liquor. He looked over his shoulder at Jia. He was young, surprisingly so, especially for this area. Handsome in a very serious way, strong brows slightly stitched together despite a barely there smile on his lips.

She would have guessed finance bro, but they rarely ventured out alone. Lawyer maybe, with the stern air about him.

"Thank you for the drinks," Lizzy said. "Cheers!" She reached out her glass and Jia met hers. The generous stranger lifted both his drink and his chin in front of him, not quite reaching out to theirs for a clink. "We're celebrating my friend here! She's getting promoted at work tomorrow."

His eyes caught Jia's and locked in. He was intense in a way that made it hard to breathe. "Congrats," he said with a head nod.

"Thanks," Jia said, her response breathier than she'd wanted. "And thanks for the drink. That's really nice of you." She lifted the glass to take her first sip. His eyes followed along with the movement. She licked her lips and swallowed. The burn was intense at first, but what followed was a surprisingly smooth flow down her throat. "God, this is good," she said.

His eyes flared. Her breath caught. Words spoken. Laughter

shared. The two of them brought their glasses up at the same time and finished their drinks.

He raised his finger and circled it to the bartender, signaling another round. Jia leaned in a little closer to him, her body warm and pliant, this time clinking her glass to his as she took a sip of her next drink.

10:00 p.m.

Henry never did this. He never went down to his local bar and overimbibed. He usually nursed one glass of really good scotch and was done. He never bought strangers drinks and let his tab run out of control. He never picked someone up and brought them to his third-floor apartment in the same building.

But he was celebrating his own win.

And there was something about her. She was gorgeous in an easy way, effortlessly sexy in that silk dress and too-bright sandals. She laughed freely, and her eyes danced at the things he said. And sure, it was partly the alcohol talking, convincing him to see where this would go.

All he knew was that he wanted her.

And tonight, after a really good day and a few glasses of exceptional scotch, he was going to let himself go for what he wanted.

1:00 a.m.

Jia did not want to get up. If she didn't have such an important morning ahead of her, she'd have stayed right where she was. It had been a very good night, and she felt spent in all the right places.

She pulled the sheet up to cover herself despite it being almost completely dark in the apartment. She swung her legs off the side of the bed and bent down searching for her panties and her dress. She looked back over her shoulder at the man lying next to her.

His arm covered his eyes, and his breath was even and heavy. Jia squeezed her legs together remembering everything that they'd done to wear this poor guy out.

His chest was bare of any hair except below his belly button leading to, what Jia had come to discover over the last couple hours, was an incredible package. God, and he knew what he was doing: attentive and took his time, always checking in on her pleasure, a consent king.

As far as hookups went, this was a really nice surprise and solidified in Jia's mind that things were most definitely picking up for her. But she had to get home and get some sleep or she'd be a mess in the morning.

She leaned down and gave him a peck on the cheek. He moved a little but settled back down to sleep. She took one last look at him, all of him, and sighed. She got up, grabbed her shoes, and quietly left the apartment.

Jia hailed the first taxi that approached, got in, feeling the glorious ache of just having had remarkable sex, and smiled. It wasn't until she'd gotten home, cleaned up, and into her pajamas that she realized she had never even gotten his name.

1

Jia held the belief that pretty much everything could be solved with a kind smile and a great pair of shoes. So, with a deep breath, she grabbed the handle of the door, pulled it open with all the confidence she could muster, and stood slowly scanning the contents of her carefully and thoughtfully curated closet.

This was Jia's happy place. Bright colors, bold patterns, and every piece with a story of how it was obtained. For most of her adult life, once she'd been able to finally be out on her own, she had barely made enough money to get by. But she was an expert bargain hunter and practiced patience as a virtue, knowing exactly what pieces she was eyeing, and waiting for just the right opportunity to grab it at a steal.

Her mother bristled at Jia's loud wardrobe. And surprisingly, she found herself standing out with her often flashier clothes, even from those walking the streets of New York, despite its reputation for being a style mecca.

For as long as she could remember, the one thing Jia insisted on in life was that her clothes would match her personality. So much of society wanted to silence and tamp down someone like her. Her clothes were her own way of fighting back, refusing to be put in a box.

Jia felt her best in pizzazz.

And she needed it today.

Some of yesterday's confidence and claiming had worn off along with the buzz of smooth alcohol and great sex, replaced this morning with a bit of nerves and uncertainty. What if it wasn't good news after all? She shook her head as if the physical manifestation of *no* could will away any bad juju.

She needed to knock it out of the park today. Jia scanned the options and knew as soon as her eyes landed on her red platform sandals with yellow polka dots. These were happy shoes. Good news shoes. Reason-to-celebrate-no-matter-what shoes.

She paired the sandals with a simple white sundress so as not to distract the conversation and a yellow bauble statement necklace for just a pop of color. Jia had long gotten over the fact that she was often the only one wearing bright colors and patterns in this world. They were her armor, her confidence booster, her connection to herself. She looked at herself in the mirror and smiled. "You've got this," she said softly. "Nothing to worry about."

She would not invite the anxiety. Whatever was in store for her, whatever news she was going to receive, good news (likely!) or bad (possibly?), she'd take it in stride.

She didn't think about the mere two hundred and forty-six dollars in her bank account, nor the rent that was due the following week, nor the inevitable look of disappointment on her parents' faces punctuated with the deep sigh and *Not again, Jia.*

She willed herself to believe that today was going to be a

great day. She tried to muster some of the confidence she had last night and grabbed her stuff as she left for the train. Smile on, shoes buckled, ready to take over the world.

"I'm sorry, Jia, but we're going to have to let you go."

Jia stared into the eyes of Genevieve Gordon, human resources manager, as she processed the words. She liked Genevieve. She had great style—understated and classy. She told her so just this morning as she arrived at the HR office at two minutes past ten, two mugs of steaming hot coffee in hand. It was why she was late. Jia had unloaded the dishwasher in the employee kitchen so that there would be mugs available for everyone as they came to work that day. Then she'd prepared Gen's coffee as she'd often noticed she liked it, black with one Splenda. Jia had hers nice and sweet, two creams, three sugars.

She'd walked in, commented on Gen's black shift dress with the dropped waist, how the fit was impeccable and, paired with the small gold hoops, timeless. And when Gen struggled to smile in return, Jia knew it was not going to be good news. Genuine compliments usually made people smile bigger.

She'd barely taken a seat before Gen dropped the bomb.

The words took her by surprise.

"Oh" was all she could think to say in response. Jia brought her coffee mug to her lips and took a sip. What an odd time to drink your coffee, she thought to herself, as she brought the mug back down. What was the right reaction to news like this?

Jia should know. She'd been fired before. But she never did it the right way. She always went home and thought of ten things she could have said or asked or done in the moment. But, like all the other times, her mind was currently blank.

Her thoughts went back to two hundred and forty-six dollars

in the bank, rent due, and a *Not again, Jia* waiting for her back home.

She realized that the silence had lasted longer than appropriate. "Sorry, I was just . . . thinking," she said.

"Look, Jia, um, there have been some issues with your performance," Genevieve's voice sounded almost apologetic. Jia felt bad that Gen had to be the one to tell her.

Gen wouldn't lift her eyes. She just stared down at the papers in front of her and continued. "Ultimately, you weren't meeting the standards of the job. So we'll be terminating your employment immediately. You'll find a box on your desk to borrow. Return it by Friday at five o'clock or twelve dollars will be subtracted from your final paycheck. Please leave your laptop and key card on your desk. All access to the systems has been revoked. Do you have any questions?"

Whoa. That was a lot.

Did Jia have any questions?

Had she done something wrong? Where was her performance lacking? Those boxes cost twelve dollars? She had to leave right away?

All good questions to ask at that moment. But she couldn't get herself to say anything. She didn't want to make Genevieve uncomfortable.

"Nope, not a one!" The answer was too loud. Too forced. Too upbeat. Not at all appropriate for this moment.

But such was Jia.

"Fine. Then, here are some papers we need you to sign before you go."

Jia looked down at the stack of papers before her and briefly wondered if *there/their/they're* were misused as they always were in the documents she corrected on the regular.

There were three signature lines at the bottom of the document, each with a name and title typed below it, one with a red flag sticker next to it. She signed where she was directed, next to the blank spots listed and waiting for the signatures of *Genevieve Gordon, Human Resources Manager* and *Henry J. Shin, Esq., Senior Counsel.*

"You'll receive a copy of the countersigned document along with an exit survey we'd like you to fill out, couriered by the end of the day," she was told. Jia had never received anything by courier in her life. She wondered if the courier rode a bicycle or simply took the train. These were the random thoughts Jia would later recall from the morning she got fired.

The rest was a blur.

"Have a nice day, Genevieve. I'll miss working with you," she said on her way out. And she meant it.

Jia was—at least she had been until ten o'clock that morning—the assistant to the chief of staff at Bakerson's Group, a financial company of some sort, though she never really knew what they did. The office was on the twelfth floor of a building just off Bryant Park, and the company was in the top fifty on one of those lists with letters and numbers on it that everyone in New York seemed impressed with. It was—at least it had been until ten o'clock this morning—the most serious job she'd ever had in her life. One she was, at the time of hiring, completely underqualified for. But if they were going to give her the job, she was going to do the best she could. Apparently her best wasn't good enough. Again.

She didn't know what she was now.

Jia wasn't even thirty, yet she already had a string of professional failures in her wake. Let's just say her résumé was not going to knock anyone's socks off. She had, at times, suspected this job wasn't for her, everyone in their black or gray or navy attire, quietly working, speaking in hushed tones, smiles rare. But she was willing to stick it out at least a little longer. At least until she could find a job that *was* for her.

Because for the past three months, two weeks, and four days, she wasn't the screwup everyone made her out to be her entire life up until this point. True, at the end of the day, bartending brought in more cash and being a Pilates instructor was a lot more fun. But this *fancy corporate job*, as her mom put it, had garnered the respect of her parents and offered a brief reprieve from their incessant nagging.

Now this former fancy corporate job was further proof Jia couldn't cut it in adulting.

The office manager came around and handed Jia the unmarked twelve-dollar box. "Thank you for always having the supply closet stocked. It helped a lot," Jia said. For some reason, it was important she knew that someone noticed. Jia should have told her sooner.

As she placed her pictures of the girls' trip to Cancún last summer, three tubes of e.l.f. lip gloss, and the six Post-it pads she had collected in her top drawer, Jia realized she didn't have much here at her office desk. Unlike her tiny apartment that was cluttered with knickknacks and mementos and screamed *Jia*, she'd kept this six-by-six cubicle void of any real personality. Guess past Jia had done current Jia a favor: less to pack up upon termination. She knew the drill.

"Did you hear the new girl got fired?" Jia heard the voice of someone from down the hall where a group of young women gathered standing around a copy machine.

The assistants were all women. And the executives were all men. And of course Jia felt a certain way about that. But she realized early on there was nothing she in this position in the company, or in her position in life frankly, could do about it.

She quickly crouched below the cubicle wall so she would not be seen.

"Already?"

"Usually they last at least a year."

"Not in that department they don't."

"Which new girl?"

"Jia, the one with all the bright clothes."

"The one who talks too loud all the time?"

"Yeah, that's the one."

"Too bad. I really liked her. She was nice and always made sure there were clean coffee mugs."

That was nice of her to say.

"Nice doesn't get the job done. She was never gonna make it here. Too soft."

Guess that was considered a bad thing, being soft.

Jia needed to get out of there before she was caught eavesdropping and they'd send someone over to embarrassingly escort her out of the building. She hoped the ladies would all be okay now that they were one person down and would likely have to pick up some of the slack until they'd hired a replacement.

She placed the lid on the comically oversized box for the limited contents and took one more look around her cubicle as she contemplated her next move.

First, walk out of the office with her dignity intact. Second, figure out her financial situation and how long she could survive without this paycheck. And third, finish off the pint of mint chip Talenti she had in the freezer. Ice cream at 10:12 a.m. felt totally valid in times like these.

Twelve minutes past ten.

It had taken all of twelve minutes for her life to be turned upside down . . . again. And after having to break the news to her parents, she'd be reminded, again, how disappointing her life had become. She'd be pressured, again, to move back home. They meant well. They were just too protective. Too quick to sweep in and control Jia's choices. She was their miracle child, after all. Problem was she was now twenty-seven and needed them to let her live her own life.

All problems she would deal with once she left.

She let out a deep breath to compose herself.

Well, here went nothing. She stood tall, raised her chin, and straightened her back. Well-practiced posture from years of walking with books on top of her head around the house as a kid as her grandmother beamed and excitedly declared her the future Miss Korea.

The route to the elevators was clear and in sight.

And as she awkwardly carried the overpriced bankers box toward the exit, past the conference room currently filled with high-powered men wearing bespoke suits who likely had no idea who she was and how they had just ruined her life, she had only one thing on her mind . . .

Jia might be soft, but she would not let them see her cry.

2

Henry took his seat at the cherrywood table in the executive conference room. It wasn't his first time at one of these meetings. But he'd usually been included when something needed reporting on or to explain a situation to the powers in charge. In the past, he'd been told to be there. Today he'd been invited. And he knew the difference was monumental.

He looked around the table where the all-white, all-middle-aged male executives of various shapes and sizes sat. Likely all Ivy leaguers connected by family, school, and job history in ways Henry couldn't ever achieve. But he'd worked ten times harder than all of them and by sheer determination had ended up here. He listened as the CFO gave a quick recap of the financials. He took notes as they discussed what would be on the agenda at the next board meeting. He nodded and laughed at all the right places, like when Mr. Bakerson commented on his wife's latest attempt at cooking dinner. "Why she insists on giving the chef Sunday nights off is beyond me. Is she trying to poison me?"

Henry nodded where he was supposed to and didn't offer words unless he felt it would add to the conversation.

As the rest of the executives laughed and commented, Henry was briefly distracted by something bright and colorful in the corner of his eye. In an entire office space full of grays, it was hard not to notice.

He turned just a little as she walked past the glass wall of the conference room down the hall toward the elevator . . . a white dress and bright red polka-dotted shoes. He didn't get a glimpse of her face. Just a young woman, head held high, steely determination set in her posture, a bankers box balanced on her hip.

"I can't believe you let that one go," he heard someone say, bringing his attention back to the room full of high-powered men. "She looks like she'd be the life of the party."

Henry looked over at Edison Wainwright, a smug look on his face like he'd just done something noble. "Great to look at. But," he said with a pause, "she was difficult to work with." A practiced response, if Henry ever had heard one. And it was the exact quote anonymously stated in the case file Henry had reviewed for this morning's termination. An anonymous complaint meant no one would dig further without having a name attached, yet would certainly still stain an employee's performance.

One thing Henry was sure of was that the documentation for the termination was airtight. He was the one who had prepared it all.

Another thing Henry was sure of? Edison Wainwright was a Grade A jackass.

He would have to try hard to forget that smug look . . . and the bitter taste it left in his mouth.

★ ★ ★

Henry knocked twice on the door before ducking his head in. He raised his eyebrows in question.

"It's done," Genevieve said. "She's gone." She did not look happy.

Of course, he'd already known it was over. Genevieve was reliable and good at her job. If it needed to be done at ten, she would do it at ten without question. Plus, Henry had seen the former employee walk out.

"Any issues?" he asked.

"Other than the ones I have personally?" Genevieve asked.

After reviewing the email he'd received yesterday with all the details of the termination for Jia Chung, executive assistant to Edison Wainwright, chief of staff, Henry had immediately messaged HR to make sure they'd take care of the face-to-face meeting Monday morning. He wasn't a coward. He just wasn't a people person. And termination meetings were technically under their purview.

"Wanna tell me why this had to be taken care of first thing on a Monday? She can't possibly be a threat to anyone."

Henry had wondered the same thing himself. Quite frankly, even looking at the cause of termination, he couldn't figure out why everyone seemed especially interested in getting this taken care of so quickly. But it was neither Henry's place nor his business to have an opinion. His job was to make sure it got done in a way that wouldn't end up in litigation for the company.

He shrugged. "The higher-ups wanted it done. The rest is above our pay grade," he answered. It was a cop-out. Of course, when—and hopefully soon—he hit the C-suite, he wouldn't be able to use that excuse any longer. Henry looked forward to that day.

"But why? What's the big deal? What's the rush?" Genevieve kept pushing.

"I don't know." They were all fair questions and ones he'd asked himself. But his job wasn't to question the *whys*. It was to question the *hows*. "I looked over all the paperwork. And it seems to check out. Wainwright discovered an error on an expense report. He believed it was foul play, but I couldn't find enough evidence of that. Still it does seem she made some costly mistakes. And then there's the anonymous complaint. All in all, it's an easy break." Was it the cleanest termination Henry had ever signed off on? Probably not. But it was enough to stand up in court.

"That hardly feels like a big enough mistake to, one, fire her and, two, do it first thing on a Monday morning. She must have pissed someone off. *Anonymous complaint*, my ass. I just can't imagine anyone having a beef with Jia. She's so nice."

Henry wished Genevieve would just stop talking so they both could sign the separation agreement and be done with it. The only question Henry concerned himself with was whether the company had cause for termination. Whether it was the right thing to do or not? Not his problem. Fact was Jia Chung did not fulfill the duties of her job. Since when did being nice have anything to do with it? Being nice was not a skill needed in the corporate workplace. Henry was proof of that.

In just two years, Henry J. Shin, Esq., had already been promoted to the senior legal counsel, reporting directly to the general counsel, at Bakerson's Group, a financial powerhouse based out of New York and currently squarely in the top fifty on Nasdaq and the S&P 500. He worked long hours and did everything asked of him, most of it their own work others were too lazy to do themselves. They trusted him with all the hard stuff. Which included, at this point, working with human resources on employment issues.

Henry had become a lawyer because, well, as cheesy as it sounded, he believed in the letter of the law. He believed in rules and following them. And being held accountable to them. He'd grown up in chaos. His whole life no one had had to atone for their failures. He didn't like that one bit.

Following rules scratched an itch in his head that felt satisfying. So as cruel as it was, an employee termination felt like a win. Someone wasn't doing their job, they faced the consequences. And Jia Chung had not been doing her job.

HR could worry about the other stuff.

"Gen, let's not question this one. They wanted it done, it's done," he said.

"Yeah, but Jia was harmless. She was a genuinely sweet person." Regret was written all over Genevieve's face.

"That's neither here nor there. And not our concern." Henry meant it. This was too much thought to be put toward someone at work. And he wanted it to stop.

Because he didn't know Jia Chung. And he didn't want to. But yesterday, when reviewing her case, Henry had spent more time going over the details of her employment than he had on anything other than his own concerns in a long time. And that rabbit hole had led him to notice the list of the past three assistants to Edison Wainwright. All of them terminated within short tenure at Bakerson's. Henry had never worked with or met any of them, but he now knew their names: Stephanie Novak, Taylor Ann Graff, and Jia Chung. All women. All young. And considering the man they worked for, likely all attractive.

And for some reason or another, they were either all bad at

their jobs, making mistakes along the way, or they had pissed someone off enough to get them fired. And if the latter, knowing Wainwright's ego, it probably hadn't taken much.

All of this was what niggled at the back of his brain. And he didn't need the distraction.

So he tucked it away, where it would stay if Genevieve Gordon would stop asking all the right questions.

Instead . . .

"What I don't understand is this is the third assistant that he's fired in less than a year. It's not a great pattern."

"That sounds like an HR thing, not a legal thing. As far as I'm concerned, I have to look out for the best interest of the company. And in New York, we are an at-will state, so we have grounds for termination."

"God. You're such a prick sometimes. Always by the book." Genevieve wasn't wrong. "I'm just curious why he goes through all the effort to hire them if he's just gonna turn around and fire them."

"Again, Genevieve, that sounds like an HR thing," Henry replied. If he didn't engage with her, the quicker he could get this over with.

"Fine. It's not even worth it, digging deeper. This company would likely find a way to bury it if there were something there."

If Henry had a heart, he'd actually feel bad for how discouraged Genevieve sounded.

"He's a creep, though. You have to agree," she said. She narrowed her eyes at Henry daring him to disagree.

Henry lifted his hands in surrender. He did not want to get further involved in this conversation. He agreed with Gen on all of the above. And something didn't feel right with these assistants being let go. But he also was right when he told her that there was an error in her performance, grounds for termination in an at-will state. That's all they needed. "Let's just sign the papers, Gen. I have a ton of work to do."

"Okay, fine. Sucks, though. I really liked Jia," she grumbled, as she put pen to paper.

She'd said that already.

That was the problem. People wanted to work with people they liked more than with people that got the job done. Henry couldn't say he actually liked a single one of his coworkers. Though, he'd have to hang out with them and actually speak to them to figure out if there was anything to like in the first place. And that was not something Henry was comfortable with.

He was more of a stick-to-himself-and-just-do-the-job kind of guy.

Henry quickly signed on the line next to Genevieve's signature and walked out of her office.

3

"Not again, Jia."

Her mom dropped her shoulders, the air of exasperation and disappointment coming through the phone screen. Jia wasn't sure what she dreaded most: telling her mom the news or running out of the gelato she'd been comfort-eating all morning.

"It wasn't my fault, Mom," Jia tried to explain. But she didn't have the words. As she replayed the meeting in her head, she was certain that there had been a mistake. But it was all too overwhelming to process.

"Jia, companies don't just fire employees without cause, even if they can." Her mom was coming in with the combination parent-talk and lawyer-speak. Great.

Both Jia's mom and dad were lawyers. Not just any lawyers, but Harvard Law lawyers. Elected-officials lawyers. Our-reputation-is-everything lawyers.

And Jia? She was their free-spirited, can't-hold-a-job, doesn't-know-what-she-wants-to-do-with-her-life, just-looking-for-a-good-time daughter.

She didn't have the energy to get into it with Mom right now. She needed time to think. And she needed to come up with a plan before . . .

"I think it's time for you to move home."

Too late, there it was. The words that were always waiting anytime Jia screwed up. A safety net that might seem comforting to some but to Jia felt like a cage.

Jia was tired of being rescued. And their help and support always came with expectations and requirements.

No, she didn't want her parents' money or their demands. She wanted to show them she was able to take care of herself, while living life the way she wanted to, doing what made her happy.

She just wasn't sure what that was yet.

Jia was, as her parents put it, a miracle. They'd struggled with getting pregnant, and after multiple miscarriages, they'd finally conceived via IVF. Her mother described her pregnancy as *the hardest time of her life*, and it didn't help that after Jia was born she'd had early health issues.

Her parents raised her with the kid gloves of two people desperate to have a child and the iron fist of Korean expectations . . . an odd and confusing combination. They wanted her to succeed, but they wanted her to do it their way.

But Jia was twenty-seven now. She was healthy now. She was out on her own now. And they had to let her live her life now. If only Jia could convince them of that by, you know, *not* getting fired from her job.

"Florida isn't my home, Mom. It never was." This was the truth. Jia had grown up in New York. Her parents only moved to Florida a few years ago. But they tried to make her believe it was heaven on earth. She wasn't buying it.

"Jia, do you understand the gravity of your situation? You don't have a job. No income. No health insurance, for god's sake. Your credit is a mess."

"How do you even know my credit score, Mom? Do you know how intrusive that is?"

"I wouldn't have to meddle in your affairs if I could trust you to handle them. How do you expect to afford to keep living in New York? You simply are not capable of taking care of yourself there on your own. It's like you're on a merry-go-round, making the same mistakes over and over. But what you do now in your life impacts what you're able to do later. At this rate, you won't be able to get bigger jobs. And you can forget ever being able to purchase a house for yourself. Come to Florida, work for me and Dad, build the skills you need to succeed, then get back on your feet."

Her mother loved a plan. Especially when it involved controlling Jia.

Everything sounded so reasonable.

It all sounded so stifling.

Maybe bigger jobs and buying a house weren't what Jia wanted for herself. Maybe it never would be.

But Jia was just as tired of letting them down as they probably were. Surely, at some point, she would prove to her folks that she could figure out her own life on her own terms and that would be enough to make them proud.

Right?

"I'll get a new job," she said with more confidence than she was feeling. With every failed job, her résumé made her look more and more unhirable. She wasn't sure she'd have many more opportunities. If only she could find a job she loved doing, something that satisfied her.

And wasn't that the dream?

"Jia, the reality is, as a woman, and an Asian woman at that, you don't have the luxury to make mistakes. You have to work twice as hard with half the amount of support and acknowledgment others receive. That also means you're not afforded time to figure things out."

Jia closed her eyes and let out a deep sigh. She knew her mother was right, but it just didn't seem fair. Was Jia supposed to be on this hamster wheel for the rest of her life?

"Mom . . ." She didn't know what she wanted to say.

"I'm going to have to put my foot down. You're being irresponsible, and it won't be tolerated. If you don't find a new job, one that will pay all your bills and afford you to stay in New York, then I'll have to insist you come and live with me and your father," her mom said with her lawyer voice activated. "I won't allow you to permanently damage your future by making bad choices."

"Just, give me thirty days, Mom. One month. And we'll reassess. You can't make me come. But I don't want to be unreasonable either. So yeah, let's meet halfway on this." Surely her mom could appreciate Jia's negotiation skills.

Her mom's jaw ticked as she narrowed her eyes at her daughter. Jia held her breath.

"Thirty days, Jia."

Jia saw her future play out in her head. Florida. Suburbs. Living with her parents until she was fifty. Dressing in Talbots like her mother. She shivered at the thought.

This would be her last shot. She wouldn't be able to outnegotiate her lawyer mother after this. It was either find a job and get her life on track or lose the little autonomy she had to live it. One thing was for sure, Jia needed a plan. Her entire life depended on it.

"Jia, honey, we need to talk."

The trauma from anyone coming at Jia saying *We need to talk* was real. Only very bad things came from a *We need to talk*.

We need to talk—we're moving to Florida, leaving all your friends behind. High school will be miserable.

We need to talk—you need a new battery, air filter, and carburetor. It'll cost a fortune.

We need to talk—I met someone else. It's not you, it's me. You'll struggle to trust any man again.

We need to talk—you're fired.

Jia sat up on her bed, pulling her threadbare Sailor Moon blanket with her, and looked into the eyes of her very best friend. Lizzy stood in the doorway looking . . . concerned. Was she worried Jia wouldn't be able to make rent? Because Jia was worried. But she didn't want to let that roll over on her friend.

Jia had been racking her brain on how to find a new job and stabilize her income.

Maybe she could start selling her clothes or something.

For someone who didn't make a ton of money, Jia knew how to make use of what she had and find the best deals. Her most prized possessions weren't fine jewelry or first edition books—they were pieces of clothing. Dior black wool slacks she'd found on consignment, a vintage Hermès silk scarf, and of course her Burberry trench coat bought at an estate sale of an heiress who passed away and her family who had no idea about the treasures that they were selling for a steal from her Upper East Side townhome. And don't get her started on the shoes in her collection.

But she couldn't part with any of it.

Jia was well-known for her particular sense of style.

The way Jia dressed impacted how she felt about herself and how she went about her day. And right now, she was wearing a ratty Hanes undershirt that had been left behind by some guy she'd hooked up with last St. Patrick's Day—Sam? Scott? Steve?—and plaid pajama bottoms from when she was fifteen years old. Comfort clothing. Sad clothing. I've-given-up-for-now clothing.

Lizzy sat down, grabbed Jia's hands, and squeezed.

Jia braced herself.

"Darcy has asked me to move in with him, and I have officially said yes."

"Oh my god, Lizzy, that's amazing!" Jia wrapped her arms around her best friend and sent her as much love as she could through the embrace. Look, you didn't have an Elizabeth and a Darcy dating each other and not expect an HEA. C'mon. As if. "I'm so, so happy for you guys. One step closer to that dream wedding in Montauk. But if you two could take it a bit slower so I have time to save up some money for a gorgeous bridesmaid dress, that would be appreciated."

She pulled back to see Lizzy with only a sixty-percent smile on her face.

"I don't want to pressure you, but what are your plans?"

Jia closed her eyes. She didn't have plans. She just had problems. She'd applied to some jobs she found online today. But she wasn't hopeful.

"The super said there's already someone looking for an apartment in this building," Lizzy explained. "Do you want me to tell him it's available? Or find someone to take over my room on the lease? Or . . ."

Or Jia could take over the lease herself? Not happening.

Or Jia could move out and look for a new place? In this market? Impossible.

Did Jia have any other options left?

"Darcy said he has a friend who may need a roommate for the summer. He could ask for you? Or maybe we can ask Jenny's coworker who just bought that place with the extra bedroom?"

"In Staten Island?" She tried to cover up her disdain. Beggars couldn't be choosers, and Jia was most definitely the beggar in this scenario. But still—Staten Island? "Don't worry, I'll figure something out."

"Or, don't hate me for suggesting it, but you could take your parents up on their offer and maybe go home for a little bit? Just until you get on your feet," Lizzy suggested. Lizzy's shoulders were up to her ears, and she'd forced out every premature wrinkle on her face as she grimaced. It pained her to even say it, Jia could tell.

"Florida is not my home," she said. "And that's just not an option. It's signing away my freedom."

Lizzy nodded in understanding. She'd met Jia's parents. She knew what a lifetime of their disapproval and disappointment had done to Jia.

"Well, let's not worry about it tonight. I have the coupon for the half-off pizza at Joey's. Pepperoni and jalapeños sound good?" Lizzy suggested, changing the subject. "It's on me."

"Sounds perfect," Jia said, trying not to let the stress and sudden concern for where she was going to live in the near future overwhelm her. Not tonight when she wanted to be celebrating her best friend's good news. "But I can cover my half. That way we don't have to fight over who gets the leftover cold pizza in the morning." Jia tried to smile. Her life had been reduced to wondering if she could afford half-price pizza split between two.

As Lizzy went to the other room to order the pizza, Jia pulled the covers over her head and blocked out the rest of the world. She hated feeling low and desperate like this.

When was the last time that Jia had actually felt like herself? Free? Truly happy?

A memory of her first two-piece swimsuit, a grape Popsicle in hand, palm trees in the skyline, laughter with a loving face with tiny, beautiful crow's-feet around her eyes accentuating the joy. Mimi.

There wasn't one memory tied to her grandmother in Palm Springs that didn't make Jia smile. Her grandmother loved and accepted Jia for who she was. Never tried to squeeze her into any box to contain her. Always wanted her to explore, be loud, question, enjoy.

Jia quickly sat up in her bed and scrolled down her Contacts list. She hadn't been back to Palm Springs in years. Holidays and family gatherings happened mostly in Florida now. She missed it so much. And maybe this was the exact sign she needed.

She could either stay here in New York and wallow in her failures, paralyzed over what to do next as the clock ticked down, or . . . she could escape to the desert. She could go and regroup, breathe, relax. She was too emotionally constipated right now. She needed to get away.

Jia pictured herself sitting by the pool, the smell of coconut sunscreen filling her nose, the vitamin D of the sun's rays energizing her, inviting all the good juju to come her way. A full inbox with job offers once she let go of the pressure and stress of needing one. Make it so!

She pressed the Call button before she could chicken out.

She needed to ask before she could tell herself she shouldn't be burdening her grandmother. She'd burdened enough people as of late.

Mimi's voice answered after only one ring.

"Jia, how's my best girl doing?" Mimi asked.

"Mimi, I'm sorry to bother you. But I was wondering if I could ask a favor?" Jia said.

"Well, okay then, right down to business. Lay it on me. Anything for you. You know that."

"I was wondering—is that spare bedroom of yours free? And if so, how'd you like some company for the next few weeks out there at The Sunset?"

4

Henry rubbed his chest where the sharp pain had awakened him.

The panic attacks had been rare enough up to this point that he avoided taking the anxiety medication that had been prescribed to him. He loathed the side effects and found that if he managed his stress levels and caffeine intake, it helped keep them at bay. But this was the third one he'd had this summer.

Why now? There was nothing stressing him out more than usual. Work was . . . work. But he was making moves. In Henry's mind, that was a good thing. And, well, there wasn't anything else happening in Henry's life other than that. He couldn't figure out what could possibly be triggering this. And this, apparently, made the pain even worse.

The doctor assured him that he wasn't having a heart attack. But it always felt like one. Henry actually wished it was one because at least he could get something for the pain. A panic attack? Opioids actually increased the anxiety. So the only hope was that he could calm himself down and wait for the pain to subside.

Henry was not the type to be calm, at least not on the inside.

As the waves of pain increased, he curled up into a fetal position on his bed trying to breathe through them. It never worked. It was, unfortunately, just a waiting game. And after what felt like hours but was likely mere minutes, the piercing had subsided. He got up and shakily walked to his kitchen to get a glass of water.

Henry looked down at his phone on his kitchen counter. He always had his phone within arm's length. Had he forgotten to bring it to bed with him? On the screen was a Missed Call notification and a voice mail. A work emergency. They were the only ones that would call him. Unless . . .

The screen read *Dennis*. His grandfather. Shit. He didn't often call in the evenings, and though he was three hours behind, by the time Henry had gone to bed, it would have been late for his granddad.

Henry's heart rate quickened as he fumbled to check the message.

"Hey, Hank, it's your gramps. How you doing, kiddo? I miss you. It's been too long. Anywho, not a big thing, but . . . well, I think I might've gotten myself in a pickle. I'm selling the house and just get a weird feeling about the real estate guy. Gimme a call when you get a chance. Tomorrow's fine. I just drank my warm milk and will be asleep in a few. Love you, kiddo."

Okay, at least it wasn't a health emergency. Henry's worst nightmare.

Since when was his grandfather selling his house? Henry tried to remember if he'd mentioned anything the last time they'd spoken. When was that? Henry had called him to wish him a happy birthday in . . . March. Fuck, it was June already. He tried to check in at least every couple weeks. But he'd been so focused on work lately, he'd let it slide. Just long enough for Dennis to get into some trouble.

His granddad, Dennis, had a home in Palm Springs, and Henry had spent summers there as a kid. More like he'd been dumped there as his only option for a roof over his head and some adult supervision. But his granddad never made him feel like a burden. He loved over him as much as Henry would allow. In any case, it had been a couple years since he'd visited out there. Even then, the house had shown its age.

But more striking to Henry was how many of the old neighbors seemed to have moved out of the area, selling their homes and letting builders come in, the newer, hipper, more gentrified part of Palm Springs creeping up on their once sleepy, residential street.

Dennis had mentioned possibly wanting to move away from the hustle and bustle of the downtown area, up a few blocks north to the retirement community of Sunset Hills. Henry thought it could be a great idea. Be around more people his age and with the various levels of support the HOA costs provided, it would put Henry's mind at ease a bit, being all the way on the other side of the country and all.

But he hadn't realized that Dennis had made the move to do it so soon. And the voice mail was not what Henry wanted to hear. He'd get the realtor's number, put on his official lawyer voice, and make sure no one took advantage of his granddad.

Henry rubbed his chest where the pain from the earlier panic attack was focused. He was supposed to be managing his stress levels. Work brought enough anxiety into his life. He wasn't expecting family stuff to pile onto it all. Maybe he'd need to start taking the meds, along with the brutal side effects, more regularly after all.

"Granddad? Hi, how's it going? I got your voice mail," he said loudly and as clearly as possible so his granddad could actually hear him.

"Hi, Hank. Thanks for calling me back. Everything good out there in the big city?"

Henry smiled. His granddad was the only one he'd let call him Hank. Like he could stop him. He'd asked him many times to . . . not. But he was a stubborn old man. And the only family Henry had. That he cared about, at least. In fact, Dennis was the only person other than himself that Henry paid any mind to period.

"Yeah, all's good. Why didn't you tell me you were selling the house?" he asked.

"I thought I did. Maybe I forgot. You know I don't like bothering you if I don't have to. You're too important to be pestered by an old man."

"You aren't a bother. And I'm sorry I haven't checked in in awhile. But it's important you keep me updated when stuff like this comes up." Henry felt like he was reprimanding a toddler.

"And that's why I called. You see, there's a nice little home down at Sunset Hills, remember the old folks community I told you about? And I wanted to put an offer on it. So the guy selling it said he'd work with me to sell my home too. Some kind of trade or something."

Henry did not like the sound of this. He wasn't an expert in real estate law, but he didn't like someone with competing interests trying to take advantage of his grandfather. How would Dennis even know what kind of offer to make on a house? He was exactly the type of trusting person that would get swindled. Henry had witnessed this firsthand when he'd found out his granddad had given a huge part of his retirement away to grifters, otherwise known as his parents.

"Granddad, how far have you gotten in the process with this guy?"

"Well, I didn't sign anything. You taught me better than that," he said, laughing.

"That's good to hear," Henry said. "So can you tell me exactly what the agent told you?" He'd need to try to pull as much info out of his granddad as he could to get the lay of the land. This was not going to be easy.

"Well, you see, it's like this. This guy is real slick, ya know? He's the one that's been going around trying to convince everyone in the neighborhood to sell. And I guess my and the Billingses' houses are the last ones standing."

"Wait, I thought it was the nice lady from your church, Mrs. Hobbs, that wanted to help you sell your house once you were interested." Henry had had his doubts about this woman and her abilities, but at the very least, he knew she wouldn't try to screw his granddad over. He just wasn't confident she could get him top dollar for his home. Sure, it was outdated and needed major upgrading and renovations. But it had strong bones and even stronger memories. And the land itself was what was valuable.

"Some other guy at her office stepped in. Like I said, slick. Not even one hair out of place, and I have never once seen him sweat, not even when it was up in the one teens last week."

Jesus, just the thought of hundred-and-ten-plus-degree weather had Henry feeling the heat. And Henry knew the slick type. Heck, some might say he was the type.

"And is he pressuring you to do whatever he wants?"

"Yeah, that's what it feels like. I wanted to see if the price to buy the house was fair. And also the price he was talking about for my home seemed kinda low. I was gonna do some poking around on the Zillow. But he's saying we gotta act fast or prices and some kind of rates will fluctuate. I didn't understand everything he was saying. It was stuff they don't even talk about on HGTV," he said.

"Yeah, I bet it was confusing. I don't even know all of that stuff," Henry said.

"I mean, I know I'm ready to make the move. I just want to make sure it's on the up-and-up. Plus, I wanna talk to the Billings family and see how they feel about being the only ones left of the old neighborhood. They might get lonely."

Lonely, sure. But more likely they'd get the pressure put on them to sell and give up the land as the last remaining original resident.

"Anyways, Hank, you know I don't know about all that smart-guy stuff."

It was bullshit, and they both knew it. His grandfather was sharp as a knife, despite his hearing and his mobility deteriorating. It was more likely his granddad wanted—

"So I thought if you weren't too busy, maybe you could come out here and help me work through all of this. Just wanna get myself a nice little home at The Sunset and sell my house for enough to live on until I kick the bucket. Oh, and you can help me move all this stuff to the new place. You haven't been out this way in years."

There it was. His granddad would use any excuse to try to get Henry out to the desert to visit him. And it was happening less and less frequently as he got busier at work. The pangs of guilt began to creep up into his chest. He let out a sigh while opening his laptop and signing in to take a look at his calendar.

It wasn't a bad time to go. Summers were slow at work and in the city as a whole. But Henry was not a take-time-off kind of guy. Still, now that he had the two junior attorneys working for him, he could leave for a week or two or just check in remotely as needed. All the other executives were gone for the summer; he could sneak away for a few. Not that he was an executive . . . yet. But it was coming.

Shit, maybe he shouldn't go.

This was the problem with having responsibilities for anyone other than yourself. Demands on your time, along with priorities for your attention got muddier.

But the desert always helped Henry relax for some reason. Henry rubbed his chest and then reached up to massage the crick out of his shoulder. It could be good to get away.

"Okay, let me check my schedule. I can probably sneak in a few days, maybe a week . . ."

"See if you can ask for two. By the time you fly out here a whole day will be lost, same as when you go back. You'll need at least two weeks, Hank. I got a lot of stuff to move."

Greedy ol' man. Henry smiled at his lack of subtlety.

"Fine. I'll see what I can do. It is kinda slow around here. I'll let you know. And Granddad, don't take any calls from the slick guy until you hear from me tomorrow. I'll be the one talking to this guy from now on."

"Sir, yes sir," his grandpa said as he always did when Henry tried to tell him what to do. "I knew my successful lawyer grandson would come to the rescue."

Henry let out a huff. "I'll call you tomorrow."

"Looking forward to it, Hank."

Henry looked down at his calendar as he hung up the call. A few recurring meetings that he could move around. Everyone else's calendars blocked off for the Hamptons likely. Henry had overheard Bakerson telling Wainwright and Sword to *steer clear* for a few weeks. It was an odd thing to say. He'd really hoped it had nothing to do with the recent employee terminations.

He shook his head. Nope, not his business. He did as he was told, and he made sure it was on the up-and-up.

Henry shot off a quick email to his boss knowing he'd get the Out of Office message. And then he emailed his team asking for quick updates on their projects. If he was going to get out of town, he'd need to make sure everything was in place for him to do so. If nothing else, he'd be reachable remotely at any time.

They were competent and capable. Things should be fine.

Guess he was heading out west to the desert. It was like a string tied in the tightest bow was yanked and suddenly unraveled. Henry felt like he could finally breathe. So he did.

He took a deep breath, let it out, and opened up the weather app on his phone to see exactly how hot it would be.

5

Jia's memories of her grandmother's home in the Sunset Hills retirement community were of hot-as-Hades summer days where barefoot on the pavement was not an option and plenty of eggs could be found in driveways frying due to curiosity and childish experiments.

Off-season was what they called the months at the height of the summer, where locals fled, tourism dropped off, and the rules of Sunset Hills were loosened. The neighborhood was for people fifty-five years or older. But in the summers, at least while Jia was growing up, kids came and visited grand- and great-grandparents for months at a time. No one questioned it, and no one complained. The summers came, and with it, so did the kids. At least those who could handle the extreme weather.

Jia loved extremes.

The extremes were where she thrived. She always had. She never complained about hundred-and-fifteen-degree temps.

Instead, she spent her days creating synchronized swimming routines with her cousin Somi in the nearly empty pool of Sunset Hills. She even encouraged her grandmother to wade into the pool and participate as well. By the time she had her neighbors Betty, Mildred, and Edith joining, she'd created an entire synchronized swimming team and choreographed a routine for them all.

If nothing else, they had the cutest swim caps.

Jia loved those summers. She loved interacting with the residents. She loved hearing their stories about life and heartstrings, about families, about war. She didn't love that each summer, a familiar name was no longer with them. Edith had passed when Jia graduated high school. Mimi had told her of a few others since, but Jia took Edith's loss hard.

Maybe that was why Jia hadn't been back in so long.

As the plane began its decent into the Palm Springs airport, Jia hung on the best memories of The Sunset. She felt hopeful for the first time in days. Maybe even longer if she were being honest with herself. The desert might not have all the answers she was looking for, but it would buy her some time. And that, in this moment, was the greatest gift of all.

Jia was hit with the heat the moment she stepped off the plane onto the stairs of the jet bridge leading down to the ground. She took in a deep breath of the dry desert air, tied her hair back into a knot, and descended into the past.

That was how it always felt when she came here.

The Palm Springs airport was small and dated, fewer than twenty gates total. But like most of the city, that was part of the charm. There was only one direct flight from New York to Palm Springs each day. Jia was lucky there was even one on this day as the air traffic significantly slowed down during the off-season.

It was all a stark difference from JFK where she'd just flown from.

Also different, the people. Brightly colored shirts, flip-flops, mismatched patterns. And smiles everywhere. Some oohed and aahed at the palm trees that lined the walkways around the terminal. Others finally released a breath as they prepared themselves to slow down while they were here. Such was its magic.

Jia had packed carefully. She brought the Zimmerman sundress that she'd bought off ThredUp for a Miami wedding she went to last year. And the gorgeous Alice + Olivia tank dress could not be left behind. It was made for Palm Springs. Though there wasn't likely anyone around her age to even try to impress, she still brought some of her favorite summer staples just in case. Her one large suitcase with her favorites, along with a few pairs of shorts and tank tops and sandals, the cute ones of course, came with her, and the rest were jammed into Lizzy's storage unit in the city. Bless that girl. She made a mental note to bring her back a huge bag of saltwater taffy from the candy shop downtown.

So as she stood there watching the baggage-claim carousel, one of only three in the whole airport, go round and round a few times, she began to panic. Not a bright yellow roller bag with butterflies splashed all over it in sight. She told herself and others that she'd bought the loud children's bag so that it would be easily noticeable among the sea of all-the-same black zippered bags. But in all honesty, she just loved it. It made her happy.

And now that it hadn't arrived, she was sad at the thought of never seeing it again, along with everything inside.

"No sign of your bag? Do you think someone may have picked it up by mistake?" The deep voice dragged Jia from her own thoughts of doom and mental cataloging of everything she'd now likely have to buy and replace with money she did not have.

"I doubt it. It's a standout. I think maybe it might just be . . . lost."

"Excuse me," he said back to her. "This one's mine." A large hand grabbed the handle of the bag on the baggage belt right in front of where she stood, the respective arm lifting it as if it weighed nothing.

Well, okay then. Her mouth suddenly went dry.

Damn desert air.

She pretended to have an itch on her cheek that she'd rub with her shoulder so she could sneak a peek at the man with the sexy voice.

Please be hot. Please be under sixty. Please be single. The chances were slimmer and slimmer just based on the demographic of Palm Springs. She slowly turned around and was met with a smiling, chiseled face of a very handsome man who couldn't possibly be a day over thirty, forty tops. No ring. And not a gaudy pattern on any item of clothing.

"Looks like mine was the last one out. Do you need help dealing with customer service?" he asked, lifting his chin in the direction of the desk where an airline employee sat on the phone.

"No, I should be okay, but thanks." Jia looked down at his small, efficient carry-on, wondering why he'd bothered to even check the thing in. Didn't he know the percentage of bags that were lost by the airlines? She knew, since she handled—well, used to handle—all the travel for the execs at her previous job.

And, well, because she was now one of those people with lost luggage after all.

"Quick trip?" she asked, nodding to his bag.

"Something like that," he said, not giving an inch. "You?"

"Unclear, keeping my options open," she said, trying to sound flirty and fun.

"I'm Matthew," he said. Nice, a solid name Matthew. She liked it. He held out his very large hand, and Jia reached hers to meet it.

"Jia," she said back as her hand enveloped in his.

"Nice to meet you, Jia. I hope we run into each other while you're visiting. The Del Rey has a really good happy hour if you're into that kind of thing," Matthew said. Was that an offer?

"Oh, I am very into that kind of thing," Jia responded, raising the intonation of her last word to keep it open-ended. Damn, she'd better get her luggage and that Zimmerman dress back in time. It showed just enough cleavage to keep a man interested.

He nodded and flashed that sexy smile again. "See you around. And good luck with your bag," he said, turning to walk out.

That was it.

Shoot. She should've flirted a little harder, left the door open a little wider. But it had been a long flight, her pink seersucker romper was a bit rumpled, and it kind of matched how she was feeling after a long travel day and an uncertain future ahead.

So she brushed off the failed opportunity and went to report her bag lost along the way . . . much like her life, apparently.

Jia walked up to the Arrivals curb and immediately saw her grandmother's Camry waiting for her.

Mimi Chung was a small Korean woman with short hair in

curls and beautiful bright pink lipstick highlighting her face. She wore matching pink drawstring linen pants with a flowy floral blouse in the brightest shades of green and purple rounding out the ensemble. She stood smiling by the car, arm waving in excitement. No traffic cop would have the audacity to shoo her away from the No Stopping loading zone. Not that anyone was in a hurry here in the desert.

"Jia, honey, over here," she yelled.

Jia ran to her grandmother. As she got closer, though, she noticed that Mimi's gray roots were growing out. The wrinkles framing her face looked a little deeper. Her signature pink lipstick was worn off at the corners. Jia tried not to be alarmed, despite the fact the Mimi she knew would never leave the house unless she was one hundred percent put-together.

She bent over to give her the heartiest but gentlest hug she could. Her grandmother's arms wrapped around her and squeezed, a little more fragile than she'd remembered. Was Jia overthinking it? Or did Mimi just seem much older than the last time she'd visited?

"Mimi! It's so good to see you. Thank you for letting me come and stay. And thank you for buying my ticket. I owe you."

They released the embrace, and Mimi held on to Jia at arm's length, inspecting.

"Nonsense. You don't let me do stuff for you nearly enough. You think I'm not going to buy a ticket to get my granddaughter out here to visit? And you're not to worry about anything while you're here. This is a time for you to rest and get back on your feet."

Jia felt emotional. Mimi's reaction to Jia losing her job couldn't have been more different than her parents'. She didn't deserve Mimi. She wished her mom and dad could be as supportive.

"But, Jia, honey, you're too skinny. We're gonna need to fatten you up while you're here."

Jia supposed the recent life of unemployment and uncertainty and a very empty bank account had stolen her appetite and made her eating options almost nonexistent.

She couldn't wait to be spoiled by her grandmother. Mimi loved a good restaurant, always insisting on sharing a desert after every meal. Jia was suddenly reminded of her lack of fashion choices.

"They lost my luggage," Jia said with a frown.

"Don't worry, honey. They'll find it soon enough," Mimi said.

Simple as that.

And Jia believed her.

"Get in. Let's rescue you from this heat," Mimi said.

So Jia opened the passenger door, and just as she stepped in, her grandmother reached over, grabbed her hand, and squeezed, drawing her back.

"I'm so glad you're here, honey. We're gonna have the best time ever," she said.

"We always do," Jia said back. And she buckled her seat belt and got ready for the ride.

Mimi poured Jia a glass of lemonade and led her to the guest bedroom. "Okay, so this is where I keep most of my old clothes. Why don't you rummage through and see if there's anything you can wear until they find your suitcase."

Jia's eyes widened as she saw a stuffed-to-the brim closet full of color and possibilities. She pulled out a yellow dress that caught her eye. The tag read *Givenchy*. "Mimi, this is incredible. It's stunning!"

"Not quite so practical for an eighty-year-old woman living in the desert," she said, laughing.

And there was more where that came from. Balmain. Dior. Pucci. Saint Laurent. "Um, you do know you're sitting on a gold mine here, right?"

Her grandmother just shrugged as she smiled at Jia, pleased she was finding things that she fancied. "If you're not gonna wear this, you should totally sell this stuff. You'd make a fortune."

"Who has the time? Not me. And definitely not the energy. It's all just taking up space. I bet all the ladies in the neighborhood have much the same in their closets too," she said.

"If you guys wanted to, I could help organize it all while I'm here. We can think of a way to market the vintage luxuries. Could be fun and a nice chunk of cash for you to take a vacation or something," Jia suggested.

"Well, whatever you like is yours. So feel free to sell it or keep it."

Jia hugged her grandmother. "You're the coolest, you know that? Thanks so much for letting me come out and stay with you. I know I owe you an explanation—"

"You owe me no such thing. When you're ready, you can tell me whatever you feel comfortable with. For now, I'm keeping you here where no one, especially not your parents, can take you away to some godforsaken southern state."

Jia laughed. "What trouble should we get up to tonight, Mimi?"

"Oh, well, I don't drive after dark anymore," she said as she looked out the window, gauging how much daylight they had left. "And not much going on here at The Sunset."

"Really? I remember it being such a happening place," Jia

said. Jia was starting to feel like she'd entered an alternate universe. It had only been a couple years since she'd been back. But it had changed so much.

"Maybe, at one time. But it's slowed down a lot. We're all getting old. Not much we're able to do with the ailing bodies and minds."

Jia hated hearing this. She didn't doubt aging was hard. But it didn't mean they couldn't have fun and live full lives. "Well, how about we go for a walk around the neighborhood? You can fill me in on all the gossip."

"I suppose a short walk can't hurt."

Jia offered her arm, and Mimi hung on as they walked around the block. The pace was slow, but Mimi was animated as she caught Jia up on who still lived where and all the new names that had recently moved in.

"There's a lot more turnover than I expected," Jia said sadly. Sunset Hills felt different. The yards of the houses, though maintained with pride, looked duller, simpler landscaping taking the place of the more vibrant ones she remembered. Fewer cars lined the streets. No one was out and about, despite it still being somewhat light out. It wasn't what Jia had expected. And she started to worry that her memory had oversold what she'd find here.

"You remember the community center," Mimi pointed to the large single-story building on the right. "And the pool, though no one uses that anymore. We're voting at the next HOA meeting to see if we should just fill it up and make it into a desert garden."

"What? Get rid of the pool? But—" Jia stopped herself. All of this change made her sad. But she didn't want to put that onto Mimi. Maybe Mimi was sad about it too. Jia couldn't tell.

She just couldn't fathom it. So many memories in that pool. And pools were great for low-impact exercise like aqua aerobics. The seniors here should be taking advantage of that.

They stopped at the next corner. "Mimi, you doing okay? You want to rest?" She looked tired. And Jia felt tired. Lack of energy was contagious. And maybe all the self-loathing and feelings of failure Jia had been putting herself through the past days were catching up to her.

"I wanted to show you this." Mimi pointed up to the sky.

Jia lifted her eyes, and her breath caught. It was like a painting. The entire sky was colored with shades of pink and light orange, the horizon sprinkled with the outline of palm trees and wind turbines. She'd forgotten how stunning the desert sunsets were. "It's beautiful," she whispered.

"Never, ever gets old," Mimi said.

They continued on until they reached Mimi's front gate. Mimi seemed a little out of breath. She'd once been so active. Jia made a mental note to try to casually ask Mimi about her overall health. She was starting to worry.

"There's a new neighbor moving in across the street. A Korean man, if you can believe it," she said. "I'm excited to meet him."

"You should throw him a welcome happy hour," Jia suggested.

Mimi laughed as if it was the funniest joke. Mimi used to be in charge of the neighborhood welcoming committee. She used to be the one to suggest a party.

"Mimi, I'm serious. And I can help, if you tell me what to do. It will be fun. Plus, I'll get to see all the familiar faces and meet some of the new ones. Please let's do it." Jia wasn't sure why this felt so important to do. But she should at least make herself useful while she was here, right?

"Well, what if you take on the planning?"

Planning a party for a bunch of seniors? Jia's confidence had taken a hit with the loss of her job. She wasn't sure she would be able to take on any amount of responsibility. But this didn't seem too hard a task. It could be easy enough.

"Will you help me and tell me what I need to do to make it the best party ever? I need it to be of Mimi-level proportions. I have a family legacy to live up to."

"You betcha. That's what I'm here for. But I have complete confidence in you," Mimi said with a smile.

Jia hugged her grandmother and led her inside.

Sunset Hills might not be what it used to, but Jia knew there was still life left in it. And she was determined to help everyone tap back in.

6

Henry packed up for a couple weeks away from the city and jumped into the Uber to JFK. The traffic was heavier than he expected, and he made a mental note to revisit his calculations of when would be the right timing to leave for the airport before his next trip.

He went back and forth in his head talking himself out of going. Sure, it was quieter in the office during the summer months. But his boss and all the executives were gone. Someone should be in the office to make sure things didn't all go to shit. But that someone didn't *have* to be Henry. This was one of those things where the upside to being responsible was little to none. No one that mattered would see him staying tied to the office. Analysis concluded. He decided to go.

If he wanted to be an executive, he should start acting the part. Dump some of the menial work on those reporting to him and go about with an air of entitlement, privilege—not something Henry was used to. He'd worked his whole life, harder than anyone else around him, to get to where he was today. And he didn't have plans of stopping.

But his grandfather so rarely asked for help, and when he did, there was just no way for Henry to say no. He was the most important person in his life, and the only family he had left in the world. At least, who mattered to him. And with him being eighty now, he wasn't sure how much longer that would be.

Instead of flying into the rinky-dink Palm Springs airport, Henry had decided to fly into LAX, secured a first-class seat with his frequent-flier points, and rented a car to make the two-hour drive to the desert. His latest audiobook played through the SUV's speakers. Henry preferred audiobooks to podcasts. And he enjoyed consuming fictional stories to keep his mind occupied.

The rental car had made a mistake with his reservation, trying to give him an Escort instead of a Bronco. But Henry had insisted on an SUV as he'd have to carry around his granddad's walker if they ever ventured out from the house.

With the rough commute to JFK, the bumpy flight to LAX, and the rental-car mix-up, Henry wondered if this trip was cursed. At least he'd managed to get that real estate agent off his granddad's back. He'd worked out buying the new house from him but secured a different agent, one referred to him by a trusted friend, to sell Dennis's home. It had all happened smoothly and fairly, and now Henry was heading out to help close the deal. And it allowed Henry to be there when all the boxes were being moved to the new house.

The drive into Palm Springs was long, barren, and droll, but something about it put Henry at ease. The San Jacinto Mountains sprawled out before him, huge hills that looked like singular pieces of stone. The wind turbines turned and signaled a different world, really.

Henry had mixed emotions when it came to the desert. On one hand, he'd loved coming to visit his grandfather as a kid in the summers at his house with the huge pool and a slide. On the other hand, it signified yet another time his parents had left him so they could pursue whatever hare-brained idea they'd had again. Whether it be living off-grid in Costa Rica for a year or traveling across the US in a van they'd converted themselves and camping in BLM land, Henry's parents were free spirits. And being free didn't include taking care of an uptight kid with a myriad of health and emotional issues.

Henry would miss his grandfather's old house. But with Dennis's health declining with his increased age, it made more sense for him to move into the retirement community of Sunset Hills where he could be close to people his own age and pace and where medical support would be nearby. He'd prefer his granddad move into a nursing home or an assisted-living facility at least. But the stubborn old man refused. It was one of the few times his grandfather had really dug his heels in, and Henry had eventually let it go. For now.

He connected his phone to CarPlay and pressed the Contact for his granddad.

"Yello," the sandy voice said on the other end.

"Hey, Granddad. Just wanna let you know I'm about ten minutes out."

"Hank? Shoot, was it today you were coming in?"

Henry held back the sigh and the accompanying worry creeping up his neck. He'd told his grandfather multiple times the date and time he expected to come. The information just didn't seem to stick.

"Yes, just as I told you. The eighth of August. That's today."

"Well, hot damn, it'll be good to see you."

"Granddad, do you remember what today is? Do you remember me telling you when I was coming?"

"Yes, Hank. I'm just being an asshole because I like riling you up. Of course I knew you were coming. I even tracked your airplane to see if you were gonna be on time. Had a whole plan to fuck with you if your plane was delayed. But I'll hang on to that one for another day." His grandfather laughed like all of this was hilarious and not incredibly infuriating. The hearty laugh turned into a hacking cough ending in a wheeze.

"Real funny," Henry managed to get out.

"Oh, don't be mad. I'm just happy you're almost here and I get to see you. Ten minutes, you say? I'll get a beer out and pop it open for you by the time you walk in the door. See you soon," he said.

Henry let out a deep breath and couldn't help it—he smiled toward the phone. "See you soon," he replied.

The house was filled with boxes labeled in his grandfather's shaky scrawl. Henry didn't want to know how he'd packed them or what he'd find broken or intact once he opened them. He'd told his granddad to wait till he arrived so they could pack up the home together. But again, he didn't listen.

"Has the hip been giving you any trouble lately?" Henry asked. Dennis had gotten a hip replacement not too long ago. He had a walker to help with his mobility, and they'd been monitoring all his other organs to make sure the surgery didn't have any additional negative effects on his health. Henry had been so busy with work recently, he hadn't checked in with the doctor in . . . months?

"Hank, that was a while ago. I'm good as new now. You

haven't seen me since I've been all patched up. New hip works better than the old one ever did," Dennis said.

Henry took one look at his aging granddad and knew that couldn't possibly be the case. But as long as he wasn't in any pain or imminent health danger, he wouldn't press the issue.

As the movers loaded the truck up with his granddad's entire life, and part of Henry's for that matter, Henry couldn't help but feel a sense of being untethered. He'd built a life for himself, steady, successful, and different from the one he'd had growing up. But that didn't mean it didn't feel odd watching the last of what he remembered of his childhood become space between four empty walls.

An unexpected lump formed in his throat. He would not get emotional. Henry did not do emotional. It was impractical and unnecessary. A house was just a building.

A hand slapped him on the shoulder. "It was a good home for us for a long time, isn't that right, Hank?" his granddad said. "Maybe we should take a last picture outside and send it to your par—"

"Let's get going, Granddad," Henry interrupted him. He did not want to think about what his parents might say about the move and whether they would ask his granddad for any extra cash he might get from the sale. Luckily, Henry had made certain to handle all the financial specifics and put everything into a separate trust account that fed into his granddad's personal finances each month. Henry would handle all the bills and let his grandfather have enough for whatever incidentals he'd need.

No telling what his parents would do if they smelled any bit of what his granddad had made off the sale of his house to a move to a much smaller one.

"We'll let the movers finish up here and meet them at the

new house," Henry suggested. A part of him wanted to stay and oversee the rest of the packing up. But with one mention of his folks, he itched to get out of the past and move his grandpa into his new future, however short it might be.

"The movers will be there in an hour, so we'll need to go and collect the parking permit and owner's guide over at the community center office. Granddad, are you listening to me?"

"Sure, sure, Hank. Whatever you say." He had his headphones over his ears. His grandfather had issues both with hearing and with attention span. So the headphones helped focus him on what was being said. Unfortunately it made it difficult for him to hear the actual words.

Just one of the many things reminding Henry that Dennis was old and aging. He seemed to age a decade every subsequent time he saw him.

Henry made sure to set up his granddad's recliner and television before anything else. That would keep him occupied as he watched *Crash Landing on You* for the hundredth time. Henry could focus on directing the movers for all the other boxes. Henry had seen bits and pieces of the K-drama in passing while his granddad had it on the screen: an over-the-top soap opera from what he could tell. He wasn't sure what made Dennis love it so much, but it was definitely not the type of show Henry watched himself.

Henry shook off the brief distraction and reminded himself of what needed to get done.

Boxes in.

Guest pass secured.

Parking pass registered.

And then he could plan what to feed his grandfather for lunch.

Henry's muscles felt tired from the lifting and moving. He insisted on helping the movers in order to direct the boxes into the right rooms and, honestly, to keep an eye on their progress. Plus there was something about using your body for something natural versus working out at the gym that made it feel both harder yet more satisfying.

"That's the last of the boxes, sir." The movers were efficient and fast.

"Thanks, appreciate all your help," Henry said. He shook the mover's hand and passed him an envelope with a generous cash tip.

"Hank, make sure you give them some money for lunch too," his grandpa called out from the living room.

Henry gave him an awkward smile and dug into his wallet for an extra hundred dollars. It was easier than arguing with his granddad about manners and the lack thereof from the younger generations these days.

After the movers had gone, Henry reached for the first box to begin the task ahead of him of unpacking.

"Hank, whattaya say we wait till tomorrow to start with the boxes?" His grandfather looked hopeful. Like he wanted to just hang out and put the hard work off until later.

Henry was never one to put things off till later. "Granddad, you go ahead and sit. I'm gonna start unpacking stuff for you, and if I have a question of where you want something to go, I'll ask you."

"Or we could order a pizza, crack some beers, and watch a movie," his granddad suggested.

Henry saw a glimpse of the man he grew up with, who loved to have a good time, who hung out with Henry and played Scrabble with him. Who laughed hard and loved even harder.

Who didn't need a walker to stabilize or headphones or a list of medication a mile long.

But the boxes needed unpacking. And Henry just wanted to get him settled.

"Maybe tomorrow, Granddad. For now, why don't you just rest."

It was impossible not to notice the droop of his shoulders in disappointment.

But Henry knew they'd both appreciate it when the work was all done. And that wasn't going to happen if he didn't get started now.

So Henry grabbed the box cutter and got to work.

7

"Hey, Gladys. How goes it?"

Jia ventured over to the community center to check in on Gladys, the office assistant and Mimi's best friend. It had been a week now since Jia had arrived back at Sunset Hills. She'd slept the first couple days for hours and hours on end. It was as if she'd been clenching her entire body and it needed to rest off its trauma response of the days since her termination. She woke up only for meals and to take Mimi on a walk each day.

When Jia suggested they invite some of the other neighbors to join them, Mimi mentioned moving the walks to the mornings and possibly getting a better response. So they did. And thus started the Sunset Hills Walking Club.

When Jia saw Betty, one of her grandmother's neighbors, reading the latest Kennedy Ryan book, she asked if she could buddy-read with her and meet her for tea the next day to discuss. She invited two of her neighbors who were also reading it. And thus started the Sunset Hills Spicy Book Club.

And when Jia peeked over their four-foot back fence to see Lynette repotting some of her succulents, Jia got curious and asked about the different types and how they grew in the heat. Carla on the other side of Lynette's fence peeked over to hear the answer. And thus started the Sunset Hills Gardening Club.

She knew life still existed here. She just needed to wake it up. So when Jia woke up from her slumber, she got to work waking the neighborhood up from its as well.

She'd told Mimi about all the ideas brewing in her head, and the first thing Mimi did was to enthusiastically tell Jia to have at it, to do what made her happy, and if that meant rousing all the old folks, then she was all in. Having Mimi's support meant everything to Jia. It gave her confidence that she was on the right track.

"Cute outfit," Gladys said.

Jia looked down at her ridiculous ensemble. It wasn't her normal style. But she hadn't received a call from the airline about her luggage yet, at least not that she knew of. She actually hadn't even looked at her phone in days. She also hadn't gone through all of Mimi's closet yet. So she saw the scrubs in a drawer, and when Mimi had mentioned they were a designer collab with Betsey Johnson from back in the day, she put them on. She decided to make a whole outfit around the most colorful things she could find. She even included the decorative norigae from Mimi's wedding hanbok. A homage to her grandmother's life. And truth be told, she loved it. It suited her mood here in the desert today.

"Thanks, it's Mimi's stuff. Fits perfectly," Jia said.

"Sure does," Gladys agreed. "I'm about to head out to lunch, sweetheart. Did you need anything from me?" Gladys asked.

"I was gonna ask about making a community events calendar.

You know, since there are a bunch of new activities happening, and it might be nice having something visual to help people keep them straight."

"I don't think you need any permission for that. But if you need money to fund any of it, we'll have to ask the HOA. We've got a pretty good budget to do stuff. No one's tapped into it for a while now. But everyone's abuzz talking 'bout the things you've been up to. It's 'bout damn time. Thought we were all dead in the water once Ruth left us."

Ruth had been one of the residents of Sunset Hills and the de facto community manager of sorts. Jia had heard from the others that once Ruth had passed, no one had taken up the charge to keep planning things. It was like they all wanted to do stuff but didn't know how to get it done. Jia's heart ached, considering that the residents here had gone for however long without any activities to feed their bodies and their minds and their souls. She wanted to change that if she could. As long as she was here, she might as well be of some use.

Jia wasn't normally a go-getter; you could ask her former employers. But few things motivated her more than getting a chance to see people happy.

"Oh gosh. They're just some small weekly get-togethers for the residents. Nothing needs any funding."

"Well, based on how much everyone's been talking about that book club—" Gladys gave an exaggerated wink before continuing "—I have a feeling you're gonna have a lot of interest on your hands for whatever you cook up."

"I hope it's gonna be a lot of fun," Jia said. "Can I use the computer and the copier to print up the calendars to distribute? Oh, and can I post one here at the community center?"

"No problem. All yours. Watch the desk for me while I go and make my tuna sandwich at home, will ya?"

"Sure thing. Hey, do you have garlic powder?"

"I do. Do you need some?" Gladys asked.

"Nope. But if you sprinkle a little bit on that tuna sandwich, it adds a nice little punch," Jia suggested.

"Oooh. I'll give that a try. It should be slow while I'm gone. Just hang out for a bit," Gladys said. "The guys will be coming in to play bridge. If they cause a ruckus, threaten to kick them out with a loud voice so they can hear you. That should settle them down."

Jia smiled and nodded and sat down at Gladys's desk to get to working on the calendar.

It was currently quiet in the community center, so Jia got up and decided to walk around and check out what was available, get some ideas of what she could do to reach more of the residents.

From what she noticed with Mimi, she was in good health, but aging was hard. It was hard on her joints, her lungs, and her attention span. Jia just wanted to help stimulate their minds, muscles, and need for community. It was a no-brainer. It just took someone willing and with the time to organize.

And that was exactly what Jia had right now. Time.

The exercise room was spacious and clean. There were no machines, which felt like the right call with the potential safety hazards. But there were some mats and free weights. Maybe Jia could organize some group movement classes. She'd taught Zumba back in New York for a few months. It was low impact and a lot of fun. She made a mental note to do some research about modifications of the dance moves for people with limited mobility. She wanted to know what some of the nuances would be for teaching an older class. She could also check in with Mimi and some of the neighbors about their favorite tunes and songs they'd loved from their past. She could imagine at least ten people showing up for something like this. A retro Zumba class might just be a hit here.

Jia inspected some of the other rooms. There was a craft room and a library, a large kitchen, and changing rooms for the pool area. So much to work with. Jia's mind was working double time with all the possibilities.

She hadn't felt this energized in a long time.

She would get to know the demographic of the neighbors and see what kinds of things interested them, what they liked to do for fun. Jia might have had trouble keeping a stuffy corporate job, but fun—fun she knew how to do.

Jia went back to the office, sat down at the desk, and took some notes from her tour of the community center. Once the good stuff was done, she decided to tackle the harder things on her to-do list. She took a deep breath and did the one thing she really did not want to do: logged into her email. *Please let there be a reply to one of my job applications. Please please please.*

When the inbox loaded, there were a few spam messages, a message from Lizzy letting Jia know that they'd be getting some money back from their security deposit (yay!), a note from Bakerson's Group letting her know they'd removed twelve dollars from her final paycheck for the box she forgot to return (shit!), and a formal-looking message from a fancy legal name which had to be fake. Jia deleted it along with the other spam. That was it. No job offers. No possibilities.

She had three weeks left in her deal with her mother. Florida was looking more and more like an inevitability. Jia closed her eyes and tried to mentally push back the darkness that crept up on her. Okay, enough wallowing, she thought to herself. Get to work.

Jia spent the next ten minutes looking at job postings online. But her attention span kept shrinking the more she tried. Her shoulders felt heavy with discouragement. Every job opening seemed to be looking for the same person: organized, strong attention to detail, self-starter. But these weren't words that people ever used to describe Jia. Overwhelmed, she closed out of the search. Maybe she could find an Etsy witch to help direct her to the right opportunity. At this point, that could very well be her only hope.

8

By the time Henry had unpacked the kitchen and the main bedroom, his granddad had fallen asleep on his lounger, the sun was setting, and the community office was closed. He hated parking the rental car here overnight without a permit, but hopefully if anyone asked, they'd give them a pass, since they were just moving in.

Henry spent the rest of the night checking work emails and had finally gone to sleep himself around ten. The night had been so quiet, all lights were out up and down the street before the sun even seemed to set. When he'd looked out his window at night, only one light from the house across the way was on. Every other house on the block was darkened other than front-porch lights.

He slept hard. Harder than he'd slept in as long as he could remember.

He was up early, but his grandfather was already sitting at the kitchen table, mug in hand.

Henry looked at the counter to find a jar of Folgers instant coffee out, the Keurig he'd bought as his first housewarming gift left untouched. He didn't want his granddad heating up water in a kettle next to any kind of open flame. He made a mental note to look into changing out the stove from gas to electric, despite it looking pretty new.

"Granddad, I'm gonna make a quick trip to the community center and the office to get all your passes straightaway. Don't want to start your time here off on the wrong foot," he said.

"No rush, Hank. We can do it later."

"I'm fine just getting it over with now," he assured him.

"Okay, but when you get back, let's go do something fun, just you and me. We gotta make up for lost time. I don't get you for very long this summer, and I want to make the most of the time we've got," his granddad said.

It struck Henry hard, the words. Unlikely meant to have the ominous undertone Henry took away from them, but they still hit like a ton of bricks. He didn't want to think about one day not having his grandfather around in his life. That would leave him with no one.

"Sounds great. I'll be right back, and then we can decide what we want to do today. We should plan to hit up the grocery store and stock your fridge, though. And we can restart the meal-kit delivery service you had at the old house."

His grandfather nodded as he walked to his lounge chair and took a seat. He pointed the remote toward the TV and settled in. He'd be good for a bit.

Henry grabbed his keys and checked the thermostat on his way out. Seventy-six degrees. His granddad had a habit of trying to lower it to sixty-eight. Maybe in other climates, but out here in the desert that would eventually blow the entire HVAC system.

Okay, he'd only be gone thirty minutes, tops. Everything was in order. There were so many things to constantly be worried about. Did his granddad think of any of these things when he was on his own? Would he need help once Henry got him settled and left to go back to New York? Dennis insisted he could take care of himself. And he wasn't technically sick, at least not enough for palliative care. Henry might look into getting a private nurse for him a couple times a week. Dennis would hate that, though.

"I'll be back in a few. Call me if you need anything."

His granddad leveled him with a stare just short of rolling his eyes. Okay, so maybe he was being a little ridiculous. But as far as Henry was concerned, he could be a little overprotective, overbearing even, while he was here in the flesh. So he would be. He smiled at his grandfather, both in apology and appeasement, and walked out, locking the door behind him.

He was immediately met with a wall of intense, dry heat. It took him a second to ensure he wasn't in fact in any danger. He was tempted to jump in his car, crank the AC, and drive the four blocks down to the community center. It wouldn't be unheard of. But Henry liked a challenge, as long as he wasn't unsafe about it. It was still early enough, the sun not at its peak.

He started walking, already feeling the cotton of his chinos stick to the sweat on his legs and begin to weigh him down almost like armor. He replayed the things he needed to do today in his head.

Check in with the office so they knew his grandfather had moved in.

Get a parking pass.

Register himself as an underage visitor.

Going over the things he needed to do helped settle Henry. Focus him.

When he arrived at the community center, there was a group of older residents with white hair gathered around the entrance. Henry stopped and waited as one of them tried to use their key card to let them all in.

"Step aside, Walter. I'll use mine."

"Mine works just fine."

"Well, clearly it doesn't or we wouldn't be melting out here in the sun. Move it."

"The sun isn't even at its highest point yet, you wuss. If you can't stand the heat—"

"Get outta the desert," the group said in unison. The old men laughed and wheezed and slapped each other on the back.

Henry stood wondering if there was an entry doorbell he could ring to have someone open the door for them. He didn't have a key card for his granddad yet—he added that to his mental checklist—and he didn't want to be standing out here much longer.

He heard the beep of the lock and the click of the door unlatching.

"See, you old goat? Told you mine works just fine," the man named Walter said.

The group ahead of him walked in and straight to one of the card tables set up along one side of the room.

There was a large central room and multiple rooms branching off it. Henry saw a small gym inside one of them with some free weights on the floor. He made a mental note to ask if he could use the facilities while he was a registered visitor here.

Another room had a Ping-Pong table and still another had rows of tables with sewing machines on them. And a farther room was filled with bookshelves and leather chairs.

It was all a little dated, yet impressive nonetheless. They had something for everyone. Well, at least those residents that were younger than his granddad.

The group in front of him sat down around a table, and one of them produced a deck of cards from his pocket and started dealing while the others settled in.

Henry saw the door with the Office sign above it and headed in that direction. Sitting behind the reception desk was a young woman in what looked like a well-worn set of scrubs with a teddy bear pattern on them. She had her hair tied back with a bright pink scrunchie, almost neon, and the color on her lips matched the vibrancy. She had her feet crossed on the desk, clad in yellow Crocs decorated with charms. She was leaned back in the desk chair reading a magazine that looked to be decades old. It was as if she was a young woman dressed as an old nurse in an explosion of colors and patterns. Henry felt like he'd stepped back in time into a scene of a television sitcom.

And yet, something about her was so familiar, Henry wanted to physically scratch his brain to try to recall where he might know her from. Not knowing made him feel on his heels.

"Excuse me," he said and quickly glanced at the name placard on the desk, "Gladys?" It wasn't a name he'd recognized nor seen many younger women have these days, and it honestly didn't fit the one sitting here.

"How can I help you?" she said. She looked up at Henry, and her eyes widened in surprise. She seemed to recognize him too.

Henry quickly thought through any possibilities. He had no reason to know anyone out here other than Dennis. Had he met her at the airport? She didn't work for the rental-car company. She wasn't the flight attendant on his trip. He couldn't place her as the barista at the coffee shop. Who the heck was she?

She furrowed her brows together. It was a race to see who could figure it out first.

"Wait." She squinted her eyes as if trying to look through a different lens. "Oh my god," she gasped. A wicked smile took shape on her face. She scanned him from head toe. "Willow on Ninety-Fifth Street. A couple weeks back. Good scotch. And great, well—" she cleared her throat and winked "—you know."

Henry's jaw dropped. Of course the one time recently that he'd allowed himself a one-night stand and it turned into some weird *Twilight Zone* episode.

She smiled and shook her head. "What are the odds? Tell me, what brings you here to Sunset Hills Senior Living Community in Palm Springs, California?" She delivered the question like a marketing campaign for the neighborhood.

Henry could not believe this was the same woman he'd hooked up with. He could see traces of the stunner from that night. God knows he'd let the memory of her run through his mind enough times since. She had been so sexy and responsive, lithe, incredibly good in bed. But she looked decidedly very different now. He couldn't wrap his head around what was happening. Why was she here on the other side of the country when he was also here, and why was she dressed like that?

Henry's lawyer brain immediately ran through questions and scenarios in his head. He started with the most obvious possibility.

"Are you the . . . nurse here?" Henry asked, nodding his chin toward her scrubs.

She looked down at herself almost surprised at what she found herself wearing. "Ha! No, not a nurse. Just found these in Mimi's closet from her working days and decided to wear them today. These too," she said, pointing at the hair scrunchie and then down to her shoes.

He had no idea who this Mimi was and wasn't sure he wanted to ask. "So you don't live in New York? I'm sorry, I'm just confused."

"God, I'm confused too," she said and laughed. "Actually, I do live in New York. Well, I did. Maybe I still will. For now, I live here. And hopefully I won't be living in Florida. It's all kind of a mess."

Henry had been so attracted to her the other night. Regretful, almost, for not having gotten her name or her number. Maybe he was lucky he hadn't. She was a bit scattered and odd in the light of day.

He felt a headache coming on.

"Weren't you celebrating a work thing that night? A promotion, was it?"

She dropped her head and avoided his eyes. "Yeah, that was a mistake on my part. Turns out that celebration was a bit premature. I wasn't trying to mislead you for free drinks or to get in your pants or anything."

He honestly did not know how to respond. She could have said almost nothing to him at Willow and he'd likely still have been interested. The chemistry was too good. He took another look at the odd woman in front of him and wasn't sure he'd have felt the same way if he had met her here.

For now he had more pressing questions, and it appeared she was the one he needed to be asking. "Okay, well, I was wondering if you might be able to help me. My granddad just moved in yesterday, and the email with his community information said he'd need to check in with the office. I'll also need to register for a parking pass for my rental. I'll need a copy of the liability waiver for him to sign so he can ride the community shuttle when needed. And I guess, if I can do it all right now, I'll register myself as an underage visitor for the next couple weeks."

Gladys's eyes grew wide. "Oh gosh. Well, I absolutely do not know how to do any of that, so I don't think I can help. I'm sorry. Um—" she leaned in and lowered her voice "—who told you that underage visitors needed to check in?"

"I read it in the HOA bylaws," Henry replied.

Her brows lifted.

"You read the HOA bylaws?" she said, nodding. "Well, I doubt anyone's gonna hold you to those." She turned her head away from him. "At least, I hope not," she said under her breath.

"Well, you never know. And I'd like to follow the rules just to be safe. Don't want to get my granddad in any trouble for harboring an underage visitor past his welcome," Henry joked.

Gladys leaned back in the desk chair looking completely stumped. She looked him over from head to toe, head cocked to the side, assessing him. Henry refused to squirm. Why should he be concerned what this wacky person thought of him?

But then she shook her head and shrugged a shoulder as if she just wasn't going to give it another thought.

"Someone will be here in—" she looked at the clock on the desk "—seven minutes to help you. This is above my pay grade," she said.

"Fine," he said. He looked around, saw the waiting chairs, and took a seat.

"Did you say your granddad just moved in? That's great. What's his name? Would he be interested in joining us for the Spicy Book Club?" She laughed to herself. It was very loud for this small space. Henry winced.

"I doubt it. He reads mostly thrillers and memoirs."

"Gardening Club? How about the Walking Club?"

"He's older and has some mobility limitations. I don't think he'll be participating in any activities for now."

She frowned. It was like the light was suddenly turned off in the entire neighborhood.

Henry felt the need to explain. "We moved him to Sunset Hills because, well, it's a peaceful place, and he can live a slower, quiet life."

Her frown deepened. "Oh," she said, "that's a shame."

"I'm sorry?"

"It's just that, well, I see the appeal of a slower life, I guess. But even in this past week, I've met too many people not wanting the folks here living their lives to the fullest. It's like family members send their *loved one*," she said using air quotes, "here hoping that they'll just pass peacefully or something. It's so sad." She frowned slightly and sighed. "Anyways, I was thinking that since I'm here for now, maybe I'd help out and just add some pizzazz to the place, if I can." She held out her hands and shook them in some weird razzle-dazzle kind of motion. "Wouldn't that be cool?"

"Well, first of all, I assure you that's not what I'm doing with my granddad. But anyways, what's wrong with wanting someone to live out the rest of their lives peacefully?" Henry asked, affronted. "Not everyone needs pizzazz." He looked down at his own hands, forcing them not to razzle-dazzle in return.

Even thinking of Dennis at the end of his life brought a sharp pain to his chest. He held back from rubbing it. She was making a pretty strong assumption about him and Dennis after having met him for only five minutes, plus a naked night together. Who was this Gladys person?

She shrugged her shoulder like she didn't believe him.

Henry wasn't sure what to say or to make of all of this. This was why he tried not to talk to people on any personal level.

"Hi, sugar. Thanks so much for covering for me." An older woman with salt-and-pepper hair entered the office and gave Gladys a kiss on the cheek.

"No problem. Did you have a nice lunch?" Gladys asked her.

"It was fine. I sprinkled some of that garlic powder on my tuna sandwich like you told me. Delicious."

"Right? It elevates it."

An elevated tuna sandwich. With garlic powder. Sounded like a sodium problem waiting to happen. Henry was starting to think this place could be dangerous if his granddad fraternized with the wrong people. But if he just avoided the community center, he'd never have to run into Gladys and her judgments and poor dietary choices.

No chance they'd be hooking up again anytime soon. He absolutely did not feel regret over that.

"This gentleman here needs some help," Gladys said over her shoulder. "He's very set on following the rules," she added before walking out the door.

"How can I help you, honey?" the new woman asked.

"I need to get some permits," Henry responded. He looked out the window as Gladys walked past, blowing a big bubble with her gum out her mouth before it popped and lapping it all back in with her tongue. He could not wrap his head around that being the same girl he'd had mind-blowing sex with.

"Oh. Well, that would be George. He's only here from eight to ten in the morning on Wednesdays and Fridays. Can you come back tomorrow?"

Henry looked back down at the woman behind the desk. “I mean, will it be okay if I don’t have them today?”

She laughed. “Sure, it will be. We trust you.”

He didn’t feel right about waiting another day, but it seemed he didn’t have a choice. He nodded, said his goodbyes, and walked out.

Fifty yards ahead of him was the bright pink scrunchie and the woman attached to it. He tried to slow his pace, but his legs were longer, and he wasn’t going to just stop in the midmorning heat.

Gladys glanced over her shoulder.

“Are you following me?” she asked.

“I’m not following you,” he replied.

“Do you even know where you’re going?”

“Yes, back to my grandfather’s house.” He wondered if he should take a detour so that she wouldn’t know where he lived. He wasn’t sure she was entirely safe.

When they got to the corner, she turned left, just as Henry did.

“I know jujitsu,” she said.

“I’m not gonna hurt you.”

“That’s what they all say.”

Henry threw his hands up in the air in frustration. If she was scared of him, why was she even talking to him? That didn’t feel like a good form of self-preservation. Plus, they’d seen each other fully naked. Seemed she’d trusted him just fine the other night.

“I choose the bear,” she suddenly shouted as he’d moved up behind her to pass her.

“Uh . . .”

A woman in a rocking chair in her screened-in porch craned her neck. “Sweetie, you okay?” she called.

"I'm fine. Thanks for checking, Myrtle."

"Cute outfit," Myrtle called back. "The lipstick suits you."

"Thanks, it's Mimi's," Gladys replied.

"Why are you wearing Mimi's clothes?"

"Because the airline lost my luggage, and I haven't heard from them yet."

Well, that explained the wacky outfit. What was the explanation for the wacky personality?

Henry stepped off the sidewalk and picked up the pace as he crossed the street. He got to his granddad's house ahead of her, but she was still in sight. Henry stopped, contemplating whether to give away that this was his destination. She was odd, but harmless, right?

She stopped at the house directly across the street, seemingly contemplating the same thing. She squinted her eyes at him and stared. They were in a standoff.

Who would move first?

"Do you live here?" he said. Henry felt a drip of sweat make its way down his back. He wouldn't last out here in the heat much longer.

"None of your business," she replied, wiping the sweat off of her forehead with the back of her hand. She looked at the house and then back at him and then up at the sky. She let out a frustrated growl. "It's too hot for this," she muttered. "Just so you know, we have a security system," she yelled as she walked through the small fairy gate and into the well-kept house across the street from Henry's granddad's new home.

Henry shook his head and did the same.

9

Jia scanned the shelves looking for everything she'd need for the soiree this afternoon.

They were having a happy hour at three o'clock.

Honestly, as many late nights as she'd had in New York, there was something about how everything happened earlier out here that made her feel so relaxed. Sure, why not a happy hour at three? Then they could have dinner by five. Grandma would be in her pajamas by six, and Jia would face her favorite time of day, seven o'clock, just as the desert sun started to set over the mountains. The entire neighborhood tucked in, and it was just her outside staring at the sky as it changed colors from day to night.

She grabbed the bottle she was looking for, and a second one just in case.

"Malibu rum. Now I know you're definitely here on vacation," the deep voice said behind her.

She turned around to find the very handsome guy from

the airport baggage claim, Matthew, there at the small grocery store.

Jia realized she was wearing her grandma's cotton rose-patterned pants that were about six inches too short and a white polo shirt. Maybe she'd been around Mimi and her friends a little too much lately, because this morning in the mirror she'd convinced herself that the outfit was desert chic. Seeing herself through Matthew's eyes, she likely looked like someone planning a retirement party who borrowed an outfit from her grandmother's closet. Which was exactly what she had done.

She really did need to get to the airport and pick up her luggage with her own clothes. The airline had called yesterday afternoon letting her know that they'd found her suitcase and she could either have it delivered to her address or come and pick it up. She told them she was in no rush. Apparently that was very true, since she had no issues borrowing another outfit from Mimi today. It was almost like a game she played while she was here in Palm Springs. What could she put together from the treasure chest of clothing that was her grandmother's wardrobe?

This was very unlike Jia. In New York, she took fashion very seriously. But since she'd been in Palm Springs, it didn't seem to matter as much. It wasn't a priority.

"Happy hour at The Sunset. You're welcome to join," she said.

"Sounds like a good time." His smile widened, and Jia's heart rate sped up. Man, he had a very good smile.

"Oh, it will be. The old-timers know how to party," she said. This time she gave him a sexy little smile herself. She'd have to use every weapon in her arsenal if she was going to get his attention while dressed like a Golden Girl.

He laughed. "I bet."

Jia had heard rumors and urban legends about what happened behind the gates of some of these senior living communities. Sunset Hills wasn't one of those party places, however, where swingers supposedly resided and STDs ran rampant.

Still, it was one of the most fun places she'd ever visited. Jia had very quickly made herself right at home. She was embraced by the surly older residents, and she loved them right back. They were fascinating and told the best stories. They never seemed to judge her like people her own age did. Or look at her with disappointment like her parents did. And, after seeing how eager they were to have a good time, Jia basically inserted herself as the event planner to the stars, the stars being the old folks who wanted to live life to the fullest for as long as they could.

"I didn't get to ask at the airport, but what brings you here to Palm Springs during the off-season?" she asked.

"I actually live and work here part-time. The other half in LA. But I tend to be up here for weeks, months on end if necessary."

"And what makes it necessary?" she asked, genuinely curious. If someone their age could make a living here, she wanted to know. It felt like a tempting possibility.

"I'd say, the number of happy hours with Malibu and pineapple." He nodded to the bottle in Jia's hand and the other one in her basket.

He really was cute, and the banter was not bad. Maybe Jia could have some fun while she was out here. She couldn't tell if he was interested or not. But she had a happy hour to get to, so she didn't have the time or energy to figure it out now. "I gotta get going," she said. "Don't want to make the party crowd wait."

"Hope I'll be seeing you around again?" he said.

"It's a small town," she said. "I'm sure you will."

"The Malibu and pineapple drink station is all set up. Louise is on the blender for the frosé. And the cooler is stocked with White Claws and water. How's it going in here?" Jia asked her grandmother and the small army she'd amassed to come help set up for the happy hour.

It's like the residents had been starving for a reason to get together. And all they needed was someone to say *Let's do it.* Jia was happy to be that person. To be honest, Jia's social life felt fuller and richer here among the septua- and octogenarians of Sunset Hills than it had living in New York among people her own age. More meaningful, at least. And she had fewer hours in the wakened day to work with here, so she made them count.

"Pigs in a blanket, check. Chips and guacamole, check. And Chester is bringing his world-famous charcuterie board. That just leaves the gimbap I'm gonna make, and we're all good to go." Her grandmother looked up at her with a smile.

"Amazing. It's shaping up to be quite a shindig," Jia said.

"Thanks to you. You're really good at this, ya know?" Mimi leaned back into Jia, and Jia placed a kiss on her cheek. She had no skills that made her employable. But a happy hour she could do.

"If only pigs in a blanket looked as impressive on a résumé as they do on this platter," Jia said. She tried not to get discouraged. But it had been a couple weeks with tons of applications filled out and résumés sent into the world. And not one response, not even a rejection.

"Don't stress over your work situation, hon. We're here for a party. The rest can wait." Mimi's words comforted her. She was right. Nothing was going to get solved tonight anyways.

Jia watched as Mimi laid all the ingredients for rolling gimbap out on the limited countertop space. The kitchen was wide enough, but the layout was so outdated. Mimi enjoyed cooking so much she deserved a better workspace. "Hey, Mimi, what would you think of doing a little renovation of your kitchen? Maybe some fresh cabinet doors? Move this table here and put an island in the middle? You've always wanted an island, right?"

"I have. I even have some money put aside to do work on the house. But it's been sitting there for decades. Your dad doesn't want me to fix it up lest the value go underwater."

Jia didn't know what that even meant. But if Mimi wanted an island, and she had some money to get one, why not? "We just won't tell him. When was the last time he came out here anyways? They're always making us come to Florida for holidays. What if I called around and got some quotes?" Jia offered.

A huge smile spread across Mimi's face. "I like the way you think, kid."

Jia's heart warmed knowing she was going to help Mimi do something that would make her happy.

"We haven't done one of these welcome parties in a long time. This is a hoot," Louise called out over the blender. "Great idea, Jia."

"Why haven't we done one of these in so long?" Betty asked as she stirred together her pasta salad.

"'Cause we're old and tired," Gertie said from the sink where she washed and peeled the potatoes. "Thank goodness for Jia."

"You guys are the ones doing all the work. You really know how to roll out the welcome wagon," Jia noted.

"Yeah, we used to never let a new resident move in without a get-to-know-you celebration. We loved making sure people felt good about their new home here," Mimi said. "Change can be so scary, unsettling. It's important to take some of that away from new residents. I guess we forgot that for little while. Glad you're here to remind us, Jia girl."

"You sound a little like a cult leader, Grandma," Jia teased.

"Well, you know what we say around here at The Sunset. Once you arrive, you never leave—"

"Unless you're dead," Louise called out from the other side of the kitchen.

"Yeah, that's morbid," Jia replied as the two older ladies laughed at their joke.

"Yoo-hoo, anybody home?" a new voice called out from the open doorway.

"Come in, come in! What did you bring?" Grandma asked the new arrival.

Jia turned around and saw Sally Mae Jackson enter, the smell of her promised mac 'n' cheese filling the space. She'd met her during one of the morning walks, and it was all anyone would talk about. "Ms. Sally Mae, let me grab that from you," Jia said as she took the foil serving tray from the rolling desk chair she'd apparently used to bring the food from her house to theirs.

"Careful with that, hon. It's hot. And I also brought some deviled eggs. Those are never as popular among the oldies here at The Sunset as they were back at my home neighborhood, but I'm gonna win people over eventually," she said. Sally Mae had originally lived in a senior community in the south, the east south, not the west south like they were in now. She liked to talk about it as *home* so she could pretend this place in Palm Springs was her *vacation villa*. Jia appreciated the approach.

"You really pulled out all the stops to welcome the new guy," her grandmother commented.

"Well, if he's a looker, I gotta get a jump start on winning his heart," Sally Mae replied.

Jia smiled. She was gathering priceless life advice during her time here.

"Hello? May we come in?"

"Dennis, you're here! Everyone, the guest of honor is here!" No one would ever accuse Jia's grandmother of lacking enthusiasm. "And as your designated New Neighbor Buddy, let me officially say *Welcome home!*" Everyone clapped.

Jia looked to see the guest of honor in the doorway. He was a slightly hunched older gentleman, his face lined with a map of many generously given smiles. Handsome in the way old men were when they'd obviously lived a life of warmhearted kindness. Jia wanted to hug him. So she did.

He let out a hearty chuckle as he wrapped an arm around her shoulders and patted her back.

"Welcome, Dennis," Jia said, delighted.

"Well, thank you, sweetheart. Mimi has already told me so much about you, as have the others. I've already got my sights set on the new aqua aerobics class you're starting and—" he leaned in to whisper "—the Spicy Book Club." He laughed heartily, and Jia smiled. She wanted to keep him forever.

"That's amazing. Those are two great choices," Jia said, feeling proud.

Dennis stepped to the side and coming up the walkway behind him, dragging a walker, was the man from the office the other day. "Just leave that there, son," Dennis told him.

He left the walker off to the side of the porch and stepped up to the front door, looking uncertain if he should come in.

Jia still couldn't believe her one-night stand from New York was here in Palm Springs. She'd felt guilty about the way she'd treated him the other day. She'd just been so caught off guard when he mentioned the HOA bylaws and restrictions for underage guests. Honestly, it scared her a little that someone might notice she wasn't supposed to be here and tell her to leave. She wasn't ready to get kicked out just yet.

But she shouldn't have taken it out on him.

"Hi, welcome," she greeted him warmly. She leaned in to give him a hug, and his back stiffened immediately. Oh shit. Was a hug not appropriate in this situation? They technically didn't even know each other, even though they did *know* each other, biblically.

This was all very weird. And by the grimace on his face, he thought so too.

"This here is my grandson, Hank," Dennis said.

Hank. His name was Hank. Huh. He didn't strike her as a Hank. Hank was more of a dog's name.

Jia brought herself back from her thoughts to see all eyes on her. Oh shit . . . Did she say that out loud? "It's just that here at Sunset Hills alone, there's Mitzi's shih tzu, Gerald's yellow Lab, and, of course, Mr. Burgess's bulldog with incontinence—all named Hank," Jia said.

"Henry," he said, sharply. "It's Henry. Only my granddad calls me Hank."

"Oh, okay. Yeah, you seem way more like a Henry than a Hank," she noted.

"Nice to meet you, Henry," Mimi said. "This is my beautiful and talented and smart granddaughter—"

"Gladys. Yes, we've met," he said.

Mimi's brows raised. Dennis laughed. And Jia . . . she blushed. In her stress yesterday, she'd forgotten to point out Henry's error. "About that. Um, I think there was a misunderstanding, and I didn't get a chance to clarify. My name isn't Gladys."

"Well, this is all very confusing," Mimi said. "Let's start over, shall we? Let me introduce you two properly, especially since we're all neighbors now." She grabbed Jia by the shoulders and pushed her so she was face-to-face with Henry.

"Henry Shin, this is Jia Chung. Jia Chung, meet Henry Shin."

The two of them stared at each other, recognition forming, yet not moving as they processed what they'd just heard. "My grandson here is a fancy lawyer at the Baking Group, some financial company in the Big Apple. We're very proud of him," Dennis said, looking at Henry, beaming.

"Bakerson's Group," Henry corrected him, not taking his eyes off Jia.

Jia's heart began to race as the familiar words from her recent past invaded her head. The safe bubble she'd been hiding under to protect herself here at The Sunset had been cracked . . . with a sledgehammer.

"Henry Shin from the Bakerson's Group," she said. It wasn't a question. It was a confirmation.

"Yes, that's it. That's the one. Jia, do you know of it?" Dennis asked.

"The Bakerson's Group? Jia? That sounds like the company that—" Mimi stopped herself, realizing she might be oversharing.

Jia couldn't believe what she was hearing. All the pieces of a puzzle were fitting together she didn't know she was working on.

Clinks of glasses filled with scotch. Heated kisses in an elevator. Frantic hands taking off clothing. Lips and tongues on the most private body parts. A formal, straight up-and-down signature on termination paperwork delivered by courier.

Jia's jaw dropped when she'd connected all the dots.

Holy shit.

This was Henry J. Shin, Esq.

10

Growing up, Henry knew drama. His parents fought all the time. They also had makeup sex all the time, with their door open. They would leave him for two to three days alone with some frozen dinners in the fridge as they took off to who knew where. He wasn't even ten years old. If the duration was longer, they'd drop him at his grandparents' house without even a phone call warning, and Henry would stay there for weeks or more. They'd missed his elementary school, middle school, and high school graduations. He never invited them to his college ceremony. Henry learned quickly that he hated drama, and when he was finally on his own to live life the way he chose, he decided to avoid it at all cost. Being a loner made that a lot easier.

Staring at the face of the woman he'd had a one-night stand with, who was the same woman he'd fired from her job the next morning, and who was now the woman making it her personal mission to care for every single elderly resident at his grandfather's new senior living community, Henry could not fathom how he found himself in this position, here, face-to-face with Jia Chung, knee-deep in drama.

He couldn't look away.

Her face wobbled and her mouth trembled as she quietly said, "Will you excuse me?"

She walked away leaving Henry, Dennis, and Mimi standing in her wake.

"Excuse me," Henry said as he went after her. He heard the voice in his head: the command *Don't go*, the plea *Leave it alone*, and the warning *Do not get involved*. But Henry was involved, and he couldn't leave it alone. He had to go and talk to her.

He needed to know why Jia Chung was here, apparently living comfortably at Sunset Hills, a neighborhood with an age limit that she most definitely did not meet and that his grandfather had just moved into. How had she landed here and why?

The facts were that Jia Chung had allegedly been bad at her job and, if he gave the anonymous complaint a grain of salt, difficult to work with. How was that person back in New York the same person now acting as social director for a bunch of elderly residents here in the California desert? And what—out of the goodness of her heart? What did she stand to gain?

She was either the salt of the earth or a grifter of some sort. And he needed to find out which for Dennis's sake.

He found her outside in the backyard. She stood with her arms crossed, back to the door, eyes staring at what, he didn't know. Her shoulders lifted in a deep sigh, and he could hear it when she let it out.

"Jia Chung?" His voice came out deeper than he'd heard from himself in days. It was the voice he used as a New York lawyer. Serious and stern. Henry only just realized how he'd somehow softened how he spoke while he'd been here.

She lifted her hand and wiped at her eyes before she looked slightly back over her shoulder. "Yup, that's me. Wild, huh? Guess we probably should have started with the exchange of names with that first drink. Could have spared ourselves all of this." Jia waved her hand in the air as if trying to figure out how much *this* entailed. She wiped away another tear from her cheek. "I'm not upset, I promise. I think I'm just in shock, maybe, and that's why I'm crying? I'm still not even sure I can wrap my head around what's going on."

"Me neither," he said. God, Henry hated tears. He usually found them manipulative, people using emotions to impact an outcome. He himself never cried. He refused.

But there was something so broken about the woman in front of him, like a scared and injured animal, that haunted him.

Henry's body had the odd compulsion to step forward, reach out to her, offer her comfort. But that wasn't something Henry did for anyone . . . ever. He needed to understand what was so upsetting to her. Was it coming face-to-face with the person who'd fired her? Or was it that she was caught hiding here where she shouldn't be?

So he stayed where he was, far enough away to not touch her. The safe zone. Because all Henry really knew of Jia Chung was that she pissed someone off and couldn't keep her job. That she wore crazy clothes because she couldn't get her luggage. That she was loud and wacky and couldn't be serious. That she was ticklish at the base of her neck, moaned at the touch of her hip, asked for what she wanted and generously gave in return.

She turned around and faced him, eyes red-rimmed, cheeks flushed, wearing absurd floral polyester pants and a white polo shirt. She was ridiculous. She was stunning. He was angry that he even took notice.

"Well, it's official. The Universe hates me," she said, forcing a smile.

"I'm sorry, what?"

"I mean, this would only happen to me. I am such a disaster." She laughed, throwing up her hands and shook her head.

"It's a freak coincidence. I guess as far as randomness goes, it could have happened to anyone," he said.

Or maybe it wasn't. She couldn't possibly have targeted him in some way and schemed to be here the same time Henry was, right? Had he read too many thrillers? Or was he just being cynical and refused to believe that someone was just a nice person doing kind things for people who needed it most? He couldn't be sure.

"I don't know. I kind of feel like the choices we make lead us to where we are. I chose to celebrate what would be my pending termination the night before. I chose to sleep with a man I knew nothing about. Though, I have to say I did clock you as a lawyer that night." She forced a smile. "I fucked up somehow at work, leading to me getting fired." She shook her head as if she still couldn't believe that had happened. "I fled to my grandma's to hide from my parents and from life and from consequences—" she lifted her eyes to meet his "—and ran into the one person who could bring me back to reality."

"I . . . I don't know what to say to that."

She held his gaze, assessing him, searching for something. He didn't know what it was about this woman. But her judgment, or whatever it was she was trying to conclude about Henry, bothered him, like he could hear her taunting him in his mind. *How could you fire me so easily, overlooking your own questions and doubts? Did you ever wonder what happened to the person whose life you turned upside down by signing those papers? Do you really think I'm capable of running some sort of grift here?*

"So you're Henry J. Shin, Esquire," she said.

It was a simple statement, but each word felt like an accusation.

It was the way she said his name that unraveled him. As if he'd heard the gavel pound in his head, judgment served. In the simplicity of how people saw things here, Henry was a bad person, doing bad things. And for once in his life, he experienced shame.

The first wave of pain radiated in his chest. He quickly turned to walk away. He needed to go back to Dennis's house, back to New York in fact, as soon as he could. He didn't need this bullshit. The sharp, piercing pain grew stronger. His vision blurred along the edges. He needed to get out of here before the panic attack fully hit.

As he found his way to the side gate to escape, he thought he heard her say, "Henry, are you okay?" And then, even dimmer, "I'm sorry."

He made it to Dennis's house and to the bathroom before throwing up in the toilet. He sat with his back against the wall, head between his knees, trying to breathe through it. When the pain subsided, he managed to stand and find his medication, swallowing two pills down dry. He crawled into his bed and slept.

The bright light felt like it came straight through the window and pierced Henry's skull. He'd forgotten to close the blinds when he passed out last night and the morning sun announced the start of a new day. His body ached all over, and a fog felt like it took residence around his brain. He'd slept through the night. His anxiety meds did that to him. He hated it.

He looked for his phone. It was plugged into the charger on his nightstand next to a glass of water and a bottle of Tylenol. His bedroom door was ajar. Dennis must have checked in on him last night.

He took a deep breath and decided to rip off the Band-Aid. He threw the covers off, swung his legs over the bed, planted his feet, and stood. He wobbled a bit, but there was no dizziness, no stomach issues, and best of all, his chest felt fine. It was almost as if he'd been drunk last night. That's what feeling things would do to you. To Henry, at least. Never again.

He tucked any sign of emotions back into his hardened heart and locked it up.

He went to the bathroom and washed up before going out to face Dennis and what were sure to be a barrage of questions about last night. Shit, Henry had probably ruined Dennis's welcome party. Nope, no guilt or shame. Lock it up. A memory of Jia Chung's face flashed through his mind. But he quickly tamped it down and put it behind the iron door. Fuck all of this.

Henry needed to get Dennis settled and go home. As soon as he could.

He heard the voices as he turned the corner. Sitting at the kitchen table were Dennis and Mimi.

"Good morning, Hank," Dennis said with a smile. No lifted brows, no curiosity in his voice.

"Hi, Henry. Want some coffee?" Mimi stood up and walked past Henry, gently squeezing his arm, as she reached up and grabbed a mug. She pulled out a Keurig pod and started the brew. "How do you take it?" she asked.

"Um, black, please."

"Mimi came over to bring some leftovers from the party and to drop this off." Dennis passed a piece of paper over to Henry.

CALENDAR OF EVENTS, it read. There was something in almost every box. Walking Club. Gardening Club. Pool Party. Spicy Book Club. Mystery Book Club. Sewing Club. Chair Yoga. Zumba.

"Pretty cool, huh?" Dennis said. "Jia did all of this. Can you believe it?"

"She's only been here a couple weeks and got right to work," Mimi said. "She's on FYA, as the young folks say these days."

"She's amazing. An angel," Dennis said.

"And to think, she's had such a hard time in New York. Hasn't quite found her purpose out there yet. Her parents are kinda tough on her, and I think it makes her uncertain of herself. But she gets out here and lets the desert work its magic on her. Suddenly she's transforming a whole community."

Henry thought about how the people at Bakerson's, himself included, thought and spoke about Jia. *Failure. Incompetent. Difficult.* Other than Genevieve, no one bothered to say anything nice about her or in defense of her. She added no value to the company by being a good person.

Not your business, he reminded himself.

Plus, something about Jia had sent Henry into a panic attack last night. And that was bad news. He needed to avoid her at all costs while he was here.

"Looks great, Granddad. But remember, you can't push yourself too hard. You just had your hip replaced not too long ago."

"It's been almost a year now, Hank."

Had it really been that long? "Well, you can't be putting too much stress on your heart or your lungs either. Take it easy."

"Nothing wrong with my heart or lungs," Dennis muttered.

"You just don't have to do every single thing on here is all I'm saying." Henry lifted the calendar in question and tossed it back on the table. Henry hated the way his voice sounded. He hated the sudden quiet in the kitchen. Most of all, he hated being here having to worry about this.

He turned the key in his mind and locked it.

11

Jia leaned into the door, using her pinkie to pull the handle while shoving her foot in and then her hip to push her way through. Her hands were currently full with a hazelnut latte with sweetener and extra cream and a matcha latte with oat milk she'd brought for Gladys and herself.

She was meeting with Gladys to review the entire events calendar and discuss where she might need to request funding, what liabilities they needed to consider, and what attendance maximums they should put on each. Jia hadn't thought of any of these details until Mimi and Gladys had pointed them out. She was so relieved for their direction because if she was going to do this, she wanted to do it right. She was learning so much from everyone.

Needless to say, the calendar had caused quite a buzz among the residents. Everyone was excited to go to everything. Jia had to make sure that people were being responsible in how they were spending their time and exerting their energy. She didn't want people pushing themselves too hard.

"This one's for you, and this one's for me," Jia said, handing Gladys her coffee.

"Oooh, where's this from? Is there another new coffee place downtown?" she asked.

There likely was, considering how quickly businesses were opening along the main strip especially. "Nope, these are special for Sunset Hills residents only."

Gladys raised an eyebrow in question.

"I was walking past Gordon's place on the way here, and you'll never guess what. He actually did it—he set up a coffee cart in his driveway." Jia had been so startled but thrilled when she saw it.

The people here amazed Jia. They were experienced in ways only time and years could make you. They were determined in ways only knowing how to overcome hardship could teach you.

Jia had come to know Gordon as one of the gentlemen who played bridge on Tuesdays. And he'd mentioned to her that when he'd lost his wife a couple years back, he was in a bit of a brokenhearted rut. Then one day, he decided he was ready to start the new chapter. He wanted a job. But no one was going to hire him at sixty-eight years old. So he passed his time teaching himself how to make froufrou coffee drinks from some viral barista on YouTube.

He'd invited Jia for a tasting, and it was one of the best things she'd ever put in her mouth. She told him so and encouraged him to open his own coffee business right there in the neighborhood.

He'd asked Louis from two streets over, who had formerly

been a carpenter, to help him build the cart stand on wheels. And this morning, he rolled it out onto his driveway and waited for neighbors to walk by. There was already a line by the time Jia had arrived.

"This is yummy. Jia, you're such a good influence on everyone here. You're kicking all our asses into gear, making dreams happen," Gladys said.

A lump formed in Jia's throat as tears welled in her eyes. "Gladys, you can't say nice things to me before I've filled up with caffeine. I'm not able to process it," she joked. She blew an air kiss to Gladys, and the two of them got to work.

Jia needed Gordon's mojo to rub off on her. She needed the strength and determination of all the residents here to motivate her. She needed to believe that she could pick up the pieces and make something of her life like many of them at The Sunset had done time and again in their lives. She needed a Jia 2.0.

And she had two weeks to do it or she'd be back under her parents' control.

A waft of hot air entered the office as the front door of the community center opened.

Jia looked over her shoulder midsip to see the large presence of the very handsome Matthew, the guy from the airport, the grocery store, and now, curiously, the Sunset Hills Community Center. He stood there in linen trousers, perfectly creased down the center, and a thin navy silk polo shirt. He looked expensive. And irresistible.

When he saw Jia, his face spread into a very sexy smile.

An audible intake of breath followed by a croaky *Oh* coming from Gladys snapped Jia out of her own stupor.

"Hey, there. What brings you to this neck of the woods?" Jia greeted him.

"Well, I didn't expect to see you this morning. It's a nice surprise. Starting my day off on the right foot," Matthew said.

"Should I leave you two alone and close the blinds on the way out?" Gladys asked.

"Gladys," Jia said with mock offense.

"Actually, I'm here to see Gladys, I think. Hello, I'm Matthew Singleton," he said, reaching around Jia and over the desk to offer his hand to Gladys. Gladys looked down at the very large hand presented to her. Jia remembered seeing that same hand at the airport baggage-claim carousel. It was definitely something to behold.

"Me? I can't imagine there's anything I could help you with that Jia wouldn't be better at," Gladys said with a wink.

Matthew's cheeks pinkened. Cute.

"Well, I was told to come to you to get a parcel map of the community," Matthew explained.

"Oh, that's usually reserved for residents. Is there a reason you need this, hon?" Gladys said.

"I'm actually the agent for Isabel Lennon," he answered.

"What kind of agent?" Jia asked.

"A real estate agent."

"Isabel is moving?" Gladys and Jia asked at the same time.

"I don't know all the details," Matthew said, "but my assumption is she's going into some kind of assisted-living facility. At least that's what her family tells me."

"Well, that's too bad," Gladys said.

"No, actually, that sucks," Jia said.

"Jia, now watch that language in front of our visitors," Gladys reprimanded her.

"But she was doing so well after her surgery. Her mobility

was getting better. And she's still smart as a tack." Jia let out a frustrated sigh. "Why would she need to be moved?"

Matthew lifted his hands. "I don't know all the details. I'm so sorry. I was just brought in to help facilitate the selling of her property."

Jia's shoulders dropped. "Sorry. I didn't mean to yell at you. It's just that I get attached easily. And usually when it's time to move, it's not for the best reasons. I didn't realize there was something to be concerned about with Isabel." Jia hated that she'd missed the signs.

"No, I get that. I'm sorry. I didn't mean to upset either of you," Matthew said.

"No, no, dear, you're fine. And I will get you that map. It will take me a bit to pull it out of the files. Do you have a fax machine I can send it to?" Gladys asked.

"Would you be able to email it to me?"

Gladys looked to Jia, brows raised in question.

"Yes, we can do that. I'll show you how," Jia answered.

"Great, here's my business card. You can email me right there." Matthew pointed to the email address.

"Sure thing, hon. Will do," Gladys said.

"Okay, well, I'm taking off. See you later, Gladys," Jia said. "Bye, Matthew," she added.

"Jia, hold up, I'll walk out with you. Thanks for your time, Gladys," Matthew said.

"You bet," she said.

Matthew held the door open as Jia walked through.

It wasn't the most unbearable day Jia had encountered, but it was still most definitely hot. Jia took off the hand-knit cardigan she'd found in the community center's lost and found last week and wrapped it around her waist as she walked toward her home. The jumpsuit she was wearing was technically a pajama onesie, but she'd cut the legs down to shorts and the sleeves off to make a cute romper with little flowers on it. At this rate, by the time she actually went to pick up her lost and now-found luggage, she'd be heading back to New York.

Oddly, Jia was finding she didn't miss her own stuff. Not like she thought she would.

"My car is parked in the lot," Matthew said. "Need a ride home?"

"Thanks for the offer, but I like walking. I like to be able to walk past everyone's home, just making sure everyone's okay, saying hello."

"Wow. You've really made yourself at home here in short order. Seems you're taking care of everyone," he said.

"No, hardly. They're the ones that take care of me. This has been a soft place for me to land for a little bit." She didn't know why she was admitting this to him. But it was all true.

"That's great," he said. "Okay, well . . ." Matthew stood by his car fiddling with his keys. It was the first time she'd seen him seem uncertain about anything. "Hey, do you think you would wanna grab a drink or dinner sometime?"

Jia very much liked the sound of that. She'd barely stepped out of the neighborhood the entire time she'd been here other than to pick up coffee. "Oh, uh, yeah, sure. That sounds fun."

"How about tonight? Is it too short notice?" he asked.

"Oh, you mean with my big social plans here at The Sunset?" She smiled and he laughed. "Tonight works. But can we make it after seven?" Jia liked to watch the sunset around seven, and she hated to miss it even one night.

"Eight o'clock?" Matthew suggested.

"Sounds perfect. See you then," Jia said.

* * *

The Del Rey was a new tapas restaurant bar in the Villa Royale hotel. With Palm Springs's quickly changing landscape, new bars, renovated hotels, and swarms of visitors looking for the hottest thing, it was sometimes hard to determine which would stick. But Jia had heard good things about this place from the locals around town. And that made her have some hope. So when Matthew suggested they meet there, she was in. It was time to let the old Jia out, wherever the night would take her.

Jia opened Mimi's guest closet and rummaged through the treasures. She'd already set aside two bins full of vintage clothes she knew would get a lot of interest when she was ready to plan the sale. That was next on her list of things to do.

Mimi helped her pick out the vintage Chanel lime-green plaid sleeveless minidress that she paired with pink kitten heels her grandma had stored away in the back of the closet as they were now *much too high* for her to wear anymore. This might have been too bright a combo even for Jia back in New York. But in Palm Springs, she could pull it off. Jia wore her long thick black hair in heatless curls. Though, it would be up in a top knot before she finished her first drink, guaranteed.

They labeled the outfit *geek chic*, high-fived each other for a job well done, and sent Jia off in an Uber that her grandmother insisted on getting for her instead of letting a complete stranger come and pick her up from their home. Mimi also slipped her two twenty-dollar bills in case Matthew ended up being a cad and not paying for their date. She really thought of everything.

Jia wanted to do something to thank Mimi for being so generous to her both in opportunity and financially. She tried not to be a burden, not to cost Mimi much, while she stayed here. But Mimi insisted on spoiling her whenever she could. Jia decided that tomorrow, she'd offer to color her grandmother's grays. It was overdue and something Jia could help Mimi cross off her to-do list.

Matthew was in a white linen button-down with jeans and leather flip-flops. His hair was mussed, and the whole vibe was *vacation sexy*, even though Jia knew he was here on business.

"Still haven't picked up your luggage, I see," Matthew said, as he leaned in and gave Jia a kiss on the cheek in greeting.

There was something about the comment and the observation that rubbed Jia the wrong way. It felt . . . judgmental in a way that she hadn't felt since she'd left New York and been in the desert. She shrugged it off. "I like shopping my grandmother's closet. She's got great style." Jia smiled and tried to make it a real one.

Truth was Jia wasn't sure why she hadn't gone to get her stuff. The airport was close, her stuff right there. Jia had often thought of fashion as her armor, protecting her soft center with a loud and bold exterior. But she now wondered if, in fact, it hadn't been more a disguise. Or a way to tell people that she knew they made fun of her for being loud and overly enthusiastic and odd. Maybe she dressed up that side of her to seem like she didn't care.

Dressing in Mimi's clothes may have started out feeling a bit like a challenge. But she'd come to really love not caring as much about what she wore where or how she wore it. No one else had noticed up until this point. And frankly, Mimi did have fantastic taste in fashion.

Matthew pulled out the chair for Jia, and she took her seat.

"The happy hour here is great," Matthew said, changing the subject. He'd mentioned the same thing to her when they'd first crossed paths at the airport. Jia wondered if it was a practiced line he used often.

He raised his hand to get the server's attention, and they ordered one of each of the things off the shared-bites menu. Jia got herself a glass of sauvignon blanc, and Matthew ordered a beer.

"So you're a real estate agent?" Jia asked.

"I am. I specialize in homes in this area," Matthew replied.

"Palm Springs?"

"Specifically North Palm Springs. I target older communities, investment opportunities," he clarified.

Jia thought about some of the homes recently sold at The Sunset and the people displaced from them. There was a discomfort brewing in the back of her mind about Matthew's target customer. *Target* being the word she just couldn't seem to get past. She shifted her weight in her seat, trying to get comfortable.

"I like helping older people, seniors who don't have anyone there to advise them." Matthew smiled at her warmly, and though the words were the right ones and the delivery seemingly earnest, Jia couldn't escape a gut feeling that something was off.

"That's really nice of you," she said.

"My grandmother passed a couple years ago, and we were really close. I think about how important it was to her to get all her assets in order so that everyone would be taken care of. I hated that she had this on her mind, and I just want to make those kinds of decisions easier for people in their last years," he explained.

Okay, so maybe he wasn't an asshole after all. Maybe his intentions were good.

"I'm so sorry for your loss. But I'm sure your grandmother was grateful that you were there for her. My grandmother is the most important person in the world to me, so I understand how you feel," she said.

"That's great that you're close," he said. "You seem close to a lot of the folks there."

"My parents, well, they have very different ideas of what life should look like for me . . . and my grandmother. We're kinda living together in solidarity and rebellion. Everyone else, they're my cheerleaders," she said.

Matthew laughed in response. "You two make quite the team."

"We do. In fact, I feel a bit like the team mascot for a lot of the residents. Betty, Gladys, Mildred, Gordon, Starla . . ." Jia thought about so many of the neighbors who she had grown to love, especially the ones without families actively involved in their lives.

"I'm actually helping Starla sell her home," Matthew said.

"What? Starla's moving too? This is all so . . . sudden," Jia said, shocked. "They used to go years between people leaving The Sunset." Jia hated the reasons why that was so. People usually didn't leave until they'd passed on or could no longer live alone. But it seemed more people were leaving prematurely these days.

"Property values are skyrocketing in the desert. A lot of people from LA and San Diego are looking for weekend and vacation homes they can renovate. The houses at The Sunset have the best value because they're older and primed for a flip. My clientele are in the fifty-five- to sixty-year-old demographic. It used to be you didn't move into senior communities until well into your sunset years." He winked at his play on words. "But now people much younger are finding they can afford homes in neighborhoods like Sunset Hills. By rotating the demographic, I'm really helping the older residents set themselves up financially to leave their families quite a healthy inheritance." He squeezed her hand, and she felt trapped. Jia pulled hers away, masking the move by grabbing her wineglass and downing half of it.

She didn't like any of this even one bit. Jia knew she was extra protective of the residents at The Sunset. But just because she didn't agree with some of their choices didn't mean she would question any of their abilities to make them. As long as the choice was still theirs to make.

She put on her best smile and finished her wine, raising her hand to signal to their server she'd like another.

By the end of the evening, Jia was nicely buzzed with a belly full of yummy bites. She and Matthew had switched topics of conversation, and she found him to be quite hilarious and spirited when they started talking about *Survivor* and *The Real Housewives*, he believing Beverly Hills the best city while Jia knew without a doubt that Salt Lake City was superior.

Was she warm in other places besides her belly? Not really. Matthew was nice and charming, but she didn't feel an attraction there. Two weeks ago, she might have considered hooking up with him if he'd offered. But for some reason now, she was just looking forward to getting into her pajamas and being in bed by ten.

"Will you excuse me? Gonna go to the ladies' room," Jia said. She got up and walked around the corner down the hallway toward the restrooms. The lighting was dimmer back there, and Jia found herself almost going in the wrong door. That would have been embarrassing. As she turned to change direction, a hand grabbed her arm.

She was startled but not frightened. If this had been New York, she would likely have been on higher alert. Instead, she turned toward the man to see why he'd stopped her.

"Can I help you—"

But when Jia looked up, it was Henry there holding her.

And by the look on his face, he was not happy.

12

"Can I help you—"

Jia's eyes widened in surprise. There was a hint of fear. She looked down at the hand wrapped around her arm. Henry followed her line of sight and considered what this must look like to her.

Shit, he'd grabbed a woman in a dark hallway like an idiot. He quickly dropped his hand. "Sorry," he said.

"Henry?" She composed herself. "What are you doing here?"

Henry didn't actually know why he stopped in at the Del Rey for a drink. It wasn't like he was even in the mood for being social. He just needed to get out of the Sunset Hills bubble and find a place that reminded him of New York. Reminded him that he was a high-powered corporate attorney. That he dealt in facts. That a hardened heart had served him well. It was like everything, and everyone, at The Sunset, from his grandfather's constant encouraging words, the neighbors' generosity of spirit, and one young woman's bright eyes, warm smile, and best intentions had thrown him off his game. He was uncomfortable.

And he needed space away from his grandfather for even just an hour to prepare himself for a time when he'd have to leave Dennis on his own and trust that he'd be able to take care of himself.

Henry had started to forget himself in the short time he'd been out in the desert. So that was why he'd gone looking for a trendy bar with expensive alcohol and glitzy people he cared nothing about.

But if he had known he'd run into them, he definitely wouldn't have come.

"What are *you* doing here?" He lobbed the question back to Jia because he needed to know. What was Jia Chung doing here with that guy?

As far as Henry was concerned, the jury was still out on Jia. He'd let go of his suspicion that she was in the desert for something nefarious. It seemed unlikely she was running some kind of grift trying to swindle the elderly residents of Sunset Hills. She was way too kind and caring with everyone, and no one was that good an actor. Plus, she'd have to be a real asshole to scam older people. His parents were proof positive of that. And in his gut, he knew she wasn't. She was clearly beloved by the community, and from what he'd seen, she really was just a good person.

But Matthew Singleton? Henry had firsthand knowledge that he was bad news. Maybe not illegal in their direct dealings, but borderline unethical and most definitely predatory. And when Henry saw the real estate snake, the one who'd tried to pull one over on Dennis when he'd sold his old house and bought the new one, out on what looked to be a real cozy date with Jia, it triggered something in him.

"I'm having drinks, um, with a friend." She looked over his shoulder back out toward the bar area.

"You have bad taste in friends," Henry said.

Her eyes snapped back to his.

"What's that supposed to mean?" Her brows furrowed together like she was seriously offended by this statement. "My best friend, Lizzy, you met her at Willow that night we, uh, you know—" Jia waved her hand between the two of them, apparently encouraging Henry to finish the statement in his own head "—she's amazing. She's loyal and funny and successful and badass. And Mimi, well, she's the kindest soul in the whole world. And . . ."

Oh god, was this woman going to list all of her friends and defend their honor by telling Henry every single one of their positive traits?

"Well, beyond those two, I don't really have any other friends. Maybe Gladys, I suppose. And Betty and Sally Mae. Is that weird that most all my friends are in their eighties?"

"Jia," Henry said, trying to get her attention back to the topic at hand. "How do you know this guy?"

"Matthew?"

Henry very much did not like the way his name sounded coming from her lips.

"Snake," he said.

"I mean, I barely know him at all. So maybe referring to him as a *friend* is being generous. More like an *acquaintance*? We've just run into each other around town a few times, and he asked me out. But now, well, he's got business to do at The Sunset." The corners of her mouth turned down, and Henry's hackles rose.

"What kind of business?"

"I don't know if I'm supposed to say. In fact, I'm not sure he was supposed to share any of it with me either. Are there, like, nondisclosures you have to sign in real estate? It just . . . Never mind."

"Jia." How many times had he said her name? Her attention span was minuscule, and he needed to bring her back to the present conversation. He stepped forward, closer, closing off the rest of the world, blocking any competition for her attention, their bodies almost touching, the heat radiating off each of them and mingling in between. The nearness forced her to lean against the wall. She lifted her eyes up to meet his.

He barely knew Jia Chung, and who she dated should have been none of his business. But it enraged him that she was here with this guy. Maybe he was a little jealous seeing her enjoying herself with him. Guys like Matthew Singleton didn't deserve easy nights out on the town with women like Jia. And this all mattered to him more than it should. It mattered enough for him to ignore every alarm bell going off in his head in this moment and to let Jia know exactly how he felt. He did not want them together. At all.

"Listen to me," Henry said, lowering his voice. "That guy is bad news. Stay away from him."

"That's not very nice," she whispered. "What if someone said you were bad news?"

His eyes lowered to her lips. The tip of her tongue peeked out to lick her bottom one.

He leaned in closer to whisper in her ear. "It shouldn't be a surprise to you, but no one has ever accused me of being nice," he said, "and I am most definitely bad news." He watched the pulse point in her neck quicken. He wanted to lick her there.

But he pulled back and stepped away from her.

Everything about this was a bad idea.

"I mean it, Jia." Henry pointed his finger at her. "Stay away from Matthew Singleton. He's exactly the type of person that would try to take advantage of someone like you."

"Someone like me? What's that supposed to mean?"

Someone soft. Kind. Easily taken advantage of. Easily eliminated by the signature of a stranger and the whim of a high-powered executive. "You're in over your head," he said.

But maybe it was Henry who was the one in over his.

He soaked in one last look before turning and walking away back to the bar, leaving her behind.

"I can take care of myself," she said after him as he walked away.

God, he wished that were true. And he was angry at himself for caring either way.

Henry signaled the bartender and asked for his check. He'd come for a drink to try to get away and was leaving more entrenched in this weird desert life than ever before.

He walked past Jia and Matthew's table on his way out. He tried to keep his gaze on the door. He didn't want to see that snake's swarmy face and Jia's big, innocent eyes buying into all the shit being spewed at her.

He would ask himself a hundred times on the short drive home why he even cared. But for now, he bit down, clenching his jaw, willing himself to keep walking.

Out of the corner of his eye he saw Jia's head turn, watching him as he passed. He caved and looked. He was met with a small smile and almost imperceptible nod.

He nodded back and kept walking.

"Do you know him?"

Henry heard the question asked between the two behind him.

"I do. He's a friend," she said in response.

The words caught Henry off guard. A one-night stand, yes. A work foe, most certainly. But a friend? Henry didn't have friends. He didn't want friends. Yet there was something about those words coming from Jia that made him wonder if maybe he actually did.

An unfamiliar feeling arose in his chest. He braced for the tight piercing of a panic attack. What he experienced instead was a warmth bubbling up inside him. And he wasn't sure which would end up hurting more.

13

"So did you have a nice time?"

Jia had a spoonful of Cheerios halfway to her mouth when her grandmother walked into the kitchen. She'd gotten home well past Mimi's bedtime and had quietly snuck in and put herself to bed shortly thereafter. But Jia couldn't sleep. She'd been playing the date over and over in her mind. Not so much the date itself but the run-in with Henry. The heat in his warning to stay away from Matthew. The heat from his body as he'd made his wishes known.

The look on Henry's face when he'd walked past her and out the door.

Was he mad at her? She couldn't think of one thing she'd done to possibly make him upset. But he was clearly irritated last night. He wasn't jealous, was he? No, it couldn't be that. And it bothered her. Jia really didn't like it when someone took issue with her. Maybe she could reach out and make it right.

She shook her head.

No.

Jia was a grown woman and could decide who to spend time with. What was with that warning? And shouldn't she be the one who was irritated with him? He'd fired her, and now he was here as a reminder that she was a failure at life. She got here first. She should be the one that was mad. She didn't even get the chance to march out of the restaurant with a sour look on *her* face.

"Jia? Honey?"

Jia looked up from her Cheerios and saw her grandmother staring back at her.

"Oh, sorry, Grandma. I was spacing out," Jia said.

"So how was the date?" she asked again.

"Oh my god, Mimi, we have to go back to the Del Rey. The food was incredible. It's right up your alley. And the vibes were immaculate. I had this cocktail—" Jia stopped. Did she have that cocktail before she went to the bathroom and ran into Henry? Or was it the one she had at the end of the night when Henry was leaving the restaurant and walked right past her?

"What's with the scrunched nose? The cocktail wasn't good?" Mimi asked.

Jia shook herself out of her memory. "Oh, no. The cocktail was amazing! But Henry Shin was there. And he was being all macho-caveman telling me to be careful. And I was like, what business is it of yours? And he was like, *growl* and *grunt*. And he said I had bad friends! Can you believe that? Well, he didn't exactly say those words, so maybe I won't put that on him. But still."

Mimi sat there, staring at her granddaughter, nodding her head as if totally understanding where she was coming from. Yup, Mimi and Jia were of the same cloth. She probably felt the same way about Henry.

"Jia, honey, I've been meaning to ask you this. And you know I don't like to pry."

Jia slid her gaze over to her grandmother. "Since when have you not liked to pry, Grandmother? I seem to recall you've been prying about details in my life and everyone else's for as long as I've been alive. And don't get me wrong, I love that about you. It's because you care. And I like to believe I inherited this very trait from you as well," she said.

"Well, that may be the case. And you're right, I care. So tell me right now why this young man has gotten so far under your skin. What did he do?"

"What young man?" Jia asked. "Oh, Matthew? I mean, he's not under my skin exactly. He did say something that kind of raised a red flag last night. And I don't know how I feel about him helping people sell their homes . . ." Jia wondered if Matthew had sold the home that Dennis had moved into. Is that how Henry knew Matthew? Maybe Henry was just projecting his bad feelings about Matthew onto her. Okay, this made her feel a little bit better.

"Not Matthew, my dear. Dennis's grandson, Hank," Mimi clarified.

"Henry," Jia corrected her. She could never see him as Hank again. She could barely see him as anything other than Henry J. Shin, Esquire. Jia was so preoccupied by the fact that he was here this summer—what were the odds?—that she didn't even realize she'd just googled *Esquire* on her phone to see why lawyers used those letters in the first place.

"Exactly," her grandmother said, bringing her out of her thoughts.

Jia raised her head from her phone. Mimi's left eyebrow lifted high to her forehead. Jia's shoulders dropped as she conceded.

"Urgh," she let out. "I don't know that it's even worth going over. It's just, he confuses me is all."

The corner of her grandmother's mouth lifted. Jia could see where her mind was going. It was time to set her grandmother's errant thoughts and assumptions straight. Let her know how she and Henry were acquainted. Jia couldn't have her thinking otherwise.

"Okay, Mimi, here's the tea." Jia grabbed both of Mimi's hands and held them so that she'd be braced for the news. "Henry and I know each other . . . from before Dennis moved to Sunset Hills," Jia admitted.

Her grandma stared at Jia for a second, examining her the way that she did when she thought she needed to be reading between the lines. She nodded once, as if coming to a conclusion. "Wait one second," she said, holding up a finger while walking to the back slider door.

"Mildred," she called out to the house to the left of them.

"Yeah?" a voice called back.

"Gather the ladies and meet at the bench in ten," Mimi instructed.

"I'm in my bathrobe. Can we make it twenty?"

"Ten minutes. No one's paying any attention to an eighty-year-old woman walking around in a bathrobe," she said.

She went back into the house.

"Did you just call the troops in? Grandma, I don't want this to be a big Sunset Hills ordeal. I don't want everyone gossiping about it," Jia said.

"If you're this torn up about a boy, especially one that we know personally, we need the troops, my dear. We've got hundreds of years of heartache and wisdom between us. We'll get you through this."

"Grandma, you've got this all wrong. I don't have feelings for Henry other than maybe annoyance and irritation," Jia protested.

"And that's exactly why we need the big guns."

Ten minutes later, five women were gathered at the northwest corner of the neighborhood park, where a bench dedicated to Mr. Charles K. Lee sat beneath a huge palm tree. Jia being the youngest among them by fifty years, she allowed two of them to sit, while her grandmother sat in a foldable camping chair she'd made Jia bring with them, and Betty rolled up in her electric scooter.

Mildred did indeed show up in her bathrobe, complete with fuzzy slippers and a bonnet over her curlers.

"What's the emergency, Mimi? Mildred said it was a *code red*. I was about to drink my morning Smooth Move tea," Betty announced.

"Oh, Betty, I'm so sorry we interrupted teatime. It's not actually an emergency," Jia said.

"Jia says Henry irritates her," Mimi said.

The women all nodded in unison.

"So, how is he in the sack?" Gladys asked.

"Gladys!" Jia was shocked at the forwardness of these women. "I cannot disclose that information," she said.

All eyes widened in shock. Jia slapped her hand over her mouth. "I mean, not that I've slept with him or anything. But if I had, a lady never sleeps and tells. At least not to her grandmother and her friends. Oh god."

The women all nodded at Jia with knowing smiles.

"It was just a matter of time, honey. You're the only two young ones here. You're both lookers. And he makes you feisty. That's the spark," Mimi explained.

"Well, just to clarify, it happened before either of us got here," Jia admitted.

"Well, all right then. Tell us everything, hon. Was it mind-blowing? Did he give you the big O? Did you have a crush on him? Or was it a wham-bam-thank-you-ma'am kind of night just to get it out of your system? You don't have to love him to have sex with him. We all know that's how it works these days," Betty said.

Jia's mouth dropped open, and her cheeks warmed to a cherry pink. How did Betty understand her sex life better than Jia herself?

"You ladies are a lot looser than I realized," Jia joked.

"Please, have you seen him jogging in the morning? I went out to my driveway to get the morning paper just to watch him go by in his flimsy shorts with his shirt off. And I don't actually even get the paper delivered anymore," Mildred admitted.

"It is definitely a sight," Jia had to agree. "I don't have to like the man to admire what he's got."

"He's blessed in all the ways."

The ladies all giggled.

Jia wasn't sure how she felt having this conversation with her grandmother and her friends. But just thinking of how Henry would likely be mortified by it brought her a little bit of joy.

"You ladies are wonderful, and I love you all. Thank you for the advice. But there really isn't a problem. It's more of an inconvenience. A coincidence. An annoyance."

"That's a lot of *-nce*s," Betty said. "In my experience, the more a woman protests with big vocabulary, the more likely it is she's trying to convince herself she's not interested."

Jia needed to get the women up to speed before they started planning some rendezvous between her and Henry. "Okay. So remember how I got fired from my job and escaped the city to come hang with Mimi to figure my life out?"

They all nodded. It was well-known around The Sunset that Jia was in hiding from her reality and they were to handle her with the softest gloves possible. Maybe that was why they all showed up to the stuff she planned for them and were so effusive and complimentary to her about her organizational skills. Jia liked to believe it was more than that, though. She hoped it was because they were all enjoying themselves as much as she was.

"Well, he was the one who fired me from my job back in New York. Technically, I guess, Genevieve in HR fired me. But Henry's name was the signature that sealed the deal."

Silence.

Jia would let that soak in. She'd let them realize that she and Henry were fated to be against each other. And maybe that made it okay for him to be mad at her. And for her to be mad at him back . . . a little. She'd give them a sec to change their tune.

"Well, praise be," Mimi said.

"Good boy," Betty chimed in.

"He's good-looking *and* has sense?" Gladys added.

"I bet his handwriting is all stern and hot and demanding," Mildred said.

What did demanding handwriting even look like?

"Hey, wait a minute. You're all supposed to be on my side." Jia pouted, feelings hurt.

"We are. And this guy saved you from a miserable job that you hated and that didn't treat you right," Mimi said, rubbing Jia's back from her chair.

"He did you a favor. And basically ended up giving us at The Sunset a gift," Betty said, reaching her hand out and grabbing Jia's. "You."

Jia was shocked at their responses. A tear welled up in her right eye. This was equal parts sweet and kind of twisted. They celebrated a guy who fired her because she hated her job? That was weird.

"Don't give him too much credit. He wasn't actually my boss. He just signed the paperwork. I didn't even know it was him until I put two and two together at the happy hour."

"So before then, you were down to jump his bones?" Gladys asked.

"Scotch might have been involved. The expensive stuff," Jia answered.

"Well, I'm sure he had a good reason for signing the paperwork. At least he wasn't the creepy boss. That makes me feel better about him," Mildred said.

"And we should all be so lucky to find a man who knows how to fire us up," Gladys added. "He really presses your buttons. And girl, that's a gift."

"No need to look deeper than we have to. Henry and I have a weird history. And because of it, it's hard to know how to act around him is all. So maybe it's best we just avoid each other for the time that we both have left here. And then he'll be gone. Poof. No longer to be seen." She shrugged her shoulder. "Anyways, ladies, the sun's getting higher. Let's get you all indoors before it's too hot. How about I make us all breakfast? Acai bowls?"

"Sure, honey. But can you make your blueberry pancakes instead? I love those," Betty said.

"You betcha," Jia said. She turned to start the walk back home.

"We'll be right behind you, love," Mimi said, waving her hand to encourage her on.

When she was a few steps ahead, Mimi turned to the ladies

and tapped her right shoulder two times, rubbed her nose, and pulled her left ear three times. She ended the pattern with a snap and a nod.

The ladies all snapped and nodded back in response.

The signal was put out there, and they all knew what they were going to do.

They were going to make sure these two young lovebirds (shoulder taps) did the nasty (nose rub) within three days (ear pulls). If nothing else, the people at Sunset Hills were romantics. They believed in true love. And maybe these two just needed a little push in the right direction.

Operation Hookup had begun, and the troops had been activated.

14

Henry had just returned from his morning run. He thought getting his workout in before eight o'clock would be enough to beat the heat. But with the sun already bearing down on the desert neighborhood, he was dripping in sweat. He reached for the door just as it opened from the other side.

Standing in the doorway was his grandfather in a green tracksuit that looked about twenty years old and a bit too snug in the belly.

"Granddad? Where you going?" Henry said. He took a quick look around, taking stock of the order in the house. His grandfather's walker was off by the back door. The TV was still on, but Henry believed that might be intentional.

"Just gonna go out for a bit. I left the cereal box out on the counter. Eat yourself some breakfast, and I'll be right back." His voice was a bit too controlled. But Henry could tell from the ghost of a smile on his granddad's face that he was excited.

"Off to do something fun? Someone coming to pick you

up?" Henry assumed that was the case, considering the walker being left behind.

"Nope, just gonna head over to the community center. There's a Zumba class at eight thirty."

"Zumba?"

"Yes, it's a very fun exercise where you shake your hips and dance the pounds away. It's one of the most popular new classes at The Sunset, and I wanna make sure I get a spot. So gotta walk over a little early. Catch you later, kiddo."

"I don't think that's such a good idea with your hip—"

"I'll be fine," Dennis called back as he shuffled his way down the front walkway.

"Granddad, wait," Henry called out. His grandfather was already to the sidewalk, obviously trying to hustle away from Henry. "You forgot your walker. You can't make it all the way to the community center without it."

"Sure I can, Hank. It's not that far," he insisted.

"Granddad, you're gonna walk all the way over there, do a Zumba class, and then walk all the way back? Without your walker? I don't think so."

Dennis lifted his hand to shoo him off and continued on his way.

Henry's patience was running thin.

He turned and ran inside. He grabbed the walker and quickly picked up the remote control and turned off the television. And with a tiny hesitation, doubled back to the kitchen, put the cereal box back into the cupboard, and ran outside. Henry locked the door behind him and rushed to catch up to his granddad.

"You promised me that you'd use the walker more. It's important. I don't want to get all the way back to New York and get news that you've fallen or gotten hurt. Please, for your safety and my peace of mind."

"Henry, I love you with all my heart. But I've been doing all right on my own. I love having you around, but you're a bit of a wet blanket."

Henry stopped in his tracks. So he was being a little overprotective right now. It was only because he'd seen with his own eyes how much older Dennis had gotten. If he could make things easier for him, he would. He wasn't there just yet, but Henry could see a day when he'd need a lot more help taking care of himself. And it stressed Henry out just thinking about that future. It would break Dennis's spirit if he had to be moved into a nursing home, that much he knew. He was a stubborn old goat and valued his independence more than anything. "I'm sorry, Granddad. But I'll be honest. I sometimes worry that you're not paying close enough attention to take care of yourself. You're not getting any younger. You've got to be more careful."

There. He'd said it. Dennis needed to hear it.

His granddad let out a deep sigh and dropped his shoulders. His posture suddenly looking wilted. "Fine, Henry, I'll take the walker." He stepped between the frame and used it to push himself forward. His pace significantly slowed down.

He looked and moved suddenly like a much older man.

Henry felt like shit. But he knew he was right. Better safe than sorry.

They entered the community center where the main room was already quite crowded. His granddad wasn't kidding when he said this class was popular. Henry examined the crowd. Some of the older women were in tights and leotards and had clearly got their inspiration from Jane Fonda. Others were in satiny track suits that looked more like Sue Sylvester from *Glee*. What surprised Henry was that there were a good number of men in attendance as well. If he didn't know better, he'd think there was a bit of flirting happening between many of the residents. But that was not something he wanted to be contemplating.

"Dennis, you made it!"

Mimi's voice called out from across the room as she headed toward them. Her hair was perfectly curled and coiffed as it always seemed to be, and her makeup, including the bright pink lipstick, was also all in place. Mimi wore a light blue terry-cloth set with *Juicy* written in sequins across her hoodie jacket. It was a flashy look for an octogenarian at eight thirty in the morning.

Henry was beginning to think that either he'd always had the wrong idea of how seniors dressed or the people at Sunset Hills were the outliers.

"I'm so glad you're here. And Henry, you made it too. Fun!" she said with a brightness that made Henry a little uncomfortable. Did she wake up in a good mood every day? Henry was reminded of another perpetually happy woman. Cleary it ran in the family.

Mimi gave Henry a once-over from head to toe. "Nice," she said.

Henry was still in his running shorts and tank top. He felt a little underdressed, to be honest. Not just in terms of coverage, but this was the fanciest group of exercisers he'd ever seen . . . and he lived in the Upper West Side.

"Dennis, come over here and stand next to me," Mimi suggested.

His granddad followed Mimi away, but Henry gently grabbed him by the elbow. "Don't forget your walker," he said.

"But it'll get in the way," Dennis replied.

"We can stand over here," Mimi suggested, pointing toward a corner in the back where a few of the other class participants were seated in chairs, some with their own walkers beside them.

Henry appreciated that they made room and accommodations for those who needed more help.

"Okay, okay, everyone," a very loud, very bright voice came through the sound system. "Who's ready for some ZUMBAAAA?"

He winced at the volume.

Henry scanned the room, and there standing at the front of the class, lavalier mic wrapped around her ear, in a bright pink one-piece leotard with a tutu wrapped around her waist was Jia Chung.

Of course she was teaching this class.

And what was she wearing?

"It's her old ballet outfit! Can you believe it still fits her? We found it in the back of my closet, and what with her not having her luggage, we made some adjustments, and now it's her Zumba outfit," Mimi explained as if reading Henry's mind.

"Huh," Henry said. He wasn't sure what else to say.

The music began to play overhead and the energy in the room buzzed.

"This is the start of the very best day! Who's with me?" Jia enthused over the speakers.

Cheers erupted in the room as people all stood and took their spots.

Henry wasn't sure what to do. He should leave. But he wanted to keep an eye on his granddad and make sure he wasn't pushing himself, or being pushed, into a dangerous situation.

"All right, we're going right then left, right and left, in four, three, two, one."

The crowd moved and followed her lead.

"Jia," a group of women called out. She looked over her shoulder at them as they began to point . . . in Henry's direction.

Jia's back was toward the crowd, but when she faced forward into the mirror, her eyes caught his. It wasn't hard to spot him. The entire crowd was moving.

But Henry just stood there stock still.

She narrowed her eyes at him in the mirror.

"What's the first rule of Zumba?" she called out.

"*Everybody moves*," the crowd called back, the ladies that had ratted him out to Jia answering her the loudest.

A wicked smile crossed her face.

"And when someone doesn't move?" she asked.

"*They go to the front!*" someone squealed.

"Keep it going. Step right, step left, step right, step left. In the next eight count, we're going to add a clap. In four, three, two, one!"

The room moved right and clapped. Then left and clapped. It was a basic dance. Even those sitting in chairs leaned to the right and clapped and then to the left.

Henry looked at his granddad trying to step right, but he was bound by his walker, like a cage.

"Sunseters, I spy someone not moving!" Jia called out.

"Front, front, front, front," they began to chant. Those tattlers. If Henry didn't know better, he'd suspect they were trying to make a fool of him.

But he couldn't think much more on that because, suddenly, Henry was being pushed by the crowd toward the front.

"Wait a minute, wait, oh no, I'm not going up there," he tried to refuse. But the crowd kept nudging him and pushing and chanting, "Front, front."

Next thing he knew, he was standing face-to-face with a tutu-clad Jia.

"Everyone moves in Zumba," she said.

"I gathered that," Henry said. "But I'm not here to Zumba," he insisted.

"You're here early in the morning at a Zumba class. I beg to differ," she said. Jia continued to move, right clap, left clap, while talking to him.

"Well, if I promise to move from back there . . ." Henry suggested, leaning his head toward the back of the room where he'd once stood.

"Are you gonna try to escape?" she asked.

"Maybe?"

"The class seems to like having you up front." She raised her eyebrows at him, as if asking for permission. He let out a deep sigh and gave in.

"Fine. Use me and abuse me."

She laughed and then squealed with delight. An honest-to-god squeal.

"Henry is gonna help us with our next move," she announced to the class. "The snake."

Oh, this did not sound good.

"Right, and left," Jia called out as she pulled Henry right and then pushed him left. "Now snake it out, snake it out, that's right."

Henry watched as Jia *snaked it out*, moving her upper body in a wave that seemed almost too risqué for a group of seniors. But as he looked up in the mirror and those dancing behind him, everyone was swaying their bodies in delight, including those seated.

"I don't see you snaking it out," she said.

"My body doesn't move like that," Henry tried to convince her.

There was a twinkle in her eye that matched her wicked smile. They were thinking the same thing—Jia knew very well how Henry's body moved. She laughed it off and goaded him on.

"You'd have to actually move it to try."

Henry suddenly felt two hands land on his shoulders from behind him, and before he could react, Jia was pushing his right shoulder down. And then his left. He was alternating shoulders to the beat, an awkward and choppy motion. But he definitely was not dancing.

The crowd hooted and hollered for Henry. He heard Jia laugh behind him.

This was humiliating. And for some reason, he thought maybe that was exactly the point.

"Gotta loosen up, Hank. You're carrying around too much stress for all that very important work you do," Jia said, mocking him.

A tiny twinge of guilt crept up his neck, but he tried to ignore it.

"Sunseters, let's give Henry here a little more encouragement. He needs to loosen up the shoulders and sway!" she shouted.

"Sway! Sway! Sway!" the crowd shouted to the beat.

"You can do it, Henry," someone cheered.

"You got this," someone else encouraged.

It was the most positive reinforcement Henry had gotten in his life, ever.

And though he was utterly embarrassed at his lack of coordination, he didn't like that everyone was having a good time at his expense. No, actually, everyone was just having a good time, period. The fact that he was terrible at Zumba but giving it his best shot seemed to just heighten the mood.

Jia moved to stand in front of him, facing him. She had a small smile on her face, this one not wicked or nefarious like her others. It was kind and patient. Like he'd seen her be with so many of the others here at The Sunset.

She held her hands out between them. "May I?" He wasn't exactly sure what she was asking, but he nodded.

She put her hands on his hips and pushed them from side to side. "Keep the shoulders going," she encouraged. He did as he was told and followed her directions. "That's it, there you go," she said. Her smile spread to cover her whole face like she'd seen a miracle happen right before her eyes. "You're doing it!"

Henry did not want to see himself in the mirror. So instead he focused on the faces of those behind him in the mirror. Everyone was smiling, laughing, having the best time. And people moved their bodies to the best of their abilities, dancing to the music.

He found his granddad in the crowd. He'd pushed his walker behind him, and standing on his own without any support, he'd found the rhythm. Dennis had the step, the clap, AND the sway down like clockwork.

Henry hadn't seen him look this happy, or mobile, in a very long time.

Jia had left Henry and moved among the crowd. He snuck a peek at her as she walked up and down the rows of people encouraging every single participant. She danced next to some. Hip-bumped others. Gave a high five to a few. And was met with enthusiasm and joy by every single person.

And though Henry was quite possibly the worst dancer known

to man, he did know how to follow instructions. Whatever move she called out, he tried to follow. Step right, clap, sway. Step left, clap, sway.

The women in the front row cheered him on and wolf-whistled in delight.

It was ridiculous.

It was hilarious.

And as Jia made her way back up to the front of the room next to Henry, giving him his own look of encouragement, Henry couldn't help it.

He smiled.

Jia watched as the left corner of Henry's mouth crept up slightly, despite him trying to hold it back. About as close to a smile as she'd seen from him to date.

And goddamn if it wasn't the sexiest thing she'd seen. She felt that smile down to her toes. She remembered one other time she'd encountered that same level of attraction for this man.

If he kept that up, Jia was going to be in some serious trouble. Nothing good could come from a smile that sexy.

15

Jia had accomplished more in the two weeks she'd been at The Sunset than she had probably in her last three jobs combined. And this was just for fun. Not for money. Not for title. But because she loved seeing people get the respect they deserved and have the opportunity to live their lives with joy.

Unfortunately, her parents did not see this as success.

"What's the status of the job search?" her dad asked on the phone. Her parents had basically taken turns calling or FaceTiming her every few days to nag.

"It's coming along. It's only been a couple weeks. Things don't move that quickly in this market," she said. "I still have two weeks left to find something. Please don't nag me in the meantime. You're killing the vibe."

"Jia . . ." her dad warned. "I knew we shouldn't have let you go out and stay with your grandmother while your life is in flux. The two of you encourage each other to behave like there isn't a care in the world except having fun."

"Well, let's be honest, Dad. That's exactly how Mimi should be living. She's eighty! She deserves it."

"She could be doing whatever she's doing in Palm Springs out here in Florida."

"Mimi doesn't want to move to Florida," Jia reminded him. And neither did she. But she knew better than to bring this up again. Not when she still had two weeks to get them off her back. "And just to remind you, I'm twenty-seven years old. I can come stay with my grandmother without your permission if I want to." There, she'd put her foot down.

"You are unemployed with no means to take care of yourself, Jia. When that situation changes for you, your mother and I will be less involved in the details of your well-being."

Damn, he was good at shutting her down.

"Fine. But listen, Dad, I gotta run. Important business going on here that I need to attend to."

His exasperated sigh made it clear to Jia better than any words could that he was not in the mood for her whimsy.

"Tell Mom I said hi. Love you." She ended the call.

Her parents weren't terrible. They were just . . . a lot. From the time she was in the womb and gave her mom *the hardest time of her life* to them always trying to pick up the pieces from Jia's mistakes, Jia just couldn't shake the feeling that all she did was disappoint them. And it made it really hard to feel good about herself.

If only they could have some patience and try to understand who Jia was and what she was hoping for for her life.

Maybe Jia didn't even know. But she was starting to get a better sense.

She'd left New York broke and broken. At least she thought she was.

But here, with her grandmother, with her new friends, with her community, she was building something and, in turn, was building someone within herself. Here, Jia could be her true self, a person filled with joy and wanting what was best for others, and no one had a problem with that. Go figure.

The community center felt like her blank canvas, the residents her paint colors. Since she'd been here, she'd more than tripled the amount of things available to the seniors. A once-quiet, semi-sleepy neighborhood now buzzed with life between the hours of seven and four.

She didn't know what the end game would be after her month-long stay, but a secret part of her never wanted to leave. And how ridiculous was that—a twentysomething happily living among seniors in a retirement community?

These were the thoughts running through Jia's mind as she lounged in her favorite chair by the four-feet marker of the Sunset Hills community pool. It was a quiet day.

The aqua aerobics class had finished about an hour ago, and though Jia hadn't been there today, she could tell by the robust gathering of people around the coffee machine that it had been well attended. The residents loved the new instructor she'd found who had been working part-time at the Froyo shop downtown. She was a licensed lifeguard, a dancer, and had amazing energy. How perfect was that?

The stragglers who walked laps in the pool either after class or on their own were also finishing up, leaving only Jared walking up and down lane one and his chocolate Lab Clementine swimming next to him in lane two.

Jia kept an eye on Jared as he exercised. He was blind, and though Clementine, his service dog, was obviously more than capable of making sure Jared was safe, Jia liked watching his steady pace and the dog faithfully moving beside him.

She let out a deep breath, the feeling of satisfaction flowed through her lungs.

"Jia, honey, do you need some more sunscreen? I got some here in my bag."

Jia looked up to find her grandmother in the doorway of the community center, a red-and-pink floral swimsuit on with a cute yellow sarong wrapped around her waist. What a stunner. She'd had her roots touched up, and an effervescent glow radiated from her skin. Her Mimi was back.

"I'm good, Mimi. Thanks. I brought extra," she said, raising the tube of sunscreen that lay by her side.

"Okay. Well, don't stay in the sun too long. Your skin is too precious. You don't know it now, but you'll regret it when you're my age."

"I should be so lucky looking like you do at your age, Mimi," Jia called back.

"Well, I put in enough years with my ten-step Korean skincare regimen. It better look good," she called back. "I'm heading home. See you later. Oh, and, Jia, before I forget, the contractor who did my fantastic kitchen remodel left a message on the home machine. He'd like you to call him back. Said there was some question with the invoice. Sounded important."

Jia looked up at her grandmother, but she seemed unbothered. In fact, the smile on her face made it very clear to Jia that all she cared about was that she had a brand-new kitchen island. She trusted Jia with the rest. The last thing she wanted to do was cause Mimi any stress. But the last time she'd talked to the contractor, everything was on track and all invoices had been paid up to date. This was odd.

Jia had gotten a couple estimates for Mimi's kitchen remodel and had chosen the one who was neither the most expensive nor the least. But he had great references and could get the job done in a couple days. Mimi couldn't be without use of her kitchen for too long, so that was a selling point.

Jia was kind of nervous overseeing his work and the budget. But she'd managed costs and receipts and payments in her previous job. *How'd that end up for you?* Jia asked herself in her head, suspiciously in her father's voice.

Jia's heartbeat sped up, and she found it hard to breathe. She felt real trauma from being fired from her last job over a mistake, one she wasn't convinced had entirely been her fault. In fact, the more Jia had thought about her termination, the more she believed it shouldn't have happened the way it had. And if she wasn't so happy where she ended up, she might have done something about it.

Who was she kidding? She was powerless against the big guns of the Bakerson's Group. And frankly, she wasn't interested in rehashing it all or even thinking about anything from those days. Except for maybe Henry Shin.

Jia had been thinking a lot about him lately, and she wasn't sure what to make of that.

Jia picked up her phone and walked to the picnic table shaded by a big red umbrella. She took a seat, pulled up the number for Martin, their general contractor for Mimi's renovations, and pressed Call.

"Hello."

"Hi, Martin. It's Jia Chung. I got your message about some error with the invoice? How can I help?"

Jia liked Martin. He seemed like an upstanding kind of guy. But she'd been told by some of the residents that no contractor was entirely trustworthy. She didn't want to believe that, but she had proceeded with a tiny bit of caution nonetheless.

"Yeah, Jia, hey. So I was auditing the papers and looks like the marble for the kitchen island wasn't included in the invoice. It's gonna be seventeen ninety-nine plus tax. I gave you a bit of a discount because of the countertops. Can you get me payment for that by the end of the week?"

Eighteen hundred dollars? Jia had carefully budgeted out an additional bathroom renovation for Mimi's house based on what they'd spent on the kitchen. This would screw everything up. How could Jia have missed this? She went through the invoice line by line. The total cost even equaled what Martin had originally estimated. She remembered seeing everything there and accounted for before sending the check.

Didn't she?

"Martin, I need to get home and look over the invoice again. I'll call you later, if that's okay," Jia said. She hustled back over to her lounge chair and began packing up her things.

"Sure thing, Jia. Give me a call when you can. But sooner than later. I gotta pay my marble guy," Martin said.

"Will do. Bye." Jia hung up the phone. "Jared, do you have a lot of laps left to go?"

"Just about done here, Jia. You can take off. Clementine will make sure I get out okay. Don't worry."

Jia hesitated. She wanted to stay. But if Jared said he'd be okay, she didn't want to doubt him or baby him. He knew his limits. Just as she put Mimi's old sundress on over her bathing suit, she saw Jared carefully step out of the pool, Clementine by his side.

She smiled their way, grabbed her bag, and headed home.

Jia looked through all the papers lying haphazardly on the

coffee table. It was a mess, but it was Jia's organized chaos. She knew this was the only place she kept the renovation stuff. Jia grabbed the invoice on the top of the pile and began going through each line item.

"Whatcha looking for, sweetie?" Mimi asked.

Jia hesitated. She didn't want Mimi to know she might have fucked up the budget and they might be an additional eighteen hundred dollars in the hole and that might change all their plans and Jia might just be a royal screwup after all. But it was no use trying to keep anything from Mimi's prying eyes.

"Martin says they missed a charge on the invoice and I underpaid him," she admitted.

"Well, that's nonsense. I watched you review that thing myself. You were meticulous," Mimi assured her.

"I don't know, Mimi. I could have made a mistake. I just need to check and see." Jia hated doubting herself, but after always being considered a screwup when it came to these kinds of things, she sometimes allowed herself to believe it to be true.

"We went through all of these receipts together, sweetie. So if there's an error, it's just as likely my fault as yours. Don't get down on yourself. How do we know it's not Martin's fault, huh?" Mimi squeezed Jia's shoulder as she walked past her to the kitchen. Jia watched her as she put a mug down on the kitchen island to make herself some tea.

The marble of the island was gorgeous. They'd gotten it from a slab company that had leftover pieces from larger commercial builds. A remnant piece that perfectly matched the countertops. The countertops. Jia looked at them and then back to the island. Wait, the counters and the island were cut from the same slab of marble. They were cut down to size.

There would be only one line on the invoice because they only bought one piece.

"AHA!" Jia screamed, waving the invoice in the air. "I figured it out! We didn't make a mistake after all. It's a clerical error, if anything," she squealed.

"Just like I told you, honey. Now, why would you doubt yourself? Just because some man made it seem like there was no way he was the one that was wrong?" Mimi's words pierced Jia. It was a moment of déjà vu. A man, her boss, telling her she'd made a mistake, that there'd been an error—hers—when she absolutely knew in her gut she was right. Questioning herself. Too scared to fight back to clear her name.

Jia wanted to crawl back into bed and pull the covers over her head. Justice wasn't for the weak, for those too soft, like Jia.

This whole day had started off so well. Jia was starting to feel safe, secure, and at peace. Happy. Now, because of Martin's message, all the bad memories and feelings of inadequacy crept back up to haunt her. And though she was, she firmly believed, right in both instances, she couldn't shake the frustration of so easily being blamed as the one who was wrong.

She should let it all go. Just appreciate where she was now.

If only it were that easy.

16

Henry had come to expect that things just were slower out here in the desert compared to in New York, compared to anywhere, really. But a morning of errands where each one took longer than necessary than the last had him on his last nerve.

"Tell your granddad that my Oliver likes to cut the pills up in half and to take them with warm milk to swallow easier. If he doesn't have one of those pill cutters, you can pick one up in aisle ten," the attendant at the pharmacy told him.

"We're the only grocery store that carries the lactose-free milk. How many did you have to hit up before you found us?" asked the cashier at the grocery store.

"I heard the coffee shop on the corner is gonna expand over into the next space. How long before you think they're gonna reopen?" said the driver in the car in front of Henry, to the driver in the car in the lane next to him. The two drivers had come to a halt at the stop sign, rolled down their windows, called out to each other in greeting, and started having a conversation right then and there, just as Henry pulled up behind them.

It wasn't worth it for him to get upset and honk.

But because of all of this, he'd gotten back a little later than he'd planned.

"Granddad, I'm back. I got your meds and some groceries for dinner. How do pork chops sound? I know a recipe where they're extra tender and juicy so it won't be hard to chew," Henry called out.

There was no response.

"Granddad?" he called out again. He walked through the kitchen where he'd entered from the garage and into the family room. His grandfather's lounge chair was empty, but the TV was still on and his slippers sat there beside it.

"Granddad?" he said even louder. His heart picked up the pace. The bathroom door was open, but no one was inside. He peeked into the main bedroom, where the bed was made but the room empty. He looked into the second bedroom, where he had taken up residence, and no one.

He rushed down the hallway and out the front door. He looked up the street and down the other side. No one was in sight. He didn't know what led him there, but he crossed the road and through the gate to Mimi and Jia's house. He knocked on the door, but no one answered.

"Hello? Anyone home?" he said.

Nothing.

And then he heard it. The faint sound of a familiar tune. He walked in the direction of the music. And as he approached, it got louder and louder. "*Hey, Macarena,*" the music sang, a chorus of other voices shouting along with it. And then laughter and joyful screams and, as he got closer, the sounds of splashes and voices.

A party.

At the pool.

He picked up speed until he got to the gate and noticed what looked like the entirety of Sunset Hills packed into the pool area and spilling over to the bocce ball courts where lawn chairs and wheelchairs were set up under large patio umbrellas. Every pool chair was taken with towels draped over them or residents lounging in them wearing large straw hats. And in the shallow end of the pool, a group of people dancing the Macarena in the water.

He was certain his granddad wouldn't be here. He hated the water, despite having lived with a pool in his backyard for decades. That pool had been meticulously cared for and cleaned for whenever Henry would visit. But Dennis had never even dipped a toe in. And the man absolutely did not know the Macarena. He was more a waltz guy.

"Hey, there! You're overdressed for the party," Jia said, walking up beside him. She had on a pink one-piece bathing suit with one of those frilly skirts that hid her bottom half. She also had on a swim cap with white and yellow flowers decorating it and a pair of oversized sunglasses that old Hollywood types wore. She looked like she'd walked off the pages of *Vogue*'s retro catalog.

Henry looked down at her toenails, painted a cheerful yellow. And then over to his deck shoes and socks and khaki chinos. He was overdressed. But this wasn't his party.

"Dennis wasn't home when I got back from errands, and I don't know why, but I came over here to see if I could find him. But he's not—"

"He's right there," she said. She pointed toward the deep end of the pool where a diving board hovered over the water. There at the end of it stood his granddad. He wore long swim trunks pulled up high past his belly, drawstring tied tight, and a white undershirt tucked inside.

"What's he doing?" Henry said. He stood in shock as he watched the old man walk until his toes hung over the edge of the board. He didn't even look down into the water. He looked straight ahead as if to the horizon. And then he bent his knees and jumped, pulling himself into a tight grip. Henry panicked the moment he saw the movement. His grandfather did not like the water. He was terrified of it. And he did not know how to swim.

"Cannonball!" he screamed just as he hit the water. The crowd whooped and hollered in delight.

"He doesn't know how to swim!" Henry cried. Without hesitation, he moved to jump into the pool, but Jia grabbed his arm.

"Henry, wait," she said, laughing. "Don't go jumping in with all your clothes on. The pool is only five feet deep. And Dennis is a great swimmer."

He looked over to see his grandfather emerge, a huge smile on his face. And he dog-paddled his way over to the edge of the pool.

His entire life his granddad didn't know how to swim. He never came close to the water when Henry came to visit him as a kid. He always sat off to the side and watched him play in the pool. There was trauma. From a previous life. From wartime and the navy. And that was all Henry knew about it.

"Mimi told me he's been taking swim lessons for months, even before moving over here. They'd been opening the pool up to other seniors in and out of the community. Isn't it cool when you can learn something new at any age? I can't believe the HOA thought of possibly closing the pool for a random desert garden. No way. Anyways, I hear his grandson loves to swim and play around, and he'd always wished he could join him." Jia's voice lowered, softer, kinder. "So he made sure to learn while he still could." She nudged him with her elbow.

Henry swallowed back the emotion. He didn't want to hear about what little time left his grandfather might have. And when his granddad had asked him to teach him how to swim years ago, Henry had said he was too busy. And eventually just stopped coming to visit altogether because Henry's life trajectory didn't include extended trips to the desert anymore.

It was too much. And not something he wanted to work out here with an audience, especially not in front of Jia.

He nodded once in her direction, and before his granddad could see him, he turned to leave. He'd sneak away and just pretend he didn't know until Dennis chose to share the information with him.

But as he turned to leave, he slipped on a flip-flop that was left at the side of the pool. His arms windmilled as he tried to regain his balance. He grabbed on to the only thing he could reach.

And as gravity took him in the opposite direction, he took Jia with him. Straight into the pool—boat shoes, socks, khakis and all—and dragging her into the water as well.

Holding on to each other, the two dropped all the way to the bottom of the five-foot pool. Henry opened his eyes, and Jia was smiling, bubbles escaping from the sides of her mouth. He watched one travel to the waterline. But they both just floated under the water, staring at each other.

Time stood still. It was surprisingly quiet under the water. And looking into the sparkle of Jia's eyes, he was mesmerized.

Their bodies floated closer to each other until their faces were almost touching. Though his eyes were stinging from the chlorine, he didn't want to shut them. He wanted to keep looking at her. He wanted, frankly, to do more than just look at her.

But when it was clear that each of them was going to run out of air soon enough, she gave him a wink, planted her feet at the bottom of the pool, and launched herself up, leaving Henry two seconds behind her.

Residents were gathered along every edge of the pool looking down at them until they emerged.

He heard his grandfather's voice. "Hank, are you okay? What the heck are you doing swimming with all your clothes on, and even your shoes? If you wanted to borrow swim trunks, I have an extra pair."

"Oh, did I leave my flip-flops right there by the edge of the pool for someone to trip over?" Betty said. Henry swore he saw her wink at Mimi.

"Jia, honey, you saved him! You saved Hank from drowning," someone said.

"You owe her a fancy thank-you dinner or something, I'd say," another neighbor suggested.

Cheers erupted from the crowd as Jia gracefully pulled herself up and out of the pool and people gathered around her. She did a tiny curtsy and a bow. "He was fine on his own. You know I just like to be dramatic," she said. She looked back over her shoulder at Henry, as he, very much less graceful, pulled his clothing-weighted body out of the pool. One of the women brought him a towel and quickly removed his shoes and socks.

"I'm fine, really, no harm at all," he said as he pulled away, uncomfortable with the attention.

"Hank, you sure you're okay?" His granddad was standing over him.

"Yeah, I'm good," he assured him.

"Did you catch my cannonball? Mitchell told me it was at least a nine point five. I think I might win the competition," he said, proudly beaming.

Henry, though uncomfortable dripping in all his clothes, couldn't help but smile. "It was pretty impressive, Granddad. Probably the best one I've ever seen. Who knew you had it in you?"

"Hmph! I never saw a competition I didn't set out to win, you know that. That's how I won your grandmother over."

"That's right," Henry replied, heart warmed. He missed her, his grandmother. She'd gotten sick and died more than ten years ago. She was so good at taking care of both Henry and Dennis. Now they only had each other. For all of Henry's adult life, it was just him and Dennis. He mentally kicked himself for not paying closer attention the last few years.

"Well, why don't you go back home and change into some real swim trunks?" He leaned in and whispered, "I know you were just trying to get Jia to save you and all. You're a strong swimmer, so you weren't fooling me." He winked.

Henry shook this head. "I do need to get out of these wet clothes. But I've got some work to do back home. Are you going to be here long? Do you want me to wait for you? Or do you want me to walk you home?"

"We'll all walk back together after just a little bit longer," Jia said, walking up beside them. "You go and get yourself out of your misery." She scanned him head to toe.

Henry tried not to squirm. The water was kind of cold, and he didn't want to know what she saw.

He stepped back into his shoes, shoved his wet socks into his pockets, and turned to leave. As he walked away, boat shoes squishing with each step, he thought maybe, just maybe, his granddad would be perfectly fine here at Sunset Hills once Henry went back to New York. Maybe he could trust that Dennis would be okay on his own. Because he wouldn't really be alone, would he? There would be a whole community of people supporting him.

And he suspected all of Jia's efforts had a lot to do with that.

17

Jia grabbed her slippers, gently opened the front door, and quietly let herself out onto the front porch. Mimi had already retired to her bedroom for the night, and even so, she respected that this time of day had become sacred for Jia.

Jia couldn't remember ever seeing the sunset in New York. It was either light outside or dark outside, and there wasn't much difference in her mind. The light was often blocked by the tall buildings, the dark usually brightened by the city lights. But out here in the desert, it was like the sky was announcing when it awakened or went to sleep. It let everyone know by projecting stunning and vibrant shades of reds, oranges, and pinks until it had gone where it needed to go.

It was breathtaking.

And it felt especially magical here at Sunset Hills where no one came outdoors after dinner. Where Jia could sit on the curb of her favorite corner, the one where she had an unobstructed view of the outline of the mountains to her right, the wind turbines to her left, and the sun providing the backdrop to them all as it went down, in complete peace and quiet.

She felt him before she saw him. He walked quietly. And she might have teased him the first time they'd walked down this sidewalk on this street, making him think she'd felt unsafe, but maybe she always knew for some reason that that was the furthest from the case. He was a caretaker in his own way. He worried, he took close care, he made sure everything was safe for his granddad.

"Hi," she said. She didn't turn to look at him, didn't watch him as he came up beside her.

He remained standing but looked straight ahead just like she did. Not taking his eyes off the show the sky was putting on.

"Hi," he said back.

She patted the ground next to her, inviting him to join her. Maybe he didn't want to bother her. Maybe he sensed this time was important for her to experience. She wanted him to stay.

She usually faced this time of day alone. But today, she felt willing to share.

He sat down on the curb next to her and stretched his long legs out in front of them on the street. He crossed his feet at the ankles and leaned back on his hands.

Who knew how long they sat there in silence. The yellow gave way to pink gave way to orange gave way to red, rust, brown, black.

And then Jia let out her breath like she did every time the night fell.

"Wow," he whispered.

"Yeah," she agreed.

Neither of them made a move to leave.

The streetlights flickered on, and the temperature finally felt bearable.

"It's special," she said.

"I never took the time to experience it before."

"What brought you out here tonight? Couldn't sleep?" Jia asked.

"Still getting used to that seven o'clock bedtime," Henry said.

Jia laughed. "Yeah, it's a totally different life than back in New York."

"It really is. I thought I'd feel stifled by the heat and the slowness. But there's something really calming about it."

Jia nodded, knowing he probably couldn't see her. But he'd nailed it. That was exactly how it felt out here. Calming. Though, she'd probably add that it was magical too. The area. The people. Everything. She'd known this even as a kid.

She knew it even more now. She just didn't know how she could hold on to it.

"Are you staying here much longer?" he asked.

She stiffened at the question, like Henry was reading her mind. Maybe surprisingly, no one at Sunset Hills had asked her that question. As nosy and gossipy as the crowd could be, they were experienced in life enough to have a live-and-let-live attitude toward each other.

But there was always a countdown clock over Jia's head. And it was getting perilously close to the end.

She tried not to think about it. Sure, it tried to make its way to the forefront of her mind. She'd always just pushed it to the back and tried not to worry that her stay had an expiration date.

But her parents were getting more impatient. And life,

whatever that meant, was waiting to be resumed. Jia didn't have a job. She didn't have an apartment. And she would no longer have a life of her own. She'd be moving to Florida to live with her parents, to work at their job, to do what they wanted her to do.

She worried about all the activities she'd started up for the residents here. She fretted about the relationships she'd fostered. She couldn't just leave them, could she?

"Unclear," she replied. "You?"

"I leave next week," he said.

"Important lawyer stuff to get back to," she said.

He let out a huff. "Something like that."

"Did you always want to be a lawyer? Did you go to middle school with a suit and tie and sign your name with *Future Esq*?"

"You got something against lawyers?" Henry teased.

"Something like that," she echoed. He probably thought she'd meant because of him. What he didn't know was she'd had an aversion to lawyers long before she'd ever worked and been fired from a job. It had all started in the home. "My parents are lawyers."

"Ahhh, I see. Well, the answer is *yes, I've always wanted to be a lawyer*. I like . . . order. And rules. And accountability."

"Life isn't always that black-and-white, though," she replied. "Sometimes life needs to have some color. Freedom to evolve, figure things out." This was something she was realizing for herself more and more.

Henry visibly cringed at her words.

She barked out a laugh. "Allergic to the freedom to evolve?"

"My parents are free spirits," he answered.

She twisted her mouth, nodding, understanding.

"We probably make our therapists a lot of money."

"Since I was twelve," he answered.

She raised her eyebrows as she turned to get a good look at him. "Impressive. Sixteen for me." She really liked a man in therapy. "Therapy is sexy, ya know?" She nudged him with her shoulder.

"Yeah? OCD, ADHD, anxiety, and panic attacks do it for you?"

"Talk dirty to me," she teased. But she wasn't kidding. She liked a man who'd been diagnosed. First step in learning how to manage it all.

"I'm serious, though. I think a man in therapy is sexy," Jia reiterated.

Henry didn't look her way. In fact, he didn't even move an inch. He either didn't hear her or she'd shocked the shit out of him. Unclear.

"You must think a woman in therapy is messy," she added, saying anything to break the silence.

It was then that he reacted. He turned his head toward her, lifted his hand, and placed it softly on her cheek. "I don't think you're messy." He held her gaze. She wanted to look away. She didn't want words that would make excuses for the type of woman she was. She knew she was a mess. "No." The one word from his lips spoken as law. "I think you're . . . vibrant. Enchanting. Bold. It's like you don't realize something is tasteless until seasoning is added, and then your eyes are opened and you know you'll never be the same. You can never go back to bland."

She held her breath, uncertain how to respond. Jia had rarely heard words like those before, and definitely not describing her. They felt like they carried more weight, these old-timey words here in this old-timey place, spoken about her. No one other than Mimi had ever made her feel like she made their space better.

"And I didn't realize until now how sexy that could be," Henry admitted.

Jia leaned into his hand and closed her eyes. She took in a deep breath, taking this moment in. When she opened her eyes she found Henry staring at her lips and then quickly looked away. He pulled his hand back from her cheek, and Jia immediately missed its steadying touch.

"Yeah, so my parents think I just need to relax, smoke some weed, go find myself," he said, a sad chuckle following.

"Mine think I need to focus and try harder. Oh, and move to Florida, apparently," she said.

They both dropped their heads and laughed.

"Is that why Dennis means so much to you?"

"He basically had to raise me when my parents were off exploring the world. They would just dump me at my grandparents' house without any notice of when and for how long. It was easier when my grandmother was alive. But we lost her to cancer when I was in high school, and Dennis needed time to grieve. So I figured out a way to take care of myself as much as I could. I've basically been on my own since I was sixteen."

Jia felt a pang in her chest thinking of young Henry on his own. No wonder he was so strict on rules and boundaries. He needed them to survive. "That had to have been hard."

"What about you? Mimi?" he asked.

"She's my biggest cheerleader, wants me to live my best life." Jia smiled thinking of her grandmother. "I'm kind of on the other extreme—I'm twenty-seven and my parents haven't left me alone a day in my life. Shit, I didn't mean it like that." She didn't want him to think she was downplaying his pain or struggle.

"No, no. I can see how that would be super difficult and frustrating. I don't think either of us had it easier than the other."

Jia nodded. "They just . . . worry about me. But I wish, well, I wish they'd let me live my own life. Let me breathe . . ." She let out a deep breath as if needing the physical manifestation of what she was hoping for. "Guess we're both the classic case of *Our parents ruined us.*" Jia said it as a joke, but it hurt nonetheless.

"I don't think you're ruined at all."

Jia could feel Henry's eyes on her. Instead of turning to meet them, she closed hers, trying to stop the emotions she was feeling. She liked him. She liked him a lot.

"They're good people, everyone here at Sunset Hills. I'm definitely gonna have to come back and visit more often," Henry said.

"I hope you do," Jia said. Why it mattered so much to her, she wasn't sure. Jia had the ability to love deep and love wide. Maybe that was why she was so careful not to get too attached. There was too much change that always happened in her life. Commitment caused upheaval. It was best to just enjoy the moment and the ones in it and then move on. She thought of people like she thought of seasons: She enjoyed them while they were there, but ultimately, they came and served a purpose and then left, for someone new to take their place.

Jia loved in em dashes and ellipses . . . with possibilities. But she ended every relationship with a period. Final. On to the next.

This curiosity to know more about Henry, to spend more time with him, to wonder when she'd see him next, it wasn't like her. And that scared her.

But it didn't matter. Because Jia was becoming more certain that New York was not where she wanted to be anymore. And she didn't get the sense Henry felt the same way.

Plus they were two very different people. Henry was a successful, powerful lawyer. His life was on the rise. Jia was unemployed, unhoused, with no prospects. They were going in opposite directions.

"I should get inside before Mimi sends the search party," Jia said. She needed to stop whatever was happening here.

"Yeah, me too." Henry stood up and reached down, offering his hand to help Jia.

She took the offer and let him pull her to her feet. She raised her eyes to meet his, not realizing how close they were standing to each other.

Henry looked down at her, an intensity in his gaze that took her breath away. Jia leaned closer as he moved toward her. He let go of her hand and wrapped his around her waist. Jia put both her hands on his chest as Henry drew her in against him. His face lowered to hers. She lifted her chin as his lips came to meet hers for a kiss.

So much for stopping anything.

Jia freed her arms and wrapped them around his neck. She rose to her toes and pulled him down closer to her. Henry's tongue pushed into her mouth, and she tilted her head so he could get even deeper.

Henry's hands moved to her ass, and he squeezed. Jia let out a gasp. "Fuck," he said.

"Yes, please," she whispered. "Just maybe not out here on the street corner."

His shoulders moved up and down as he tucked his head into her neck and laughed. He kissed her once on the skin just below her ear and lowered farther to the base of her neck. She squirmed.

"Ticklish," he said. She remembered he'd said the same thing to her the first night they'd been together.

It felt both fresh and familiar. And Jia could so easily give in to the desire for more. She liked him. She liked being around him. But it felt a little like the universe had put them at odds each step of the way since that first time. Were they meant to overcome the obstacles or just accept that the odds were stacked against them? She didn't know.

And she didn't think she was quite ready to try.

She stepped back out of his hold. He released his arms and let her go.

"Good night, Henry." She held on to his hand for just a second longer, before letting go.

"Good night, Jia."

"Thanks for watching the sunset with me."

"Thanks for letting me. I see now why it's so important to you."

Jia wasn't sure what he meant by that. How did he know how much she cherished this time each day? Had he seen her out here before?

Henry crossed the street, and the two of them walked parallel to each other, a road between them.

Just as Jia opened her front door, she looked over her shoulder to see Henry doing the same. He lifted his arm in a wave, and she waved back.

In her peripheral vision, Jia thought she saw the curtains of the house next door move. But she hadn't felt a breeze, and since everyone was likely already asleep, she brushed it off to the night playing tricks on her eyes.

She walked inside and lifted her fingers to her lips, remembering the way Henry's felt kissing hers. And wondered if the night was playing tricks on her heart as well.

He'd seen her out there every single night watching the sun go down. He wondered what it was she thought about in those few minutes of the day's transition. He'd wanted to ask.

He just never had a reason to join her.

Henry saw the light on under his granddad's door, so he knocked gently.

"Come in," Dennis called out.

"Hey," Henry peeked in seeing Dennis tucked away in his bed. "I checked outside about that crying cat you thought you heard? All clear. Not a cat in sight."

"Okay, good to know. Thanks for going out there." Dennis smiled and then let out a yawn. "Could you turn the light out?"

"Sure thing," Henry said as he turned off the switch and shut the door.

Dennis: Got Henry outside. He came back about an hour later.

Mimi: Way to go. Jia just came in too.

Betty: I peeked through my window, and they were definitely together out there.

Gladys: Yahoo . . . it's working!

Mimi: Night, everyone!

Dennis: Night!

18

"Good morning, Gladys."

"Henry, what brings you by today?"

"I was wondering if I could use the printer and the copier? If you can believe it, Dennis doesn't have either in his home," Henry says.

"Oh, I can believe it. What do any of us need a printer for when we're eighty? Having this one here for the whole neighborhood is just fine for all of us," she replied.

Henry smiled and nodded. He couldn't argue with that.

"Whatcha working on?"

"Just some stuff, reminders and lists for Dennis for when I go back to New York. So he has all the answers in one place," he told her.

"Sweet boy, I don't think any of us can have all the answers. But if someone did, it would more likely be one of us old folks who've been around, made our mistakes already, and lived to tell about them. Don't you think?" Gladys winked and got up from behind her desk. "Here, use this computer, since it's already locked and loaded. The other one sometimes forgets to talk to the printer."

Henry sat in Gladys's chair, ruminating on what she'd just said. He wanted to believe that we all got wiser as we got older. But his granddad often forgot to take his medicine, sometimes refusing completely to take the larger-size supplements that were harder to swallow. He was stubborn as all get-out and wouldn't use his walker. He left the TV and lights on when he went to bed or left the house.

And each time Henry caught any of these things, it brought about a spike of anxiety. And a fresh wave of guilt. Dennis had always been there to take care of Henry when he was young. And now, Henry was realizing, he'd neglected to take care of Dennis as he got older.

But Henry had a life in New York, a successful career and . . . well, not much else. But he'd been busy. Still, spending time with his grandfather these past couple weeks made it clear that he could have paid and would be paying closer attention. Starting with these lists and reminders. It was the best he could offer.

"Gordon had a special today—strawberry matchas! Now, I know you think matcha tastes like grass, but— Oh, sorry. I swore Gladys usually sits in that chair." Henry looked up from the computer at the loud intrusion to his thoughts. Jia stood there with two brightly colored drinks in her hands, a wide smile on her face.

"Jia, it *is* me, Gladys. I just borrowed Henry's body for the day."

Jia stared at Henry, expressionless.

Shit, so much for attempting humor. What was he thinking? Henry never cracked a joke. Because, clearly, he was bad at it.

Jia's entire face exploded into laughter. She keeled over with it. She barely balanced the drinks in time before they could spill. "Henry J. Shin, Esquire, did you just make a joke?"

"Not a very good one." He deadpanned back before lifting the corner of his mouth. Why was her laughter funnier than the joke itself?

She pulled herself together, but the smiled remained. God, she was pretty. She didn't look to have any makeup on. Her hair was up in a knot. She wore denim shorts and a plain white tank top. And she was the most stunning thing he'd laid eyes on.

Last night, he'd lost himself. It was dark, and he'd been mesmerized by the most gorgeous sunset he'd ever seen. And Jia was there. He'd let himself go. He'd let himself say things he never said out loud. He'd let himself explore emotions, test out feelings, even in small bite-size pieces, with Jia last night. *What if?* he'd asked himself. *Could we?* he'd wondered.

He'd gone to bed feeling raw, exposed, untethered. He hated it. But he wasn't so sure he wanted to leave it behind.

It didn't matter. Because Henry was leaving all of this, and likely Jia too, soon enough.

"Whatcha working on?" she asked, leaning her hip against the corner of the desk.

"Some things for Dennis. A calendar, reminders, just for when I'm . . ." Henry stopped himself.

"Gone?" Jia completed his sentence.

It felt odd to be talking about it . . . leaving. He assumed they'd both eventually be back in New York at some point. And then . . . what? Just go back to life as he was living it?

Yes, probably. Was there another option? Everything was very simple, ordered, and focused before. It was also empty, lonely, and repetitive. That wasn't a bad thing, though, right? "Yeah, since I won't be here to help him."

"That's nice of you." She looked at everything Henry had worked on. "That's a lot of reminders."

"He's got a lot of stuff to remember to take care of himself."

"You included a reminder to wash and fold his laundry."

"Yeah, that's important."

"He probably knows to do that, though, no? I mean, Dennis doesn't have any issues with his memory, does he?" Jia asked. "You think maybe this is too much?"

Henry looked back at the list. Everything on there felt important. He'd also cross-referenced much of it into a calendar format. "It's just for reference. I don't want him to get overwhelmed with everything he has to do and forget."

"I'm just saying. My parents do this to me all the time. Try to, well, control how I live my life. Down to the minutiae. It's stifling. I'm an adult. And, Henry? So is your granddad. Give him some credit. I know you're trying to help. But don't, in your best efforts at love, end up taking away his freedom."

Henry stared at her. He opened his mouth to respond, but he couldn't think of what to say. He battled the irritation of her overstepping with the deep pull of shame. He wanted to defend himself and his intentions while apologizing for going about it the wrong way. But also, she didn't know Dennis. She didn't know how both he and his granddad had the trauma of Henry's flighty parents always hovering over them. How when shit didn't get done, it ended up often hitting the fan.

Maybe this was why Jia couldn't cut it at Bakerson's Group. She needed to be more detailed, organized, meticulous, overprepared. But he knew that wasn't fair for him to say to her, even if he was thinking it. It would be a low blow.

"Thanks for the advice. But I know my granddad, and this is what he needs." His voice was sharper than he'd meant it to be.

Jia nodded and didn't say another word.

Henry thought about asking Jia if she wanted to meet up sometime when they were both back in the city. He thought about asking when she'd next be in Palm Springs and maybe they could coordinate visits. He considered various different ways that he could see her again.

But if this time in the desert with his grandfather and with the people at The Sunset all trying to creep into his heart had taught him anything, it was this: Life was easier without the worry, fear, anxiety, desire, or warmth of caring about anyone other than yourself.

Henry needed to get back on familiar, solid footing and shut everything and everyone else out.

His phone buzzed in his pocket, and Henry pulled it out to answer. He froze when he saw the name. *Elliot Shin.* Not *Dad*. Because as far as Henry was concerned, he didn't have a dad, or a mom. They were just Elliot and Katie, nuisances at best. Why was he calling now? But if Henry didn't answer, he knew Elliot would direct his efforts to Dennis next.

"Excuse me. I have to get this," he said to Jia. He stood up and walked out into the main room and over to the more private library.

"What do you want?" he said into the phone.

"Henry, how you doing? Good? It's been too long. Listen, Mom and I are on our way down from Toronto to hike the Appalachian Trail. Thought about stopping in the city to see you, son." It was how they did things. Acted like things were always okay and relationships had never been severed. Softening up communications before laying on the request for money, just *a little extra help*.

"I'm not in town. Can't make it," Henry answered.

"Well, that's too bad. Would have liked to see you." Henry waited for the inevitable ask. "Listen, your folks are a little short on cash this month, and we'll need to stock up on supplies for our extended trip. It's a rough journey, and we could use some equipment—"

Henry gripped the phone so tightly he worried it would break. "We're not doing this, Elliot. I'm not sending you anything. And don't even think about asking Dennis. Do you understand me?"

"Now, now, no need to get irritated. Just think about it, and give us a call if you change your mind. We could really use the help."

Henry hated how they always turned it on him, making him out to be the asshole.

"I'm hanging up now," he warned. And he did just that.

He closed his eyes and took a few calming breaths. Interactions with his parents always brought out the worst in him. Because they were the worst.

He'd have to warn Dennis, yet again, not to take their calls and definitely not to send them any money. He just knew Dennis wouldn't listen, though. Henry looked back into the office where he'd left Jia and his stupid lists and his stupid calendar and his stupid best intentions.

And he wondered when, despite all his best efforts, he had lost control of his tightly held life and considered what he needed to do to get it back again.

"Are you okay?" Jia's face had her concern written all over it.

She didn't ask if *everything* was okay. She asked if *he* was. Something about that struck him so hard he had to stop and put his hand against the doorway to gain his balance. Henry hated the vulnerability of being perceived by other people. But with Jia, he craved it.

And that had the ability to bring him to his knees. He had no doubt that she would one day kill him with her kindness if he let her.

"Yeah, I'm okay" was all he could say in response. It was all he was going to give her. But it was more than he'd ever given anyone else.

19

Jia closed out of her Zoom call and sat staring at the now-blank screen.

She wasn't sure what to make of it. When she had come home from being fired from Bakerson's Group, she'd started to allow herself to believe that maybe, just maybe, they'd been wrong. In fact, the more she played it back in her head, made sense of the situation, she was certain that she had been terminated for something that was not her fault.

Maybe she was a bit much, a little too flashy for the finance company. But was that a fireable offense? Other than that, she could not think of one error she was told she'd made except . . . the expense report.

"Mr. Wainwright, you listed here a two-thousand-dollar dinner at Le Bernadin, but I don't see the receipt for it. Can I get that from you?"

"Look it up on my credit card statement," he'd said, visibly annoyed by her question.

"Yes, but sir, anything over one thousand dollars needs a detailed itemized receipt plus a list of all attendees. I'm so sorry to bother you, but can you get that to me? If not, would you like me to hold off processing this expense until you can?" She'd tried to say it with a smile. She'd tried to remove any tone that might sound accusatory or set him off. She'd clearly failed.

"Useless. Pain in my ass," he muttered as he walked away, her questions unanswered.

The entire exchange had ruined her night. But she swore to come back the next day in a better mood.

She should have asked Genevieve for more details. She should have demanded to see proof. But Jia was not a fighter. She hated confrontation. And was it worth it to even try?

She wouldn't even know where to start if she wanted to fight it. And the thought of doing so was just too daunting for her to consider. She considered her termination a favor, truthfully. She didn't want to work there and, for now, it had brought her here.

Plus, what would she gain by it? A chance to go back to that same job that made her miserable? Or maybe redemption and reclamation of her self-confidence?

But when she received the request for a Zoom call from Stephanie Novak and Taylor Ann Graff, she had been thrown for a loop. In fact, she'd deleted the previous attempts to contact her by the legal group representing them, unaware of what the messages were even about. This one, however, came directly from the women, whose names Jia had recognized. So she accepted their invitation to talk, despite the fact that with time zones, it would be an early morning for Jia.

She'd seen them on old reports, previous files, on various

documents in her computer history. They were the ones who had been in the role before her. They were the women that Mr. Wainwright often referred to as *dummies*, *incompetents*, and *failures*, reduced to simply being known as *the girls before* and, ultimately, that he had also fired like he had Jia. And apparently now, after their own time to consider and gather evidence, they were ready. They were taking Bakerson's Group, along with a long list of names, to court.

And they wanted Jia to join them.

But it all felt like too much, too over Jia's head.

Or, if she would admit to herself, too much a Pandora's box she wasn't sure she wanted to open. Because if she went to court and lost, her parents would most definitely have her ass for shaming them and being so irresponsible and ill-prepared. But if they won? She'd have to face the real possibility that, despite proving she was capable and competent at her job and not the screwup, once again, everyone thought she was, it still might not bring her the respect, or the life's satisfaction, and definitely not the joy, she wanted for herself.

What good would it do to even try to get her story and the real facts out in the open? She didn't have a need for a redemption arc. She really just preferred to move on.

Jia looked over at the clock: 6:58 a.m. Shit.

She would review the details in their follow-up email more closely and think it through later. Maybe she'd ask Henry his thoughts on the matter. He knew Bakerson's Group better than she did. And she couldn't imagine him signing off on something that wasn't valid and justified. He'd tell her if she should pursue the lawsuit or not, if she asked his professional opinion.

Right now, she was late and had to go.

★ ★ ★

Jia waited on the corner as she did every Friday morning at seven for the rest of the crew to arrive.

When she'd first arrived at Sunset Hills, she'd noticed a lot of the residents taking their daily walks around the block, all at their own pace, some with dogs on leashes, some pushing walkers to assist them. But all were alone. And that felt kind of sad to her.

Surrounding yourself with others doing the same thing as you provided accountability—we all could use some of that, she thought. So she'd suggested a walking club. It was the first thing she'd organized for the residents here. She limited the official meetup to twice a week so as not to overwhelm them. The group would meet at the corner at seven, and they'd walk exactly one mile.

For some it was a stretch and pushed them a little harder and farther than they'd gone before. And for others it motivated them to walk up to two miles on the other days when the club didn't go together. It was their third week now and still one of Jia's favorite group activities.

"Hello, fellas," she said as Eugene, a retired salesman who had lived at Sunset Hills going on twenty years now, and Louis, a retired school teacher and newish to the neighborhood, walked up. "Hi, Jia. Looking good today in the stripes," Gordon said.

Jia had on another one of her grandmother's outfits, a striped jogging suit possibly from the eighties that she'd cut into shorts. It was soft and comfy and colorful, and Jia loved it. "Thanks," she said with a wink. Eugene blushed, and Louis elbowed him. Jia held back an assessing gaze, but she got the sense that maybe something romantic was brewing between the two. Go,

Eugene. Louis was only sixty, a good fifteen years or so younger. Nice. Jia loved a good age-gap romance.

The bark of a small dog caught Jia's attention. Gladys had her terrier, Elizabeth Taylor, strapped into her doggy stroller and pushed her along to meet up with the rest of them. As the others arrived, they had a nice group of about twenty people and at least eight dogs of all shapes and sizes.

"Okay, everyone got their fanny packs clipped? Water bottles filled and secured at your hips? Sunscreen, anyone?"

"Let's get this show on the road," someone growled.

Jia smiled. Like any of them had anywhere else to go.

Just as she was about to turn around to lead the way, she caught sight of the sun glistening off the very nice chest of a shirtless Henry Shin. He was like clockwork when it came to his morning run, and it wasn't the first time Jia had seen him looking nice and sweaty and only half-clothed. His T-shirt was tucked into the pocket of his shorts. Heroic effort to be a runner in the desert during off-season.

He looked up and caught her eye.

She lifted her hand and waved.

The others took notice and all waved as well.

"Hi, Henry!"

"Hey there, Hank!"

"Looking good there, handsome!"

Henry's smile could not be helped, and it completely transformed his face. Jia had seen that smile more and more these days, and she liked it.

Henry walked over to greet the group, taking the shirt and pulling it back on over his head.

Shame.

"Walking Club?" he asked as he reached them.

"Yup, and we're late. Are we leaving anytime soon?" Gerty growled.

"Shush, you big grouch. Not like we're in some kind of race or anything."

"Wanna join us?" Jia asked.

"I'm almost done with my run. I should go take a shower and get some breakfast ready for Dennis," he said.

Jia nodded. "Hey, ask Dennis if he wants to join Walking Club next week." She bent her head toward a couple of the folks with their walkers, trying to put Henry's worries at ease if Dennis could keep up or not. She knew he was super protective.

"I'll bring it up to him," he said.

Jia's eyebrows shot up in surprise. She hadn't expected it to be that easy.

"Hey." Henry took a step toward her.

"Watch out, Henry, there's some dog—"

Jia looked down just as Henry stepped in a fresh pile of . . .

"Poop right there."

"What the heck? Right here? In the middle of the sidewalk? Why don't people pick up after their dogs? I thought that was common practice and courtesy," Henry said.

"Sorry, Henry, it was probably Chewbacca here. He's had some stomach issues the last couple days," Harold said.

"Yeah, well, if you knew that, you should have prepared to pick up after him," Henry replied.

"Hey, I get it. It's disgusting," Jia replied.

Henry was scraping the side of his shoe on the curb.

"But maybe just consider that some of the residents here aren't as mobile as others and might not be physically able to bend down and pick up after their dogs. We're a little more flexible with the rules here. And *common courtesy* means different things sometimes," she said. She tempered her voice not to show her own frustration at Henry's outburst. Not in front of the crowd.

She understood. In fact, she felt the same way when she'd first arrived. But as she paid attention and noticed limitations and best intentions, she'd stopped harping over things that weren't that big of a deal. Not in the grand scheme of life here at The Sunset. She could relate to needing some extra grace and empathy more than she admitted.

Henry closed his eyes and shook his head trying to gather his composure.

Jia didn't know why she bothered. She liked him. But he could be so uptight.

"Okay, everyone, let's go," she said. And she didn't bother to look back. And she didn't bother to offer him the Kleenex she had in her pack. He could figure out his own shit. Pun intended.

She started off faster than she should have. She was just annoyed by Henry's lack of empathy. She understood he had a thing about following rules. But sometimes he had to understand that rules could and should be bent and broken. It frustrated her . . .

"Hey there, speedy. Wanna wait for the rest of us?"

Jia looked back over her shoulder and saw the Walking Club at least twenty feet behind her. "Oh my gosh, I'm so sorry. I was lost in thought," she said.

"Honestly, Jia. Feel free to go on and walk ahead of us. It can't be fun slowing yourself down to a snail's pace just because the rest of us can't keep up. You're young and strong and flexible. Don't let us hold you back," Eugene said.

He'd meant it as encouragement . . . to push forward at her

own pace . . . to get something out of this time for herself as well. But what he didn't realize, none of them did, maybe she hadn't either until this very moment, was that the pace Jia had been living life was too fast for her. That the pace life was moving right here at The Sunset was just right. At least for now. And she loved it. She loved the lack of judgment.

She needed the freedom to figure stuff out for herself. And maybe what she was figuring out there was that slower worked better for her.

"I like walking alongside you all. That pace is just right," she told the group. "Let's take a water break at the corner," she suggested. "Humans and furry friends all hydrate at the halfway point."

"One of us will have to remember about stopping to hydrate once Jia's gone."

The words hit her like a ton of bricks. Of course Jia had thought about eventually having to leave the desert and go back to New York. But she didn't realize that maybe her friends, the residents there, were also thinking about it. Her chest felt tight, and the sudden pressure of a timeline made it feel like she was carrying fifty pounds of stress on her shoulders.

"You guys can't get rid of me that quick," she said. She tried to keep her voice light, joking.

"We'd keep you here forever if we could," Gladys said.

A chorus of *yes*es and *yup*s and *you betcha*s followed. Tears welled up in Jia's eyes. She'd never felt like she belonged anywhere. And suddenly, after living among a bunch of seniors in a retirement community, she'd felt like she'd found a home.

But this couldn't be her home, could it? Jia needed a job. She needed a place to live. She needed a life. And none of those things were available to her here at Sunset Hills, what with age restrictions, financial burdens, and overbearing parents with their own expectations of her.

And the sense of loss weighed the heaviest on her of all.

"Hey, Dennis? Do you remember where we put the toolbox?" Henry rummaged through the garage looking for where he'd put the stuff he didn't think Dennis would need on the regular.

"Yeah, it's out in the garage. What do you need it for?" Dennis asked.

"Thought I might try to make something, an instrument of some kind. Wanna help me figure it out?" Henry asked.

Dennis's eyes lit up at the offer. "You betcha, I do," he said. He came and sat next to Henry at the kitchen table. Henry had a pen and paper and began drawing.

"Okay, so this is what I was thinking . . ."

20

The now-familiar knock came at the front door—two knocks, pause, three pounds. It was the code derived from the neighborhood watch to signal a friendly person was there. Its pattern set itself apart enough that it couldn't be mistaken for anything else and was a loud-enough combination that residents who were hard of hearing could easily make it out. Not a solicitor, a scammer, or someone with bad intentions. Henry liked the idea of a secret knock. And he really liked how everyone took care of each other and watched out for one another at The Sunset. Though, with the way the neighbors always came to visit his granddad on the regular, Henry had had a hard time concentrating on his work since he arrived.

But if he were being honest, it was the best, most relaxing, most fun time he'd had in a long time.

Henry opened the front door and there, standing behind the screen, was Jia, in a brown-and-blue checkered muumuu. He wondered if she were ever going to go to the airport to pick up her own luggage, but by this point, it was pretty obvious she wasn't in a hurry to do so. The airport was a ten-minute drive away, so it didn't seem like something too hard to do. He should ask her. Maybe offer to take her.

But the more he got to know Jia, the more he realized how deep her waters flowed. There weren't just willy-nilly reasons for how she was. She was thoughtful and emotional, empathetic and purposeful. The reasons she'd likely share about her luggage and her clothing would probably go deeper than Henry wanted or needed to know about his neighbor, so he always held back. Rather, he found it an amusing game seeing what new piece of her grandmother's wardrobe she'd be sharing that day.

But after their kiss the other night at sunset, his curiosity about Jia had only grown. He wanted to know more. Because her quirkiness, her zest for life, and her pouty bottom lip were incredibly sexy to Henry.

"Hey there," he said, as he opened the screen door. "Come in."

"I wish I could, but I have to get these invitations out for the rest of the street," she said.

Jia just stood there.

Henry stood back.

"Okay," he said, drawing it out and hoping Jia would go on with why she was here. "Did you say invitations?"

"Oh god, yeah, sorry. I've got like a hundred things going through my head right now. There's so much to do before the prom, and if I don't write this all down, I know I'm going to forget."

Henry knew he had heard her say *prom* but had no idea what she was talking about. But if he asked her, he risked distracting her and everything she was trying to remember. "Jia," he said.

"Yeah?"

"Do you want a pen and a piece of paper or something? To write stuff down?" he offered.

"No, no. I'm good. Streamers, punch bowl, step-and-repeat, photographer. Streamers, punch bowl, step-and-repeat, photographer," she chanted.

Henry let out a sigh, dropping his shoulders. They could be stuck there all day at this rate. He made a mental note: *streamers, punch bowl, step-and-repeat, photographer.* And then asked the million-dollar question. "Jia, what brings you here this morning? Did you want to invite Dennis somewhere?"

"Yes! I'm throwing a seniors' prom. Get it? A prom for seniors, not the senior class, but senior citizens," she said. Her wide smile giving away how proud of herself she was for coming up with that one.

Henry shook his head but couldn't help but let out a chortle. He was also very impressed that Jia had planned and executed so many things in a few short weeks. She was motivated and organized, and she delivered. Nothing like the person she had been made out to be back at Bakerson's Group. Henry wasn't used to being surprised by people. He was always prepared, overprepared mostly, and made sure to know what he was getting into and who he was dealing with. Realizing now that he'd believed in a narrative about Jia that very likely was untrue made him antsy. And angry.

This emotion was happening more and more with his work.

"And are you here to invite Dennis to the seniors' prom? Is there a date? A time??"

"Of course Dennis is invited. All the residents are. And so are you. You have to come. All the ladies made sure I asked you. They're dying to see you dance again," she said. "It's Friday night at six o'clock. I know that's late for everyone, so I'm encouraging afternoon naps and early dinners before you arrive. Palm Springs formal attire suggested."

"Palm Springs formal?"

"You know, anything that's clean, ironed, and can stand the heat," she said with a giggle.

"Got it. Well, I'll let Dennis know. I'll walk him down there on Friday."

"And you'll stay and dance a few rounds with the ladies?"

"No promises."

"It's gonna be a blast," she assured him.

"I have no doubt," he replied.

"Okay. I'm off, then. More invitations to get through." She waved over her shoulder as she turned and walked away.

"Jia," Henry called after her.

"Yeah?" she answered.

"*Streamers, punch bowl, step-and-repeat, photographer,*" he listed off.

She made a mental note, nodded, and smiled. "Thanks, I completely forgot all of that for a minute."

He knew she would. So that was why he'd memorized it.

The community center was decorated to the nines.

An appreciative whistle came from next to him. "They really know how to throw a party, huh?" his granddad noted.

"She really does," Henry said back, taking it all in.

The front entrance was decorated with a balloon arch in red, white, and green.

Inside, tables bordered the room with red tablecloths and plastic poinsettia centerpieces.

"Would you look at that! It's a goddamn Christmas party in the middle of summer," Dennis hollered over the music.

Henry barked out a laugh when he realized it as well.

"Dennis, Henry, you made it! Isn't it fabulous? A midyear holiday seniors' prom! Go figure!" Mimi walked up and gave Dennis a hug and Henry a kiss on the cheek.

A man with white hair and a full, matching beard walked in the door wearing a red sweatsuit with a white T-shirt peeking out from the top and bottom of the sweatshirt barely covering his large round midsection. He looked around at the decorations and down at himself. "Well, shit," he said and walked back out the door.

Henry raised his eyebrows, and Dennis shrugged his shoulders.

"Oh, that's Chris. He's gotten mistaken for Santa Claus for decades. Probably going home to change into something a little less obvious considering the last-minute theme."

Henry didn't know what to say to that.

"Henry, be a doll and go help Jia at the snacks table? She won't let any of us do any work and insists we get to dancing. Maybe you'll have better luck."

"Sure, of course. I'll be back, Granddad," he said.

"I'll be on the dance floor. Let's go, Mimi. Tell me they spiked the punch in that bowl," he said.

"This isn't amateur hour, Dennis," she said back.

Henry hoped this wouldn't quite be the shit show that his own prom had been. But no one needed to know that Henry had been dumped by his high school girlfriend who'd rather have spent the dance with the runner up for prom king. Henry had been pushed into taking a picture by himself, drinking too much spiked punch, and throwing up into the school's prized possession, their 1985 football state championship trophy.

Henry found Jia pouring a bag of chips into a large bowl.

"Hey there, I was relegated to the snacks table so as not to embarrass myself on the dance floor. What can I do?"

"Hey there," Jia greeted. Her face lit up when she saw Henry, and his heartbeat picked up like a fifteen-year-old boy. What the fuck? Get a grip, Shin.

But she was beautiful.

Jia had on what looked like a white nightgown with lace around the neckline and the hem. Over it, she wore an oversized red cardigan with her hair tied up in a ponytail with curls.

"It looks amazing in here," Henry said as he leaned in, placed his hand on her hip, and gave her a kiss on the cheek. "And you look incredible," he whispered into her ear. He didn't know what had gotten into him. He wasn't a public-display kind of guy, and this wasn't even his girlfriend. Maybe it was the surprise holiday spirit. Or maybe it was just the magic of Jia.

Jia's cheeks pinkened.

"Thanks. It's one of Mimi's nightgowns. I just thought it looked so pretty and romantic, I wore it as a dress," she said. She was surprisingly shy, and it honestly was a huge turn-on for Henry. He squeezed her hip before letting go and moving back.

They stood there at the snacks table passing out cups of spiked punch to the residents. Everyone who walked up gave Jia a hug and thanked her for such a nice party.

Henry had felt pretty proud of his accomplishments in his life thus far but hadn't had reason to feel proud for anyone else in his life. Until now. He loved every genuine and warm compliment people came to give Jia.

"You know, you did a really great job here," Henry commented.

"Yeah? Thanks. It's fun seeing everyone having such a good time," she said.

"Where'd the Christmas theme come from? You didn't mention it with the invite," he commented.

She laughed. "We had a limited budget. So it was either the extra liquor for the punch or the decorations. I made an executive decision and got top shelf at the wine store, and the sale bin at the party store. This was the best I could pull off. And who doesn't love an ironic theme?"

"Clearly this crowd does," he said. "It never ceases to amaze me how well you know the people here and what they want and need. I feel like your coming here added something special to this place."

"Well, I think I needed this place as much as it might've needed me," Jia admitted.

Henry raised an eyebrow, hoping to encourage her to go on.

He'd never really heard from her what she wanted, what she hoped to get out of being here, what she was going to do next. And all of these things suddenly seemed to matter to him.

But she closed up right away, seemingly unwilling to share. For someone so vibrant and willing to do so much to help others, Henry was beginning to see that Jia shared very little about her own needs.

"It's not really my place to ask, but do you know what you're gonna do next?" Henry asked, deciding he had to take the direct approach.

"I'm not really great at keeping a job, apparently." She snuck a peek at him under her eyelashes.

He stiffened. "I . . . About that . . ."

"We don't have to talk about it. I thought about asking your advice with something. But I realized you might be breaking some kind of rules talking to a former employee about Bakerson's stuff, right? And you don't quite strike me as a rule breaker, Mr. I Have To Get A Visitor's Permit." Jia leaned into him and gave him a little nudge with her shoulder. The small contact immediately put him at ease. "Anyways, I figured this time I should really know what I want to do before jumping in. That way, the chances are better for me not to be a total failure yet again."

"You're not. A failure, I mean. You're pretty amazing, if you ask me. I know I gave you a little bit of a hard time about it when I first got here. But I see it now. What you're doing here, for the residents, for their lives. It's incredible."

"A *little* bit of a hard time?" Jia laughed. "I thought you were gonna petition to have me removed, citing the HOA bylaws."

He lifted his hands in surrender. "I was just looking out for my granddad, making sure there weren't any rebellious rule breakers in the neighborhood."

Jia gave him a playful push. "You haven't figured out that you and I are the last people to worry about here? Miscreants, all of them."

They both looked out at the crowd of seniors on the dance floor having the time of their lives. Henry didn't know them all by name like Jia did. But he could see what her efforts had brought them. He found Dennis on the dance floor, shimmying his hips, his walker nowhere to be found. Henry smiled.

"Thank you for giving this to him," he said to her.

She shrugged. "I'm just helping them all have some fun," Jia replied.

"No, you're giving them their dignity. You're building their confidence. You're giving them reasons to live and enjoy their lives. It's pretty astounding. And, well, I've learned a lot from you. So thank you."

Jia laughed off Henry's compliment. "You make it sound like planning parties is akin to saving lives," she said.

"You know it's more than that. What you do here . . ."

Jia shook her head, uncomfortable with the words. Had no one complimented her on her work before in her life? Henry found that hard to believe.

"We're low on ice. I'll be right back." Jia turned and ran off, leaving him standing there in front of a spiked punch bowl and filled with questions about who had hurt Jia Chung and what he could do to help her see herself the way the rest of them saw her.

21

"You really don't have to come with me," Jia said over her shoulder as she made her way to the kitchen at the back of the community center.

She would just need one minute on her own to catch her breath. To make sense of what Henry had said about her. To remind herself that he didn't really know her at all.

But he wouldn't let her go alone. He wouldn't let her escape him and his surprisingly kind words.

"You said you were getting ice, and I'm coming to help you carry it out," he said.

"I'll be okay. I promise I'm capable of carrying a bag of ice." The final word caught in her throat. She wasn't sure why she was getting so emotional. Maybe because she wanted to believe the things he said about the Jia there in the desert. That maybe he was wrong about the Jia he terminated back in New York.

Henry's hand wrapped around her arm and gently tugged at

her to turn to face him. "I know you can get ice on your own, Jia. I'm becoming well aware of what you're capable of. And it's so much more than you give yourself credit for."

She shook her head as he spoke. Jia was nice. She was kind. She was a good time. She made people happy. So she could plan a party. But none of that mattered. When she met someone new, and they inevitably would ask *What do you do?* When she filled out job applications, and they asked *What's your experience?* And if she wanted to have a voice, speak up about how maybe what had happened to her when she was fired wasn't entirely fair, no one would listen.

"Hey," Henry said, blocking her path, stopping her in her tracks. He put his hand under her chin and lifted it so her eyes were forced to meet his. "Listen to me. I don't know what lies you're telling yourself right now. But I'm telling you, I see you, and this is what I know. And I don't give out compliments or even bother to say kind words to people that often." He smiled. It was shy, self-effacing, so unlike the confident and stern Henry she was so used to seeing. It made her want to listen.

"You're incredible. Possibly the most capable person I've ever met. You're capable of loving freely," he said. His voice was so gentle she almost didn't believe she'd heard it. "You're capable of making anyone feel seen and heard," he added. He lifted his hand and reached past her face, tucking an errant strand of hair behind her ear. "You're capable of giving people their value and their confidence back," he said as he stepped in closer to her. "I've never been the type of person that usually even notices these things. But with you, it's like a billboard hangs out above you with shining lights announcing that someone's here to take care of everything, everyone. You, Jia, you take care of everything."

She shook her head, trying to not let his words take residence in her brain. Jia Chung was a screwup. She let people down. And a few weeks out in the desert having some fun with old people didn't change that.

Did it?

She still didn't have a job. She still didn't have prospects to set her up for her future. She still had bad credit. She still had no health insurance. She could go down an entire list of things she didn't have.

But Henry stood here trying to convince her she was more than enough. Could she believe him?

Henry crowded Jia closer until her back hit the wall. He reached out an arm and leaned it against the wall, blocking her in. She didn't know why she'd ever said it. She was not choosing the bear over this man.

He smelled impossibly good even through the scent of disinfectant and bleach in the community center's kitchen.

"Actually, I was wrong, Jia. You're not capable."

There they were. The words that she knew would eventually come. He realized the truth.

She dropped her head and could not look at him. But his fingers gently propped below her chin, once again lifting her head up to face him. "You're so much more than that. You're extraordinary."

A tear pooled in and eventually dropped from her eye down her cheek, and he bent a little closer to her. His lips met it with the gentlest kiss. She let out a sob.

"Sweet Jia, please don't cry because someone, anyone, made you believe you were less than amazing," he whispered into her ear. "Especially if that someone was me."

He pulled back and looked at her. His gaze was tender and

pleading. His hands had grabbed her arms with just enough grip that she felt . . . grounded.

"Henry—" It was the only word she got out before his lips were on hers. They were but a whisper of a touch at first. Like he was asking for the permission to kiss her. She placed her hands on his hips and pulled him until their bodies were flush against each other. "Yes," she said as she pulled back for just a second before pressing her kiss to him, harder than he had. She had no hesitation. She wanted him.

And that was all he needed.

His mouth hungrily took over. He reached down, grabbed both her hands, and then lifted them above her head, holding them there against the wall with one of his while his other arm wrapped around her waist. His upper body leaned in, pressing her back, while his arm pulled her hips toward his.

Henry's lips moved to her neck and then her ear. Jia's head was spinning with desire, but she wasn't able to reach for him while he had her pinned. Jia didn't usually like being overtaken, but with Henry, it felt safe. Like she knew how much being in control meant for him, so giving him this felt like her own level of satisfaction.

The hand around her waist lowered, reaching down under her dress, lifting up the fabric to expose her from the waist down. She felt the coolness of the air-conditioned chill and shivered.

"Open your eyes, Jia," Henry commanded. She didn't realize they'd been closed.

"I want to watch you," he said.

Jia felt Henry's hand tug at her underwear and pull it to the side. A long finger dragged along her fold, until it reached the top and pressed against her clit.

Jia cried out at the pressure.

"You are so fucking wet and hot down here," he growled.

For a brief second, Jia's thoughts centered on how she'd never once heard Henry swear. Knowing she was the one to make him lose that control made her smile.

"You like that, do you?" he said.

"Yes," she said breathily.

The tip of his finger rubbed along her pussy until it found the opening. Henry's eyes focused on hers as she felt his finger enter her. Jia's eyes fluttered closed at the penetration.

"Open," he reminded her.

She quickly opened her eyes back up to look into his. His pupils were blown, and the look he gave her was so lust-filled she felt more wetness flood between her legs.

"Fuck," he said. He pressed his finger in again, dragging as he pulled it out. He added a second finger, and Jia felt the stretch along with the faintest burn.

She wanted more.

"Henry, I want you," she said.

He moved his fingers faster. "Baby, I'm gonna make you come just like this."

She thrust her hips to meet his hand as he pumped harder. "I want you inside me," she pleaded. She needed more. She wanted the burn of being stretched, filled.

"Not here, not where I can't take my time with you," he said. He bent down to kiss her again, his tongue pushing into her mouth, taking control, moving at the same pace as his hand. In and out.

Jia knew what Henry was capable of if they had more time. She'd had him before. She needed him again.

The mere memory of his cock inside her had her clenching,

the pulsations of desire grabbing his fingers, letting him know how much she wanted him.

"Tonight, I make you come on my fingers, and I'm gonna lick every last drop of you off them. And clean your pussy up with my tongue."

"You read legal briefings with that mouth?" she asked with a wicked smile.

Henry's eyes flared, and the corner of his mouth lifted. "I'm gonna show you everything I can do with this mouth," he whispered into her ear.

God, Jia needed more of this man. She hungrily leaned in for his mouth, and he kissed her back, all lips, tongue, teeth. No finesse, just a passionate ache to connect.

She reached down for the button of Henry's slacks and pulled them open, dragging the zipper down with it.

Henry's cock strained against the cotton of his boxer briefs, and Jia wanted to take a look. But that would require disconnecting from Henry's mouth, and she wasn't ready for that yet. He tasted so damn good.

Instead, she let her hand do the exploring.

Her fingers found the waistband and pulled, giving her space to get her hand in and find its prize.

He was long, thick. She remembered how perfectly he had fit inside her, the stretch of when he entered, the fullness of when he planted himself and then moved with precision.

Jia loved the feeling of him in her hand. She dragged her thumb across the tip of his cock. The wet of his precum making the motion slick.

"Fuck," Henry hissed at the contact.

As if Jia needed any more encouragement. But damn, hearing

Henry cuss, losing control of his carefully chosen vocabulary, charged her.

She wrapped her fingers around his shaft and applied pressure.

His breathing sped up, and so did the thrusting of the fingers inside her.

Henry grabbed and lifted one of Jia's legs and wrapped it around his waist, drawing them impossibly close at that angle. She began to pump him, and as she did, her own motion dragged across her clit. His fingers on the inside, her own fist on the outside, bringing both of them pleasure.

He angled one of his fingers and hit something inside her that triggered every nerve ending and made Jia gasp. "Oh god," she groaned.

He pressed his body closer to hers, each of them with a hand working toward the other's pleasure trapped between their bodies.

She moved in tandem with his body rubbing, pumping, receiving the thrusts. She felt completely out of control and had no idea how she was still standing.

She tightened her hold on him, and he growled in her ear, "Don't you fucking dare make me come before you do."

And as if he decided to release the secret weapon, his thumb pressed down on her clit. That was all it took. Jia felt like an explosion had gone off within her. Waves of pleasure caused her to pulse between her legs. It was as if she was outside of her body hearing her own voice scream *Yes, yes, yes* in a way that would give any porn star a run for their money.

She had no idea how she managed to keep holding on to him, but she circled his dick with her thumb and forefinger, dragging them along his shaft from tip to base. When she'd stopped pulsating, he moved his fingers from her and shoved his hand down his pants and wrapped it around her hand. His was wet from her orgasm. And the two of them together picked up the pace.

Henry quickly pulled his cock out of his briefs and his pants, turning at a slight angle as he came all over the wall next to Jia. His hand held on to her shoulder while the last of his own thrusts and squirts emptied out of him.

Next thing she knew, he laid his head down on her shoulder.

There was something so intimate and tender about the position. Jia turned and softly laid a kiss on top of his head.

Jia felt Henry shift as he readjusted himself. He pulled up and managed to zip and button his slacks and then turn toward Jia, helping straighten her skirt. He reached around her for the stack of napkins on the counter and gently cleaned their hands and wiped down the wall.

"Probably gonna need some disinfectant for that," he said.

He hadn't looked at her once.

"Um, everything okay?" she asked.

She waited the second it took for him to respond. He straightened up to full height and then bent his head to look down into Jia's eyes. The intensity shocked her.

"You and I are going to fuck, for real, soon. And I mean it, Jia. I'm not waiting. I have to get inside you again. We're figuring out a when and a where, understood?"

As if she needed the encouragement. She nodded her head enthusiastically. She liked the sound of that.

He placed a surprisingly gentle kiss on her mouth and then her cheek. "We're making a plan before the night is done. I'll fuck you in the back of my rental if I have to."

The desperation in his voice charged her. She wanted it too.

So much. She wrapped her arms around his neck and pulled him down for another kiss. A promise. Next time they'd do it for real. And soon. She shivered with the anticipation.

Jia pulled back, and Henry gave her a last kiss on the top of her head.

"We should probably get back out there," she said.

He nodded. He took one more second and breath to gain his composure, and then he opened the door to the kitchen and led them back out to the party.

22

For someone who prided himself on being in control of every aspect of his life, Henry felt anything but when it came to Jia.

His hands still buzzed as they walked out together. The electric current caused him to extend and flex his hands a couple times so he wouldn't reach out for her, wouldn't pull her back into another room, wouldn't take her fully, right this minute, like he wanted. He felt like a sex-crazed sixteen-year-old. He had to have Jia, all of her. He needed her naked and screaming, riding his cock, and taking it all the way to the hilt as deep as it could go.

Fuck it. He reached out for her hand and wrapped his around hers, leading her back to the main hall. He couldn't remember the last time he'd held someone's hand. It wasn't an intimacy Henry allowed or enjoyed. But he wanted that connection now.

The first time they'd been together back in New York, he'd taken her home thinking she was nothing more than a hookup, a one-time thing. But even then, as he'd tasted her to climax and she'd sucked him deep after, as he entered her from above and later behind, as she'd openly expressed what she wanted with *More* and *Harder* and moans that could get Henry hard right now thinking about them, he knew he hadn't gotten enough. He surprised himself by thinking of that woman the next day and even days after.

What he didn't expect was how much more he wanted Jia now that she had a name, now as he was getting to know her, now that he knew what she was capable of. Her kindness was sexy. Her enthusiasm addictive. Her selflessness, her determination, her joy . . . Fuck, he wanted to be around her all the time. And he wanted her all to himself as soon as he could get her.

There just weren't going to be a lot of places or opportunities while they both lived with their grandparents.

Henry needed a plan.

When they turned the corner from the kitchen, the party seemed unbothered, having gone on without them there.

Henry walked them up to where his grandfather and Mimi stood. Mimi glanced down at their connected hands and back up to Jia, her smile stretched wide.

"Um . . ." Jia stuttered.

"We went to get more ice," Henry said.

Mimi looked around them to the punch table where ice did not magically appear. She nodded. "I see," she said.

Jia's face pinkened. "Did you, uh, hear everything?"

Mimi shook her head. "I don't know what you're talking about. The moment you two walked off, I had everyone turn down their hearing aids and the DJ turn the tunes up. It's a party, after all."

"Thanks, Mimi," Jia said, rolling her eyes.

Henry nodded, giving a small smile to Mimi in appreciation.

They could keep it discreet and pretend like it didn't happen in front of their grandparents. Everything was good.

"Tale as old as time. Two kids sneak off and enjoy their first time together. What's a prom without someone getting lucky, am I right?" Dennis said.

Henry dropped his head to his chest. Oh god.

"Except this isn't their first time," Mimi said.

"Grandma!"

Henry turned to Jia. "You told her?"

"I was having a crisis. The man that fired me was also the man I had mind-blowing sex with? Oh, and he happens to be our neighbor's grandson? I think yes, I definitely told her. I needed Mimi's wisdom."

"Mind-blowin', you say? Way to go, Hank. I knew you had it in ya," Dennis said, patting Henry's back. His face beamed with pride brighter than when Henry had graduated law school.

"Come on, Mimi, let's dance and let these kids get back to canoodling," Dennis said, grabbing Mimi by the hand and leading her to the dance floor.

"You know, if you two want some privacy, we can arrange to stay at the prom for another, oh, say, hour or so?" Mimi called back as she was led away.

"Oh god. I think our grandparents just gave us permission to sneak off and have sex," she said laughing. The fairy lights that decorated the room sparkled in Jia's eyes.

"But apparently just a quickie," Henry teased. The offer was tempting. But he was going to make his next real time with Jia better than their first. A hand job was hot. A quickie could be fun. But Henry had something else in mind in this moment.

He pulled her by the hand he was holding and drew her close to him "Shall we?"

Jia smiled and nodded and followed him to the center of the crowd where he put his arm around her waist and drew her against his body. "I thought you didn't dance," she whispered into his ear.

He didn't. But he would.

"I can sway back and forth a little. If that's enough?"

"It's everything."

"Well, don't the two of you make a beautiful pair," Betty said as she and Herbert danced past them. Herbert sat in his wheelchair as Betty pushed and spun them around to the music.

"You two put us to shame with your moves," Jia said back. Betty's smile spread across her whole face.

"Are we voting for a prom king and queen? Because I know who I want to win," Gordon called out from the snacks table.

"Hear! Hear! They've got my vote too," Gladys said, clinking red solo cups of spiked punch with Gordon.

Henry looked down into Jia's eyes. They sparkled as if she had her own fairly lights that lit up from within. He'd never felt this accepted and embraced by people as he did by the people of The Sunset. And that included Jia. He pushed back fears of the other shoe dropping. He quieted the voice in his head that wanted to reason how these feelings were fleeting and they, as morbid as it would sound, were all on a ticking clock of some sort or another.

Instead, he allowed himself for this night to feel . . . happy. To lend his heart in this moment to someone else other than just himself.

He bowed his head and met Jia's lips. Just a soft whisper of a kiss.

And the two of them danced the night away to "Winter Wonderland" on a blistering hot summer night.

With the promise of more to come.

23

Jia was one of those types that got the postcoital gooey and mushy feelings. She didn't think Henry would love this about her. But she couldn't help herself.

"Something smells great in here," her grandmother said, joining Jia in the kitchen.

"I made a pie," she admitted.

"A pie is very nice. I hear young men love pies."

"Oh, well, it's like a belated welcome pie . . . for, um . . . Dennis. And Henry if he wants some."

"Jia, honey, the way you braided the top of the crust, that's a thanks-for-the-fuck pie if I ever did see one."

"Grandma!" Jia gasped.

"Like I said, honey, men love pies. Now, I've got Knitting Club tonight at Mary Beth's house. She said she got some new mattress for her guest bedroom, and she's not sure it's very comfortable. Maybe her granddaughter won't like it when she visits for Christmas. So I agreed to test it out. Gonna give it a practice run and spend the night in it tonight. Don't worry, Mary Beth promised to buy me coffee from the cart tomorrow morning as a thank-you. So don't expect me home until well after nine tomorrow. Hate to leave you . . . *alone* like this, but you know how I am. Gotta help a friend in need."

"Uh-huh," Jia said. She wrapped her arms around her grandmother and hugged her tight. "Thanks, Mimi. I love you," she whispered into her ear.

"Be safe and have fun . . . by yourself," she said. "Unless you want to have a friend over for your own slumber party." She winked at Jia and walked out of the kitchen.

Jia was giddy with excitement. She could have sex with Henry tonight in a bed. They wouldn't have to go park somewhere for privacy and worry about gear shifts or cops finding them. What a relief.

She placed the pie in the Tupperware container and walked out to deliver it to him—them—Dennis and Henry.

Outside she saw Harold walking his dog, Chewbacca. As the dog did his business, Harold took a stick with pincher tongs at the bottom and picked up the waste off the ground, without having to bend all the way over. One press of a button and the waste emptied into a bag attached to a hook separate from the tongs. Cool.

"Hey there, how's it going?" Jia asked as she crossed the street to greet her neighbor. Jia balanced the Tupperware in one hand as she bent to pet the head of the little pupper with the other. "That's a cool contraption you've got there. I bet a lot of people in the neighborhood would love something like that. Where'd you get it?" Jia asked.

"Oh, I don't think it's for sale anywhere. It's one of a kind. Henry made it for me," he said.

"What?"

"Yeah, he said he'd heard it was rough for me to pick up after my dog and he'd felt so bad giving me a hard time about it. He made this and asked me if it worked okay. We tried it right then and there, and it was perfect. Look, the poop even drops straight into the bag. I just have to reach out and grab it, tie it up, and I can throw it away at home. Pretty cool, right?"

"Henry . . . he made that for you?" Jia's heart felt ten times too big for her chest. He'd made it . . . to help someone who wasn't able to do what needed to be done. She swallowed. She was going to take such good care of that man tonight, he had no idea.

"He did. Good boy, that one. I hope I'll get to see him before he leaves. Or before I do."

The comment struck Jia. She'd hadn't even thought about how Henry was only here for a couple weeks. She wondered if they'd see each other when the two of them were back in New York. Was she overthinking all of this?

But also . . .

"What do you mean before you do?" she asked.

"Oh, well, looks like I might be selling my place," he said.

"Why's that?" It used to be that people only sold their homes here if they were going into assisted living. And Harold was nowhere needing that kind of support. He was perfectly capable of living here with the support of the community. She really hoped it wasn't what she thought it might be . . . that someone might be behind this, encouraging Harold to leave before he was ready.

"Well, some real estate guy reached out to my family and suggested it might be time for me to move. Told them he could get them a lot of money for my place and that, since I wasn't getting any younger, it might be the time to move me to the assisted-living place down the way," Harold explained. His shoulders dropped, and his voice sounded resigned.

"What?" Jia was livid. "WHO? Who is this guy?"

"Oh, some slick guy named Matt, or something like that. He seems to be reaching out to a lot of other families too. Like he knew which ones of us were getting a bit older or whose families weren't like you and Mimi, if you know what I mean."

Matt? Airport Matt? Date at the Del Rey Matt? "Was the name Matthew Singleton?" she asked.

"Yes, yes, that sounds like the name. Do you know him? If you do, Jia, maybe you can ask him to talk to my family again and maybe have them change their minds. They don't listen to what I want. And honestly, I'm getting a little sad at the thought of moving. How will I get my steps in if I don't have Zumba class or Walking Club? Plus some of those other places don't accept dogs. Where will Chewbacca go?" Harold's voice began to shake with the emotion.

Jia wrapped her arms around the smaller, bent man. "Harold, don't you worry about anything just yet, okay? I'm not gonna let anyone make decisions for you that you're not agreeing with. We'll figure this out." She gave him a squeeze, and he squeezed back. Plenty of strength left in him.

"Thanks, Jia. You're the best," Harold said.

"Okay, I gotta run. But remember, don't make any decisions and don't let your family pressure you into anything until we talk again, okay? I need to check on some stuff first."

"Sure, sure, Jia. I trust you. I probably trust you more than I do my own kids, I hate to say." Harold's smile was a sad one, and Jia's heart broke a little. She wasn't sure what she could do, but she wasn't going to let any of her people go down without a fight.

Jia gave him one last squeeze on the arm and jogged toward Dennis's place. She did not like the sound of all of this. It couldn't be legal, could it? Forcing older people to sell their homes? She needed Henry's professional opinion on all of this.

They would discuss it over pie.

"Hi." Henry's hair was tussled and his smile sleepy. Jia wanted to jump him right there in the doorway. Privacy and propriety be damned.

"Napping during the day, Mr. Shin? You look very relaxed. Very unlike you," she teased. Truth be told, she loved that Henry was relaxing. He could use the rest.

"I didn't even realize I'd fallen asleep. I was looking over contracts."

"Yes, that is indeed shocking. How could anyone fall asleep over contracts?" Jia teased. "I brought you a pie," she said. She held the Tupperware out to Henry, and he looked down inspecting it.

When his eyes lifted back up to meet hers, she didn't expect the emotion she found in his gaze. "Thank you," he said, voice soft.

"My pleasure. Share it with Dennis, okay?" she said, smiling.

Henry took the pie and put it down on the console table behind him.

"Come here," Henry said, pulling Jia into the house. He wrapped an arm around her and drew her into his body, still warmed from sleep.

Jia hesitated, looking around to see whether Dennis was around.

"He's at Book Club," Henry said, as if reading her mind.

"Oh, I'm so glad. I was hoping he'd join them. There are some real characters in that group."

"Yeah, I know. Someone named Farrah came over and personally handed my granddad a copy of a book called *The Love Hypothesis* and told him to read it and be ready to discuss."

Jia started laughing. Oh god, Farrah was a character.

"Jia, Dennis was red in the face for at least two hours after. But it was nothing compared to the other night when he got a third of the way through the book and I heard him whistling. I—" Henry paused and composed himself "—do not want to know what was in those pages."

"I don't know," Jia said, leaning into him. "Maybe we could find some inspiration."

Suddenly Jia was airborne and lifted into Henry's arms as he walked her over to the sofa. He sat down and dropped her into his lap. She readjusted her legs to straddle him. Jia wrapped her arms around his neck and leaned in for a kiss.

"I'm plenty inspired," he said against her lips.

She rubbed herself against him. "Yeah, you are," she teased. She kissed him again as she felt him grow harder between her legs, too many layers of clothing between them in her opinion. "Henry," she moaned. The two of them rubbed against each other, grinding in a rhythm. God, Jia loved this position. Jia moved her lips to Henry's neck and sucked. He tasted so good.

"Jesus," he said as he bucked his hips up against her. "I need to get you naked and into a bed, but I think Dennis will be back sooner than later."

"Oh, wait." That reminded her. She stopped what she was doing and leaned back.

Henry leaned forward, not wanting to lose the connection from her mouth. Jia laughed.

"We have all night!" she declared. "Mimi is spending the night at a friend's house. My bed is ours. All. Night. Long."

"Are you serious? No disruptions? Just us and a bed?" Henry's eyes lit up like a horny teenager, and Jia was living for it. Henry, this sweet, sweet man. Like when he made that tool for Harold to pick up his dog's—

"Henry," Jia exclaimed, "I need your help."

"Um, okay . . ."

"I just remembered. First." She kissed him. Hard. "You are a saint."

He lifted an eyebrow.

"The poop tool you made for Chewbacca! Are you kidding me? Genius. You softie." Jia tapped him on the chest over his heart. The corner of Henry's mouth lifted along with his shoulders. An aw-shucks shrug that Jia could not get enough of.

"And tell me how this leads to your needing my help?" Henry said, getting them back on track.

"Oh, right. That snake," Jia shuddered. She couldn't believe she'd gone out on a date with that guy. She'd given him some of her best flirty smiles. Wasted. Blech.

"Jia," Henry brought her back once more.

"Matthew, the real estate guy. You've dealt with him before, right? That's why you were so pissed off when you saw us together at the Del Rey? I thought you were kinda jealous. But now that I think back, you could barely stand me then. I mean, not like now." She waggled her eyebrows at him.

Henry grabbed both of Jia's wrists and squeezed a tiny bit. His thumbs rubbed over her pulse points. God that was more erotic than expected. "There was never a time I couldn't stand you," he said. Very stern. Very sexy.

"Oh." It was all she could think to say.

"But yes, he's a snake. And an asshole. He tried to scam Dennis. And I don't like him."

"You're hot when you get all growly like that," Jia said.

"Thanks," Henry said back. "Now, tell me why we're talking about that guy when I've got you straddled on top of my dick right now."

"Well, I've noticed more of the residents have been talking about moving out of Sunset Hills. It started confusing me. But it was always because their families were pressuring them. And guess who has been doing the pressuring?"

"Matthew?" Henry guessed correctly. Smarty-pants.

Jia nodded. "We have to stop him. We have to cease-and-desist him or something. We have to tell the families that they're wrong and that they should leave their loved ones here."

"Jia, I love that you care so much and that this matters so deeply to you. But it's not our business. It's not right for us to get involved in other people's family matters," Henry said matter-of-factly.

Jia couldn't believe how unaffected he seemed. This was terrible. What Matthew was doing was terrible. "But we have to help!"

"You're the one always telling me that we have to let the residents live their lives. Not infantilize them. Not make decisions for them. That's what you're trying to do." He was using his lawyer voice on her, and she didn't like it one bit.

"I'm trying to help. *We* should help. At least look over the contracts or whatever and see what their rights are. And then they can make their own informed decisions. Right now, I feel like they're getting pressured without knowing what they're allowed and not allowed to do." Jia's voice was getting more desperate. But she couldn't let Matthew just do this to the residents. She wouldn't.

"Jia, I'm not getting involved. Plus, I can't practice law in California. And I really don't think you ought to get involved either. Neither of us are experts in this area. I'm certain there are reasons we don't know about. The families know better. Just let it play out. Maybe, for some of the residents, this is the right move. Maybe it is time for them."

Jia's frustration and anger bubbled inside her. Henry was wrong. And he was unwilling to help. She really thought she'd seen some progress in him. But maybe not.

"I have to go," she said, scrambling to get off Henry's lap.

He held her at her waist as she stood up, making sure she wouldn't lose her balance. He stood up with her. "Jia . . ."

"It's fine. I can do it on my own," she said. She didn't care if she sounded petulant. She would do it on her own if she had to.

He let out a deep breath. "Don't be mad."

Jia dropped her shoulders. "I'm not mad. I'm just . . . worried. About Harold and Isabel and Dottie and whoever else might be next."

Henry wrapped his arms around her shoulders and brought her head to his chest. She listened to his heartbeat, steady, strong. "I know. But you can't carry the burden for everyone at The Sunset on your shoulders."

And as she continued to be lolled by the beat of Henry's heart, Jia thought to herself, *Just watch me.*

24

Henry sent Jia off on her way promising her that tonight, he was going to give her the date of her dreams: a home-cooked meal and lots of sex on a bed. She was thrilled. She was not the high-maintenance type.

He hadn't gotten much done today, but for once, Henry decided not to stress about it. Work was slow, it was why he'd been able to get away. And he was going to take the advice he'd given Jia and not carry the weight of everyone else's burdens on his shoulders.

So when the phone rang, he had a brief thought of letting it go to voice mail. But Henry wasn't going to change that easily. So he grabbed it before even looking to see who was calling.

"Goddamn it, Shin. What the fuck is going on over there?"

And that was why he was surprised by the voice of his boss on the line screaming at him before he'd even managed to say hello.

"Sir? What's going on over here? In the desert?" Henry was

trying to put two and two together in his head and was not sure what he was missing. His boss was in Saint Lucia this week. Henry was still within the two-week vacation period he'd requested to come to Palm Springs. And nothing, from what he'd heard from his team at their last check-in this morning, was happening in New York.

He'd just checked his email an hour ago . . .

"Don't you check your email? I forwarded you the message from Harrison, Mars, and Leighton. We're being sued."

Henry rushed to his laptop set up on the kitchen table and logged in. A message had been forwarded to him from his boss.

Subject: FW: What do I do with this?

It was from none other than Edison Wainwright, Jia's old boss.

Wainwright had been served papers. He was being sued for unlawful termination and a hostile work environment. The company was included in the lawsuit.

"Okay, I'm reviewing it all now. I'll get back to you when I know more. I'm on it," he told his boss.

"I don't need you bothering me with this over the weekend. Just take care of it, Henry. Jesus fucking Christ." And with that, he'd hung up. Missing were the effusive *Well dones*. No *son* at the end. Just an order to get it done.

Henry looked at the clock: 3:36. Dennis would be home any minute. And it was after close of business out in New York on a Friday.

The Henry of a couple weeks ago would have canceled all plans and immediately pored over every word of the documentation and then gone back to review everything in the employee files and his own personal Cover Your Ass file. He'd have answers for any question lobbed his way and a strategy set for how to move forward, taking no prisoners, and would be prepared to update his boss first thing Monday morning. He would have gone over it all again and again, singularly focused on it the entire weekend.

But Henry already knew what he'd find deeper in the lawsuit and in the files. He'd looked them over before, hadn't he? He had turned a blind eye to things that had been brought up and subsequently swept under the rug. And though he was confident he could figure out how to keep the company protected and get the lawsuit taken care of, he felt an unfamiliar turning in his stomach about it.

Dennis had bragged to everyone at The Sunset about his grandson the lawyer.

Mimi had patted him on the back time every time she saw him, greeting him like he was her favorite person.

Jia trusted him and looked at him like he was worth falling for. And he had fallen too, as much as he tried to deny it. Shit, and she had come to ask him for help today, to offer support to good people who needed and deserved it, and he'd refused.

There were people here who believed in him. Not like his boss did, to just get something taken care of. The people here believed he'd do the right thing.

He looked back at the email chain from his boss, from Edison Wainwright, from the law offices of Harris, Mars, and Leighton. He wasn't surprised by what he saw there. He just didn't know what to do. Was this the kind of lawyer Henry had worked his ass off to become? He closed his eyes, releasing a deep breath.

Henry wasn't so sure if he would do the right thing.

But he didn't want to think about this now. He didn't *have* to think about this now. He'd tackle it tomorrow.

Tonight, he was going to focus on Jia and making their date an amazing one. Because Jia deserved it. And in the back of his mind, Henry knew, circumstances being as they were, with the world working against them, that this could very well be their only date.

Henry took one last look at the email, took one closer look at the names of those on the claim, Stephanie Novak, Taylor Ann Graff, and Jia Chung. He wouldn't tell anyone at Bakerson's this—he wasn't bound to disclose this feeling. But damn if he wasn't proud seeing Jia's name there on the documentation. He'd hoped it would be.

Henry closed his laptop, stored it back in his workbag, and went to change for his date.

"Watching a man cook me dinner is possibly the sexiest thing ever," Jia said. She came up behind Henry and peeked around him to see what he was working on.

Henry liked cooking. Following recipes with clear directions and an immediate payoff satisfied his brain.

Jia's arms wrapped around Henry's waist, and he turned to face her. She was affectionate in ways he usually found uncomfortable. But with Jia, it felt nice. He took a quick glance at the timer on the pasta. He had seven minutes. The sauce he was putting together could wait a few. He was going to take advantage of every opportunity tonight to be with Jia in every way.

He bent and wrapped his own arms under her ass and lifted her up to sit on the kitchen island. "This is brand-new. Mimi always wanted an island," Jia said. The words came out breathy and made Henry feel feral.

"Well then, we've got to christen it, don't you think?"

Jia nodded feverishly. Henry laughed. "Oh, and, Jia? No more talk about Mimi. Or Dennis. Or Gladys or Betty or Gordon, for that matter. Let's let the young folks have some fun tonight, okay?"

Jia pouted. "But what about Ernie? He planted new rosebushes and got—"

Henry crashed his lips against hers, swallowing whatever Jia was about to say about Ernie's rosebushes. She smiled against his mouth and pressed herself harder against him.

Henry pulled back for one sec to check the timer.

"I'm sorry, am I not holding your attention, sir?" she said playfully.

"The pasta," he explained.

"Did I mention I love overcooked pasta?" she said teasingly.

"Well, in that case . . ." Henry pushed Jia's legs open, and she leaned her body back on the island. "We've got at least nine minutes, then. Plenty of time for an appetizer."

Jia had another one of Mimi's colorful, bold muumuus on. Henry realized these were quickly becoming her favorites to wear. As he lifted up the bottom of the dress, exposing her legs, it felt almost immodest, forbidden. He was rock-hard in his shorts.

Jia's hands came to Henry's head, and she threaded her fingers through his hair, gently pushing him where she wanted him to go. His impatient girl. He smiled. "Eight minutes," she teased.

It was all the encouragement he needed. Henry reached for the top of her panties and pulled them down her legs, exposing all of her to him. God she looked so fucking tasty. He could go slow, savor it, draw it out. But they were on a timer, and she was the one reminding him. He'd give it to her good, hard, and fast.

Henry's tongue went straight in lapping her folds, and Jia cried out, bucking her lower body up. He reached and placed his hand on her stomach. Bent over her body like this, he felt the burn in his legs. Better than doing a hundred squats, he thought. Still, his back wouldn't last this way.

"Baby, scoot back just a little," he encouraged her. He helped push her back farther onto the island. And then lifted her legs and placed them straddled on his shoulders. Perfect. With one hand bracing the edge of the marble, the other grabbing hold of one of Jia's legs, he propped her up just a little to give him the angle he needed. He bent his head down and went back to devouring her.

He licked up one side and back down the other. God, she tasted so sweet. "Henry," she kept whispering. Henry kissed and sucked and licked, and she took it all. He speared his tongue into her hole, and Jia bucked again. "Yes," she said, louder this time. "God, yes."

Her hands tightened in his hair, and he could tell she was already close. His responsive girl. As his tongue continued to go in and out of her, he brought his hand up to her clit, pressing down on it with his thumb and then rolling it between his thumb and forefinger. "Oh my god," she cried out.

She wriggled and squirmed, pushing herself against his face. She took without apology, and Henry happily gave her what she wanted.

She moved faster against him as he worked her clit, his tongue moving in time with her body. He felt the pulsations against his tongue immediately as Jia gave a loud moan and came, wetness coming out of her and into his mouth. He swallowed the taste of her as her body collapsed onto the island.

Henry kissed up her stomach until he reached her breasts. Her nipples were hard and pebbled. He sucked the right one and then moved over to the left. Jia hissed and bucked. "Everything's really tender after I come," she confessed.

Henry was amazed how freely Jia spoke about anything and everything. Henry was usually guarded in what he shared. He wanted to tell Jia more about his thoughts and feelings, or at least, he could try. He could start by talking to her about the lawsuit. He wondered if she would bring it up tonight. He wasn't sure if he wanted her to or not.

But it would be the biggest buzzkill. And right now, he just wanted to raise a shield around them both and shut out the rest of the world.

Henry's head appeared through the neckline of the muumuu. "These things are big enough for the both of us to wear," he joked. He leaned on top of her and kissed her just as the beep of the timer went off.

"Perfect timing," she said against his lips.

He lifted his head and looked directly into her eyes. "Perfect" was all he said back.

Henry grabbed a clean washcloth and turned on the tap until the water quickly turned warm.

"On demand water heater," Jia commented. "It's new."

He came over and helped clean Jia up before going back to wash his hands and get back to making dinner.

"But I want to return the favor," she said, hungrily eyeing the erection in his shorts.

"After dinner. Consider it dessert," he said.

Jia's lips turned down in a pout, and Henry kissed them back to smiling. He went on to plate their dinner, and the two of them sat down to eat at the small kitchen table.

"Oh my god, this looks so good. You're an amazing cook," Jia said as she shoveled a forkful of pasta into her mouth. When she pulled the fork out with her lips wrapped around it, Henry thought about those same lips wrapped around his—

"Are you thinking dirty thoughts right now, Henry?" Jia's eyes sparkled.

He loved how she wouldn't let him get away with anything.

Henry finished off his wine, took Jia's hand, and stood up.

Jia put down her fork, took one last, longing look at the rest of her pasta, and quickly grabbed her own wineglass, downing the rest of it, before standing up. "It's even better as leftovers," Henry assured her.

She smiled and nodded as he led them to the bedroom.

They stood there in the small but tidy bedroom. It had been less than a month since he'd first met her, first brought her to his apartment, first had her. A lot had changed in that time. He had changed in that time. And he wanted her now, to show her how it could be between them.

The room carried her scent, her energy, her vibe. He felt drunk off her presence.

Jia gave Henry a small push to sit down on the bed. "My turn," she said. "I've been waiting too long for this."

Henry had been half-hard all evening, so by the time Jia had unbuttoned his shorts and pulled them down, he was fully erect and ready. Henry loved a good blow job. But the way Jia carefully removed his boxers and kissed up his leg, nuzzling her nose at the base of his shaft, kissing the tip, lapping at the slit, small breaths whispering over him, it all felt so intimate. Henry swallowed. He wasn't sure how much of this he could handle.

He could stop it. He could flip her over onto the bed, crawl on top of her, and enter her. He could follow the motions of what he knew and was used to. He could avoid the feelings that were creeping up inside of him, a new kind of discomfort bordering on pain where his panic attacks usually hit him in his chest.

But as Jia wrapped her lips around him and took him in her mouth, he forgot it all. Every thought of self-preservation out of his mind. Knowing that he'd give her whatever she wanted and protect her at all costs.

If he'd just let go and let himself.

25

Jia was, on most days, a people pleaser. She liked making people happy. She rarely minded if it came at the cost of her own comfort or convenience. And the other upside was that this approach helped her avoid the one thing she hated: conflict.

When it came to pleasing Henry, it offered Jia her greatest satisfaction. She squeezed her legs together, pressed her bare knees into the thin rug at the foot of her bed, stretched her jaw as wide as she could, and took him all in. And she loved it.

"Fuck, Jia," he said as she opened up her throat to take him farther.

"Jesus Christ," he swore when she added pressure with her lips as he slid through till they met his tip.

"Baby," he groaned as she took his balls into her hand and gently massaged them to the rhythm of her mouth around his dick.

She was in heaven. Henry's pleasure was her singular focus.

"Jia, wait," he said. He pushed her shoulders gently, his cock pulling out of her mouth with a pop. "Come here."

"Is something wrong?" she asked. Her mouth turned into a frown. She was having fun.

"I'm gonna come if you keep going on that way. And I want to be inside you when that happens," he said.

"Oh," she said and turned that frown right around. "Yay!"

He laughed as he sat up and took hold of both her arms and guided her off her knees and onto the bed. He pushed her down and rolled on top of her. "Now, this is better."

He grabbed the hem of the enormous muumuu and easily pulled it up and over her head. He threw it off to the side of the bed. Henry stared down, running his gaze from her head to her toes. He was completely still except for his head moving as he took in her body, and yet his breathing labored, like controlling himself in this moment, taking his time, spent energy akin to a workout.

Henry reached his fingers down between Jia's legs. "You're so wet for me," he said. There was a sense of awe in his voice that humbled her.

"Henry," she whispered, "I need you."

Those were all the words he needed to hear. He scrambled off her and reached over the foot of the bed where his shorts had been stripped off and left on the floor. He fumbled around and came back holding a condom between his fingers. "Got it," he said, his face beaming with pride.

"Why am I not surprised that you came prepared?" Jia teased. "And thank god for that."

He tore open the package and quickly rolled the condom on himself, returning to his position above Jia.

"You okay?" he asked.

She nodded. "Yes, better than okay."

He lined himself up at her entrance and pushed slowly.

Just a little bit to start, gauging Jia's body's ability to stretch around him, to accommodate his size, to take him. And then he pushed some more. They'd only done this once before, but as he made his way into her fully, they both moaned their pleasure in unison.

She felt impossibly full.

And she needed him to start moving. She lifted her hips to encourage him, and that was all he needed.

Henry pumped in and out of Jia, slow, small movements at first. But then he picked up his pace. She wrapped her legs around him, holding on and encouraging him to go harder.

"You feel so good," he said.

"Henry, I want you deeper," she told him. She pressed down with her hands, trying to bring his body closer.

Henry was, Jia was finding, incredibly responsive to her sounds and her needs, both her encouragement and her begging. He dragged himself out almost completely before pressing himself back in, hard. He did it again, and the delicious push and pull of him ignited all of Jia's nerve endings. She felt it in her toes.

Henry lifted one of Jia's legs and placed it on his shoulder, the position causing her to rise a little onto her hips. The angle felt completely different and reached new, hidden parts inside her she didn't even know could be touched. He pumped into her at an angle, their bodies slapping each time they came together with his thrusts.

He buried himself as deep as she could take him and then slowed down to small movements. Henry moved his hand from her leg down to her clit, and with each thrust of his penis, he pressed against her most sensitive spot.

"Oh god," she cried out. "Henry, I think I'm close." He'd already made her come once with his mouth earlier. She couldn't believe she was already there again so quickly.

He wrapped his arms around her and turned them, flipping them so that Jia was now on top. "Ride me, Jia. Ride me until you come," he said.

She placed one hand on his shoulder, and with the other, she lined him up and then lowered herself onto him in one move.

He groaned so loud she felt the vibration in his chest. She lifted herself up and pushed herself back down. Over and over, each time slightly rubbing her clit against his body. The friction and the fullness were all she needed. Jia's pussy tightened as the orgasm rippled through her, wave after wave. "Oh god," she cried out. "Yes, god, yes." It felt like it went on forever, a pleasure almost to the point of pain. Jia couldn't imagine surviving it.

She hadn't realized she'd shut her eyes. But when she finally opened them, it was just in time to watch Henry's neck cord and his entire face freeze in pleasure. He pushed up into her one, two more times before he stiffened and yelled "Fuck, Jia. Fuck yes."

He was beautiful. And in that moment of completely spent bliss, she thought to herself that she would be willing to do whatever it took to see Henry's face, unguarded and completely released, whenever she wanted for as long as she could.

The first time they had hooked up, when they were nameless and unknown to one another, Jia had snuck out of his apartment in the middle of the night. She'd felt a bit of regret about it. Not because she owed him to stay longer, but because she'd actually kind of wanted to.

This time, they had all night. And she was surprised to find that Henry was a cuddler. She was thrilled by this.

Jia's legs tangled with his, his arm casually draped over her body holding her close as they faced each other. He looked at her, his expression soft, and she watched as his eyes examined every part of her face. She wiggled her toes a little, and he met her movements with his own. They sat there quietly, just enjoying each other's presence.

"I have to go back to New York in a couple days," he said, breaking their safe cocoon.

Jia knew that Henry's time at The Sunset was coming to an end. She just didn't realize it was so soon. She nodded. "I figured."

The mention of New York changed Henry's face, hardening what Jia had just come to see of his soft edges. She could spend hours, days, years, longer if he'd let her, learning all the expressions of his face, his body, his heart.

But she couldn't even let herself think of that without finally telling him what had been on her mind.

"Henry."

He raised his eyebrows and tightened his grip on her hip in reflex.

"I need to tell you something. And I, well, I need you to tell me what you think I should do," she said.

She saw it . . . the flare in his eyes, how he shut down his features and put them on lock. He knew. He must have known all along.

"Jia," he stopped her from going further. "We can't talk about this."

"But I think we have to," she said. "I'm confused, and I'm

not sure what to do. And since you've kinda, sorta been involved—"

"Stop. Don't go on." Henry moved to sit up, and she immediately missed his body on her. He lay back against the headboard and looked straight ahead. "Jia, it's a conflict of interest. I can't talk to you about this. I can't talk to you about the company. About what happened to you. About this lawsuit."

"You know," she said. Of course he knew it. But hearing it come from his mouth, knowing that they'd both held it in the entire time they were together tonight just so that they could have this before whatever happened next, broke her heart. "I'm sorry. I didn't mean to put you in a bad position by bringing it up."

He turned his face to look at her. He reached his arm out and invited her to come to him. She snuggled closer, laying her head on his chest as his arm wrapped around her, cocooning them in. She listened to his heartbeat, steady and strong.

"I don't know what to do," she whispered.

"Jia, you have to do what's right for you. Not what you think someone else wants. Not what you think other people need. What do *you* need? That's what's most important. Whatever happens, whatever you decide, that's all that matters."

Had anyone ever given Jia permission, encouraged her even, to make a choice completely for herself, without anyone else to consider? Had she ever allowed herself this choice? Did she even know how?

She turned and kissed Henry's chest over his heart. Then she rested and let his steady breathing lull her to sleep. She'd decide tomorrow what to do.

Tonight, she'd go on pretending that it didn't matter.

26

"I have all your medication lined up here in the daily dispenser. On Sunday nights, you just have to refill each one for the upcoming week. And I set a reminder on your phone that will go off each morning. Over here, I moved the pots and pans to the lower cabinet so they're easier to reach. But make sure that if you turn on the stove, you don't leave it. You stay here—"

A hand came to rest on Henry's back. It was warm and comforting. "Hank, leave it all here for now. Grab your keys. Let's go for a drive. I only have you for another day. Let's make the most of it."

Henry dropped his head to his chest and let out a breath. "Okay, yeah, you're right. Let's go have some fun."

Henry knew he was going overboard. Everyone had told him so. But all of this was more for him than it was for Dennis. His granddad could ignore all of his instructions once Henry went back to New York. But he felt helpless to take care of him from far away, and this made him believe he was at least doing something.

Leaving was going to be harder than he had anticipated.

"Okay, Granddad. Where do you wanna go?"

"Let's go see the dinosaurs."

It was such a silly thing. What had started out as a marketing ploy, a way to get people off the freeway to a local restaurant twenty minutes outside of Palm Springs, had become an art installation of huge dinosaurs painted in neon greens, sky blues, and bright pinks. They were rotating canvases of sorts for artists to come and recreate over and over again. One wore a rainbow T-shirt during Pride month. Another had *I ♡ CA* on its chest. One had daisies painted on its huge body.

Henry had been humorless as a kid, not having many things to laugh about, lacking opportunities to be carefree growing up. But the dinosaurs, over-the-top, colorful, playful, and ridiculous in a way that no one could avoid their charm, were the one thing sure to lift Henry to a place of joy.

It struck him that these were exactly the things about Jia that he liked so much.

They got into Henry's rental car. "Seat belt," he reminded Dennis.

"Henry, I've lived in California my whole life. You think I don't know a seat belt?"

"Sorry," he said back. He was glad Dennis called him out on his shit. Henry needed more of that.

Jia's voice rang in his head. *They deserve respect. Don't infantilize them. They're wiser than we are.*

She was everywhere. She'd taken residence in his head. Maybe even snuck into his heart as well. But he couldn't let himself think about that. Not while both their futures were so in flux.

"Let's listen to my audiobook on the way," Dennis suggested.

"I have Book Club this weekend and need to finish it." Henry set his granddad's phone up to the car's media system, and the two of them listened to the recording on the way.

Nations, wars, nor national disasters can keep me from you. It but your resistance to receive love . . . The narrator's words stirred a discomfort in his chest. Henry quickly reached out and turned down the volume. He felt Dennis's eyes on him, but he kept his gaze on the barren desert road ahead. Why these words hit home was not something he wanted to consider right now. But Henry made a mental note to ask his granddad the book's title for later. He might like to find out how this story ends.

Henry's favorite dinosaur had always been the one that stood the tallest, the proudest, the most intimidating: the T. rex. Today it was painted an emerald green with a red heart on its chest that said *I love you*.

"Go stand in front of it so I can get a picture," Dennis said. He fumbled with his phone trying to open the camera and then looked down his nose at the screen, squinting without his glasses. The sun had already hit a peak, and Henry could see the waves of heat bouncing off the ground. He waited patiently for Dennis to get his shot.

"Would you like me to take one of the two of you?" a woman asked. She was with two kids who were running around and screaming their heads off.

"That would be great. Thank you. My grandson is visiting from New York. He's a big-shot lawyer out there."

Henry rolled his eyes and rubbed the back of his neck. Dennis just couldn't help himself.

"That's amazing. You must be so proud," she said.

"Oh, I am. But not just because of his job. I'm mostly proud he turned out to be a good man. He's my best friend."

Dennis walked over to Henry under the shadow of the T. rex and wrapped his arm around his waist. Henry swallowed back the emotion swelling in his throat.

"Smile," the woman said.

Henry had to make sure his grandfather sent him a copy. He'd never been a sentimental man. But this picture with his granddad was one thing he knew he'd want to take back to New York with him. One thing he'd want to keep forever.

"It's been a good couple weeks, hasn't it, Hank?" Dennis bit into his burger. They'd stopped to get lunch at the In-N-Out nearby. Henry couldn't remember the last time he'd had a fast-food burger. It was incredible. "I gotta say, I've really loved having you out here. Made making this move a lot easier. Thanks for taking care of all the details, big and small."

"I'm glad I could come," Henry said. "I, well, I wish I could stay longer." And he meant it. The thought of going back to New York had dulled somewhat for Henry. He couldn't imagine his empty apartment, his endless hours of work, his solo existence, being in the center of any of it.

The moment he got back into town he'd have to hit the ground running, working with Genevieve on the investigation into the claims made in the lawsuit. If Henry had any influence, he would try to push the executives toward mediation. No one wanted this going to court. It would be damaging to the company's reputation. And even if there were substantiated evidence, with all the money, power, and resources on Bakerson's side, they'd spin it in a way that would end up hurting the women involved. Hurting Jia. Henry couldn't let it happen.

When he received the full brief, for a moment he'd hoped Jia wouldn't be listed. But ultimately, he was glad she had taken this stand for herself. It was the one thing he wanted for her.

Never mind that Henry personally was listed as one of the defendants on the claim. He was the one who'd signed the paperwork, after all. It was clear that wasn't a mistake. If this turned south, Henry could very well be the one to take the fall. Hell, he'd probably been set up for that from the beginning.

Henry pinched the bridge of his nose, pushing back the headache threatening to break through. He didn't want to ruin a good day.

"There's something I have to tell you, and I think now's a good time to do it," Dennis said. It sounded serious. Henry immediately froze, waiting for the bad news. Dennis was sick. Dennis was dying. Dennis needed help.

"I love you."

Henry pulled back, completely blindsided by the admission. Their family wasn't the type to say *I love you*s. He couldn't remember the last time he'd ever heard it spoken in his presence.

"I don't tell you that enough. I didn't tell your dad that enough, and I sense he never told you either. A book I was reading mentioned generational curses, and, well, as ominous and heavy as that sounds, this is one I want to break."

"I, um, I . . . I love you too, Granddad." Henry chuckled. The words felt almost silly coming out of his mouth.

"Appreciate it, Hank. And I meant what I said to that woman who took our picture. I'm so proud of the man you've become. You didn't have it easy. Your parents weren't that great."

Henry really didn't want to be talking about his parents right now—or ever, to be honest.

"They were shitty parents, but I do believe they're not bad people. And if I can say that after they took my money, well, I hope you can get to that point too. Not for them, but for you. They're selfish and unreliable, sure. But not evil." Dennis wiped his hands with his napkin and laid one on top of Henry's. "You know, they live in their own punishment every day by having lost a relationship with you. I'd never ask you to give them any more chances. But I will ask you to let yourself off the hook. You didn't deserve being left to fend for yourself. But you came out on top. You don't have to carry around that anger anymore, Hank."

Henry's face heated. Tears welled in the back of his eyes. "I don't know if I can let it go." He struggled to get the words out. The truth hurt too. Who would he be without his drive to succeed as a way to punish his parents for abandoning him, for never allowing him to feel like he was enough to stay?

"I think if you let yourself, you could probably replace that anger with a whole lotta love. And I know of a really special someone worth that love."

"Mind your own business, old man." Henry squeezed Dennis's hand and smiled. He didn't mean it. He could use a lot more of his grandfather's wisdom in his life. He wouldn't let months, or even weeks, go by without it again.

"And Henry. Don't worry about me. I'll take my pills. As long as you promise me you'll take yours too."

Touché.

It was Henry's last night in town, and he wanted to spend it with Jia. He'd made reservations for them for dinner and gotten a room at a hotel after. He wanted uninterrupted time to say goodbye.

Billy Reed's was a favorite among locals, an older crowd, a restaurant steeped in history and nostalgia. When he got back to New York, Henry would miss places like this—a home to generations of stories quieter than ones in the city, tales regaling of the desert's magic. They sat in a red leather booth and immediately ordered dirty martinis and steaks.

"I love this place," Jia said, wistfully scanning the large space, black-and-white photos of patrons and town history and copies of newspaper articles decorating the walls.

"So do I," Henry said. Though, he'd meant it beyond just the restaurant. He meant the town with its contradictions of old ice-cream shops and new pizza places. The streets with classic cars driving next to new electric vehicles. The mid-century modern homes and the flashy glass-faced condos. And the quiet little paradise of Sunset Hills just at the northern border of it all.

"Are you gonna miss it?"

"I'm certain I will. I'll miss Dennis. I'll miss the others. I'll miss Zumba," he said and winked at Jia. "I'll miss you."

She met his eyes and smiled, but there was a sadness behind it. "I'll see you soon enough, I guess. I just wish the circumstances were different."

Jia and Henry had agreed not to talk about the case. He meant it when he'd told her it was a conflict of interest. But he also didn't want her to back out because of him. He wanted her to do what was right for her.

The first meeting between the parties was scheduled for a week from now in New York.

"Do your parents know?" he asked.

"No. I don't think they'd take it well. I've only told Mimi. And swore her to keep it between us."

"Listen, Jia, whatever happens . . ." He wasn't sure how to finish his thought.

They'd survive being on opposites sides of a lawsuit and be okay? She'd move to Florida and they'd date long distance while he stayed in New York? They'd both give up everything and live in a commune upstate, and to hell with the rest of the world?

Neither of them had answers about what was next.

"Whatever happens . . . happens," she said.

He wanted to say more. He had the words at the tip of his tongue. A confession of feelings he'd never had toward anyone before. Emotions that excited but terrified him. But he wouldn't, couldn't let them out.

He just nodded in agreement. "Whatever happens happens."

27

If Jia thought her walk out of the Bakerson's Group offices was a walk of shame, she clearly didn't know how awful it would be to be walking back in.

She didn't notice back then how sterile the offices were. No color. No life. No soul. Did everyone always dress this bland? Did everyone always look this miserable? Maybe she hadn't realized how she never quite belonged here because she'd never actually experienced what it felt like to fit in anywhere . . . until she'd made her way to The Sunset.

It was quiet, too quiet, and the click of her kitten heels felt too loud in the space. A tingle crept up Jia's spine like she wanted to turn around and run out of this place. But she wouldn't. She was here for the others. And she was here for herself.

Jia had stopped by Lizzy and Darcy's new apartment to pick up an outfit to wear to the meeting. The emerald-green sheath dress with a ruffle hem was hers. When she put it on, it felt too tight. Too stiff. Foreign. But it was the most appropriate outfit she had for something like this. At least she hoped so. She'd been in Mimi's clothes for a month now and had grown to love the freedom to still wear bright colors and patterns, fits that weren't trying to impress anyone except herself.

A head peeked out of the main conference room, and Jia recognized the face of their attorney, Helena Wimberley, a woman she had Zoomed with along with Stephanie Novak and Taylor Ann Graff about the lawsuit. Helena had been very detailed and matter-of-fact about what they had ahead of them. It was a wrongful termination suit by the three women who had all been in the same position at the company, worked for the same man, and been terminated in ways that all felt off, never once being shown proof of their errors.

There were questionable ways about the way they'd been treated at the company as well. But the attorney decided to not take that route, since those things—creepy comments and looks and general discomfort from their skeevy boss—were harder to prove. If this didn't say everything about how broken the system was, Jia didn't know what would.

Jia had hesitated in agreeing to the lawsuit. She wasn't sure she wanted to participate. Was this something she was willing to fight for? There were times Jia would fight the world, like for the residents of The Sunset. But she found it harder to fight for herself. It was only when the lawyer made it clear that they were stronger as three plaintiffs than alone, that the other women were counting on her, that she agreed.

There was also the Henry factor.

Jia had been surprised to find that, as the one whose signature was on the termination paperwork, Henry was also listed on the lawsuit. And it was what gave Jia the most pause of all.

But Henry, in his own follow-the-rules way, had basically

encouraged her to do this, to do what was right for her. Knowing Henry supported her in this meant so much to her. She just hoped it didn't come at a cost to him.

Jia wasn't doing this to get her job back. She wasn't even doing it for any kind of justice or a settlement. She was doing it to be heard. She wanted her voice and the truth to be known.

Jia entered the room and took a seat next to Taylor Ann. She'd never met either of the two others before their phone calls, before their Zoom meeting. But she'd felt a kindred connection to them. She squeezed her hand and smiled over her to Stephanie as well. They were in this together.

Jia wasn't sure what *this* was or all that it would entail. But Mimi also encouraged her to do it for all the other girls that would get hired after her. Those that might not have a safe place to land like she had at Sunset Hills. That was what eventually sealed the deal for Jia to take part in the complaint.

Jia's hands shook, and she found it hard to swallow for some reason. She crossed her leg and uncrossed it because her foot wouldn't stop moving. Truth be told, she was terrified. Terrified of coming back to this office that had always made her feel inadequate. Terrified of facing her boss who always made her feel stupid and like a piece of meat. And maybe what she was most terrified of was seeing Henry.

She didn't want any of this to blow back on him.

But from what her lawyer had told her, as the one signing the termination contracts, both Henry and Genevieve Gordon could be liable and it was standard to include these roles in wrongful termination suits. But Helena Wimberley had pretty much guaranteed they wouldn't end up even getting that far. The risk of going to trial for the company was too great for them to not at least try to reach a settlement. And that was the goal.

For Jia, she hoped for redemption.

The team from Bakerson's Group entered the conference room. A man Jia didn't recognize came in first, holding a bunch of files under his arm. He immediately shook hands with Jia's attorney and ignored the rest of them. He was followed by Steven Sword, the general counsel for Bakerson's Group, Edison Wainwright, the accused, and behind them all, taking a seat directly across from Jia at the long mahogany conference table, was Henry.

Henry's expression was stern, his face shuttered. She couldn't remember the last time she'd seen this version of him. She barely recognized him. Was this the mask he put on every day when coming to work?

He gave nothing away, and Jia reminded herself that she expected this. She knew he was great at his job. And this was Henry doing just that. His job. Hadn't she been on this side before? The recipient of Henry's no-nonsense, just-the-facts way of looking at life? When he'd first arrived at Sunset Hills? When they'd butted heads all along the way? When he'd signed his name to her termination paperwork?

But that was before. Jia knew a different side of Henry now. And she just couldn't, wouldn't believe he was out for blood.

And then she saw it, the smallest tick in his jaw, a sign that this was hard for him or maybe even that he wished he wasn't here going against her. That was what she hoped it meant.

A part of her wanted to cry . . . for him. For this impossible position he was in.

But the other part of her? She let her mouth curl up into the smallest smile, trying to convey that it was okay. That she was okay. That maybe, just maybe, they would be okay.

"Thank you all for joining us today," the unknown man began.

"We've reviewed all the claims of the complaint and have determined that there are no grounds, no validity, and most of all no proof to any of them."

"Well, that's unfortunate. You must not have read closely enough. Or maybe take off the lens of misogyny you were reading it through, and we can discuss what you see in the documents then." Damn, Helena was good. Jia was impressed.

Jia had never seen her parents at work. But she could imagine that her dad with his loud, booming voice, always sounding a bit put-out with a slight air of disapproval, could shut any opposition down.

Her mom? A softer approach, a kinder tone, until you realized she was waiting with ten facts collected to make you feel small and beaten.

Being in this scenario, watching and listening to these lawyers go back and forth, felt a bit like pulling the curtain back on the wizard. It all was an act to come out on top. And maybe that was what everyone did in this world, especially in the workplace. They put on an act to get the job done and then went home at the end of the day, trying to remind themselves who they really were.

Jia knew she couldn't live like that.

"And Ms. Jia Chung had a number of clerical errors. She spent more time flirting with and distracting the staff than she did her actual job. She violated company dress code. She spent entirely too long in the kitchen each morning. And she raised questions where she had no business even addressing."

Jia's attention was brought back to the conference room and the voice of Mr. Wainwright. He wouldn't look at her as he accused her of behaviors that just weren't true. He didn't even acknowledge her presence. That was what they were all doing, trying to make the women feel small, unseen, insignificant.

"I see you . . ." Henry's words echoed in her ears.

Jia put both hands on the table and got to defending herself. "I was never made aware of a company dress code, nor did anyone ever make it known that I was breaking one. I spent time in the kitchen to unload the dishwasher every morning so that people would have clean mugs for their coffees, since no one else would do it. And though I never flirted with anyone in this office—" she scrunched her face thinking of all the swarmy men who worked at Bakerson's Group, and the only one worth even considering was obviously Henry, and she'd never even met him while employed at the company "—I did make small talk with other employees to help lighten the mood, since everyone was always so miserable at work. And as far as clerical errors go, I can attest that the only time my work was called into question was regarding an expense report—"

"Enough." Steven Sword's icy voice silenced Jia in her tracks. "This is not a sorority. This is a financial institution. All of this is nonsense. We don't pay you to chitchat and unload the dishwasher."

Jia folded into herself. This whole time she'd thought she was doing a good job because she tried to help people. But clearly that wasn't important at all—at least, it wasn't what they wanted from her. They just wanted her to sit and be quiet and fill out forms and do as she was told. She lowered her head.

"Just to be clear, there is nothing in the documentation or information we gathered to substantiate any claims of Ms. Chung *flirting with and distracting the staff*. And it's not part of the complaint filed against the company."

Jia turned her attention back to Henry. She'd wondered

earlier if the wide conference table, one so big that even if they both reached their arms out they wouldn't be able to connect, symbolized a divide that they couldn't overcome.

"Let's keep these proceedings to the facts at hand. The plaintiffs filed a wrongful termination case. But New York is an at-will state. And unless they can prove illegal misconduct, which," Henry said and looked down at his stack of papers, sifting through them in what Jia could see was clearly a dramatic pause, "I don't see anything here that will stand in court, then I see no reason for all of us to be here today. This is not a case you can win."

This time, Henry looked directly at Jia.

They held each other's gaze.

You did so well, she wanted to tell him.

You'll get hurt if you keep this up, she thought she saw in his eyes.

I have to at least try, to state my piece, she tried to convey through her expression.

His eyes narrowed the slightest. *You won't win this. I'm too good at my job.*

She knew it was true. And she was actually so proud of him.

"Look, Shin is right. You can't win this. But we also don't want a PR mess on our hands. So let's just cut some checks and be done with it. How much, girls? How much to make it all go away?" Edison Wainwright said across the table. The man was such a prick.

Jia hated this whole thing. Was there a price tag for her dignity? For fairness? For respect in the workplace? To bury her truth? She just wanted to be back in Palm Springs. She wanted to get all her stuff and leave New York behind. She didn't want to be here among these dregs of the earth who couldn't appreciate that all she'd ever done at this job was try to help people be okay during a miserable workday. And she was over being treated like dirt.

"Sir," Henry said, trying to stop him.

"Are you saying you want to settle?" Helena asked. "If so, make the offer by midnight, and I'll discuss with my clients. But I'm warning you, do not insult us with the number."

Jia felt the two women next to her fidget in their seats. Their lawyer had made it clear to them that they probably could not win this case. She had mentioned, just as Henry had, that New York was an at-will state. But she said their goal was not to take this to court but to get a healthy settlement for their silence.

Jia didn't feel great about that.

But she was in a bind financially, and it seemed like something she could do.

Sitting here now, watching it all play out, she wasn't so sure. They might not be able to win, but taking money to be silenced left a boulder in her throat and a sourness in her belly.

She looked back up, meeting eyes with Henry. His softened. He saw the struggle she was going through. Could it be possible that the two of them had had some of their most intense conversation here in the middle of a heated legal discussion, without even saying one word?

She wanted to climb into his lap and put her head on his shoulder and comfort him after a long, hard day . . . to be comforted by him after the emotional toil of the meeting.

She wanted a future with Henry.

And she hoped that he'd want that too, even though she couldn't possibly see how.

28

Henry sat through the entire meeting with barely contained rage. It had gotten to the point where he'd felt physically ill, his body rejecting holding his frustration and outrage in.

Some of this anger was directed at Wainwright and the company, sure. But some, he had to admit, was at himself. He'd been complicit. He'd suspected what was happening within these four walls; it was his job to know. After hearing some of the specifics of how Wainwright's behavior hurt people, people like Jia, he couldn't justify his own actions and inactions any longer. Henry couldn't explain them away as doing his job.

He knew this was what would happen—that the company would try to minimize the experience of the women present. He wasn't sure that Wainwright would out himself as the prick that he was. But apparently he couldn't help himself.

And Jia. Jia had been incredible. She'd spoken up for herself. She was brave and did what she'd come to do. He wasn't sure how she felt about the decision to settle, but he hoped she was proud of herself. Because he was so fucking proud of her.

Henry collected the papers in front of him and opened the leather folio he'd brought them in. A postcard that he hadn't seen before was tucked in the inside pocket. He pulled it out. It read *Greetings from Palm Springs* on the front. Henry turned it over and froze. On the back were small messages written in various hands.

We'll miss you —Mimi

Go get 'em Henry —Gordon

NY is so lucky —Betty

Come back soon —Eugene

Love you, Hank —Dennis

Gonna miss your morning runs ;) —Gladys

And many more. His eyes scanned them all. A message in beautifully loopy handwriting in the corner caught his eye:

I believe in you <3 —Jia

He swallowed back the emotion. Henry didn't deserve this kindness. But it was delivered to him at just the right time.

He looked up to find Jia and her team quietly encouraging each other with pats and hand squeezes and smiles. As they walked out, she looked back over her shoulder at Henry.

His heart fluttered at just that one look. He felt like a lovesick teenager. The corner of his mouth lifted in a small, reassuring smile that remained even as he watched her go.

He looked around the conference room. He'd dreamed of having a seat at tables just like this. He'd worked hard to be accepted and respected among men like the ones currently in perfectly tailored suits standing in the corner, talking in hushed tones. He prided himself on being the one knowledgeable and prepared enough to deliver the knockout blow in legal battles like he had today.

But none of that felt satisfying anymore—not like seeing Jia walk out with her head held high, looking back at Henry like he meant something to her.

He let his fingers run over the heavy card stock of the postcard. Something had changed in Henry. And the names on this card had everything to do with it. Most especially Jia's.

He couldn't sit there any longer.

He needed to see her, to talk to her, before she left New York. He had to tell her how amazing she was. He wanted to apologize that he'd never done anything to protect her from this, even though he hadn't known her back then. He had been a good lawyer, but he wished he could have been a better man. He wanted to confess to her his feelings and hopes that they could figure out how to make this work.

He couldn't let her leave without telling her everything.

Henry quickly stood, gathered his stuff, and hoped he could catch up to Jia before she got on the elevator.

"Good work, Shin. Pretty sure we buried this before it took life." Steven Sword stepped between Henry and the door. He patted him on the shoulder. He leaned in to add, "Look, I'll make sure Wainwright steps in line and we don't have to deal with this kind of nonsense anymore. But good to know that precedence was set that, even if he does, the law is on our side." He stepped back and laughed.

The laugh felt like a punch to Henry's solar plexus.

Sword and men like him, they believed Henry was on their side. They saw him as one of them. And as much as Henry had believed it was what he'd wanted too, it made him sick to his stomach facing the truth now.

The revelation hit him: Henry did not want to be like them at all.

"If you'll excuse me, sir. I have someone I need to talk to." He stepped around his boss and made his way to the elevators.

Henry's only thought was to find Jia.

He rode the elevator down to the ground floor, ran out the front door, and looked up and down the street. No sign of her. She was gone.

Where would Jia be off to right now? If they were at The Sunset, she'd be at the community center laughing with the residents, or in the office gabbing it up with Gladys, or by the pool watching Jared walk his laps. But Henry didn't know the New York version of Jia.

He looked down at his phone and opened up the text app. It rang just as he meant to type out his message. With a pounding heart, he tapped to answer it and quickly lifted it to his ear.

"Hi, thanks for calling," he let out, the relief clear in his voice to his own ear. There was so much he wanted to say to Jia.

"Hank? Hank, you there?"

"Dennis? Sorry, I thought it was someone else calling. Hey, Granddad, can I call you back in a bit?" he asked. He'd only been back in New York three days, and the old man already missed him. And honestly, he missed him right back.

So much. But he was eager to get Jia on the line and wanted to do that right away.

"Hank, I've taken a bit of a tumble," the strained voice said. Henry heard it this time, Dennis's attempt to hold back the pain and the sound of it.

"What do you mean? How? How bad is it?" Henry's voice was panicked.

"Now, don't you worry. One of the others in the Walking Club got her phone out, and she called the ambulance. We made sure it was the one my insurance covers. But I'm in the hospital now, in case you get a call from a stranger. You're listed as my in-case-of-emergency contact."

"The hospital?" Henry's voice broke. "Jesus, how bad is it? Is the doctor there? What did they say? Can I talk to them?"

"Tripped over my own goddamn feet, if you can believe it. Gordon told me that today's Walking Club would be all the slowpokes. I figured I'd be okay. That damn curb just snuck up on me. Anyways, it was a fluke accident. I was careless. But it's not too bad. It's just the wrist. Broken. I got a sweet cast on it now. Luckily it's the left side, and I hardly even use that one." Dennis laughed at his joke, but it clearly came at a cost, and the laughter turned to wheezing and a groan. "The body is a bit bruised but none the worse for wear."

The thought of Dennis in pain broke his heart. Bones healed slower on older people. He needed to know the details. How serious was the break? What were they going to do to help with the pain?

"Dennis, let me talk to the doctor," Henry said.

"He's not here right now, Hank. But I'll call you back next time he checks in. I'm getting a little sleepy now, so gonna hang up. But just in case you're worried, don't be. I got all the neighbors who came by to visit, and I called your folks."

"You did what?" Henry didn't want to raise his voice at Dennis ever. But it was impossible not to be frustrated when it came to his parents.

"Just gave them a heads-up. I figured I'd want to know if one of them got a little banged up. They said they were planning on visiting sometime soon anyways, so they're probably working their way out here. Don't be mad."

"I'm not mad. I'm just . . ." Henry couldn't let his parents be there alone with Dennis. He didn't want to even think of what they'd try to talk him into. "I'm on my way. I'll let you know as soon as I figure out how fast I can get out there."

"Now, Hank, if you're busy at work, don't make a fuss. We'll talk about it tomorrow. Gonna catch some z's now," Dennis said. He sounded weary, and Henry let him go.

Henry rushed back up to his office to get his stuff. He'd figure out flights on his way to the airport. If there was nothing direct, he'd do LAX again. He grabbed his laptop, shoving it into his briefcase, and headed for the door.

"There you are," Edison Wainwright said, blocking his way. "Fine job you did there today, Shin." He reached out a hand to shake. Henry stared at it but didn't offer his own in return. "Well," Wainwright said, pulling back his hand, "good, looks like you already got your stuff. Let's head out. We're going for celebratory drinks and cigars. Figure it's time you come along with us, now that you've proven you can hang with the big guns." His smug voice and pompous attitude made Henry sick to his stomach. "They probably won't have the sake you people like, but there will likely at least be some Japanese whiskey."

Racist prick. Henry had a right mind to sue the man himself. If he wasn't in a rush to get out of there, he could very well be pushed to throwing a punch. That was how much disdain Henry had for the man.

"Not now, sir. I've got a family situation I have to take care of, if you'll excuse me."

"Now, Shin. Family can wait. Work is the priority," he said, his voice laced with condescension. As if going for drinks and cigars was work. "You know what I like about you? You're like me. You put yourself and the job first. Everything else ranks way below on the priority scale."

"Well, considering you've been divorced three times and are cheating on your fourth wife, oh, and that you're almost never in the office or actually ever get any work done that I can see, I find this a very odd comparison." Henry had never once spoken this way to someone senior to him, to anyone at all, for that matter. And he'd never put himself at risk in the workplace like this. But he couldn't help himself. He felt lighter, relieved, free from holding in his disdain for a man he was meant to respect.

"You better watch what you say to me, son," Wainwright said.

Henry hated that word. He hated that his dad never referred to him as his own. And he hated how patronizing it sounded coming out of Edison Wainwright's mouth.

"I've got nothing more to say to you at all, Eddie boy," Henry said, patting him on the arm. "And be careful how you address me here in the workplace. Don't want me filing my own case against you. They start asking me questions, I may have to share how you've been padding expense reports and holding your assistants accountable when they've questioned you about it."

Wainwright's eyes widened, and his face turned beet red.

"You . . ." Henry was surprised steam didn't come out of his ears as pent-up as he looked.

Henry scooted past him and down the hallway to the elevators. He had no time for this man, or for this job, for that matter.

He had a plane to catch and family waiting for him to come home.

Henry had thrown a bunch of clothes haphazardly into his carry-on, trying not to think about how he'd regret the wrinkles later, and got a cab to the airport. He guessed JFK. He recalled Jia mentioning she'd flown direct from JFK to Palm Springs.

Jia. Did she know about Dennis's accident? Surely Mimi had called to tell her? Or one of the other residents? Should Henry?

He grabbed his phone to message her just in case.

Henry looked down at the text notifications waiting for him and couldn't believe what he was seeing.

Father: Yo. The old goat called us so we're heading out his way. It'll be good to see you kid.

Mother: Fuck yeah! The 4 of us together again just like old times. Shit, how long's it been?

Father: Send cash to pay us back for the plane tickets, would ya?

Henry ignored them and swiped out to get to his Contacts list. He dialed the number of the company travel agency. "Hello? I need the quickest way from New York to Palm Springs leaving immediately." He covered the mouthpiece and leaned toward the driver. "Can you get me to JFK as fast as possible?"

"Sure thing."

The car jerked and picked up speed.

Henry closed his eyes and took a couple deep breaths. The last thing he needed was to have a panic episode and not be able to get on a plane. There was no room for any delays.

He hadn't seen his parents in years. Hadn't heard from them in months. And hadn't counted on them his entire life.

When Dennis mentioned they might be coming, Henry had thought he'd have time to prepare. But seeing their texts saying they were on their way caused Henry's anxiety to rise. He had to get there first.

Dennis didn't deserve this.

And Henry wasn't sure he himself would be able to survive it.

29

"We're so proud of you, Jia. You did a really scary thing today and stood up for yourself. You're amazing. This is my best friend, everyone. She's incredible and strong and smart and—" Lizzy stood up and lifted her glass to continue her toast.

Her boyfriend Darcy gently pulled at her arm to return her to her seat. "We're all thirsty, honey. I think everyone gets the idea. Jia, to you." He lifted his glass, and Jia brought hers to Lizzy's and then Darcy's.

"Thanks, you guys. Ten out of ten would not recommend. But I'm glad I did it. And I'm glad it's over."

"Let's be real, Wainwright should be fired. Bakerson should be fired. Shin should be fired." Lizzy clearly had opinions on the matter.

"I think Bakerson owns the company, my love," Darcy said.

"And we don't hate Henry," Jia said.

"Oh yes, I forgot. We looooove Henry," Lizzy singsonged.

"Okay, dear, I think it's time we switch to water for a bit."

Darcy took Lizzy's drink out of her hand and kissed her on the cheek.

"That was my first drink! If anything, I'm drunk on Jia's good vibes!"

Jia warmed at the sight of the two of them. She loved their relationship and admittedly felt a tiny bit jealous of it. Jia couldn't have feelings for just any guy, an easy guy, a regular guy with a regular job to be in a regular romance with. Nope.

Apparently only a man who fired her and she was now suing would do. Pesky details.

But, as odd as it sounded, Jia could laugh at it. So what if she didn't have a normal life like everyone else? She couldn't keep a job? She didn't want a normal job. She couldn't keep an overpriced, too-small apartment? She was pretty sure she didn't want to live in New York anymore anyways. Jia had to stop comparing her worth based on others. She needed to start looking within and giving herself credit for what she had done.

She thought about calling Henry after she'd left the Bakerson's Group offices. She could invite him here right now for a drink. But she'd seen him getting pulled aside by his boss as she was leaving. She really hoped that that meant good things for Henry. Despite being on the other side of things, she was incredibly impressed with him today. And proud.

And call her inappropriate, but she found him incredibly sexy in his lawyer mode.

Jia's phone buzzed in her purse. She'd been so hoping it was Henry, she didn't look before answering it. "Hello?"

"Jia." It was her father.

Jia covered the mouthpiece and got up. "Excuse me, guys, I'll be right back. I have to take this." She made her way through the restaurant and out the door. "Hi, Dad."

"Apparently being involved in a lawsuit with your former employer is cause for celebration by the sound of it."

"How did you know about the—"

"Jia, lawsuits are public record from the moment you file," her dad explained.

"Okay, but unless you have my name on some kind of Google Alert, how could you have even known . . . Oh god, Dad. You guys don't have a Google Alert on me, do you?"

"Don't turn this into something you disapprove of."

"It's weird, and intrusive, and—"

"If you didn't consistently give us reason to worry, maybe we wouldn't have to track you this way," he said. No apology in his voice.

"It's crossing the line," Jia said.

"Listen to me. You don't understand what you've done. You've basically ruined your chances of a future. What company will hire you, knowing you've filed a lawsuit against your former employer? Jia, we have given you enough chances to do this on your own. Now, you will do what your mother and I tell you. Check your email—there should be a confirmation message for your flight to Florida. We'll handle moving your stuff down to our home from there. Do not go back to Mimi's, understood? We want you in Florida tomorrow morning. You've caused enough distress and hardship on the family."

"Yes, I know, Dad. You and Mom have told me enough times what a burden I've been on you both my entire life. Mom never lets me forget how hard I even made her pregnancy. God, I get it, okay? Telling me again, after what I've just gone through, isn't gonna make me any more willing to leave my life behind and go live the one you want for me." Jia buzzed with the anger and frustration and sadness of the conversation. Her parents couldn't accept her for who she was or the choices and mistakes she made. They would only be okay if she conformed to who they wanted her to be.

"I have to go now. I'm out with my friends celebrating a really big deal in my life." It wasn't technically a win on paper. But even taking the steps to fight for herself, despite it not working out completely the way she'd hoped, was worth something.

"Jia—"

She hung up on her father.

Jia woke up to a sore back and a stiff neck and a general feeling of regret and dread. She'd crashed at Lizzy and Darcy's place on their couch, tossing and turning with the fear of having truly pissed off her parents.

She and Lizzy had plans for coffee before Jia's evening flight back to Palm Springs. She had ignored the confirmation email about a flight to Florida. She knew her parents would be furious at her for disobeying them, but they were being unreasonable. She'd deal with the fallout later.

They grabbed their coffees from the café on the corner and walked a couple blocks to Central Park. Lizzy's new apartment was fifteen blocks farther south from the one they had shared just a few weeks ago. So much had changed in that short time for both of them.

This part of the park was new to Jia. Morning joggers filled the paths alongside people walking their dogs. Jia and Lizzy found a bench and took in the sights and sounds of the city waking up.

"So what's the plan?" Lizzy asked. "And how can I help?"

"I still don't know. I mean, I didn't expect this lawsuit, no matter what happened either way, to change my life. I just needed to close that chapter. Now? Well, it's been a month, and I still don't have any job prospects. I've also pissed off my parents and don't know if they'll ever forgive me. I could go back to crashing at Mimi's—maybe find a job serving tables or selling souvenirs." Jia shrugged at the lack of possibilities.

"There's got to be something," Lizzy said. Ever the optimist.

"How does it feel?" Jia asked, nudging her best friend with her elbow.

"How does what feel?"

"Being a fully grown adult. Having your shit together?" Jia smiled. She meant it as a compliment, not an accusation. She truly wanted to know how it felt not having the weight of failures and disappointments on your back.

"Listen, my life is far from perfect. And having some parts of it supposedly figured out doesn't mean other parts aren't a mess. I'm pretty convinced that life is all about pulling different levers until something works and then moving on to the next challenge. You're not behind, if that's what you're thinking. You've just prioritized some things at the expense of others for now. It'll all balance itself out." Lizzy sounded so confident in her assessment. Jia wasn't so sure. She couldn't think of one thing she'd succeeded at to date. It all kind of felt like a mess to her.

"You know, all that stuff you're doing for the residents out at Sunset Hills? It's pretty amazing. There are few people who have the motivation and the heart and the patience."

Jia smiled thinking of her friends out there. She missed them already, and she'd only been away a couple days. What a weird thing to feel so connected to and invested in people so much older than her.

"Hey, is there a way for you to make all that work you do

into an actual paying job? Like, can the community maybe pay you out of the HOA budget or something?" Lizzy was a fundraiser for a nonprofit organization. It's how her mind worked.

"They've never posted anything like that before. I don't think it's an actual *thing*," Jia said.

"Well, maybe you should ask them. It couldn't hurt. And isn't it the dream to get paid for work you love to do?"

Jia wondered if this could be a possibility. Maybe like an event planner or a community manager role? She could do some research online and see if such jobs existed. She could come up with a job description and a proposal. She could take it to the HOA board. She was starting to get excited about the possibility. Even if it didn't work out, the idea triggered something in Jia to start thinking outside the box for her next career move.

"That might not be a bad idea. I'll give it some more thought," Jia said.

"Okay, my love, I have to get to work. Give me a hug before I go." Lizzy stood up and pulled Jia to her feet. Jia wrapped her arms around Lizzy and squeezed. She loved her bestie so much. "When do I see you again?"

"I still have a few days left in Palm Springs, and then I have to see how everything plays out with my parents, but I'll call you soon just to catch up. I love you."

"Love you back. Safe flight tonight, okay?" Lizzy walked off with a wave and left Jia sitting with her first sense of hope in over a month.

Jia's phone rang, and she knew this time to look at the caller ID. She should talk to her parents and apologize for hanging up on her dad last night. But she wasn't ready for their criticism and disappointment right now. The screen read *Mimi*. Jia missed her grandmother and quickly picked up the call.

"Hiya, Mimi. How goes it?"

"Hello? Jia?"

"Mimi? Can you hear me? I—"

"Honey, there's been an accident. Dennis fell during Walking Club. It was a fluke. Didn't realize the curb on the corner of Robart and Pine was a little higher than the others. Just lost his balance, and, boom, he was face down on the ground. Bruises all over and a broken wrist. We're here at the hospital . . ."

But Jia couldn't hear the rest of it above the ringing in her ears. Dennis fell? A broken wrist? Walking Club? Jia was the one who'd encouraged him to participate weekly. In fact, she'd suggested to him, pressured him even, to give it a try. Henry had asked her not to push him too hard. But she hadn't listened. She thought she knew better what would be good for him.

She'd done this. She was the one that made Dennis think he didn't need a walker. She was the one that told all of the residents at Sunset Hills that they didn't have to listen to their families, their doctors, their naysayers. They could live the way they wanted to.

She was the one at fault for Dennis's accident.

"Mimi," Jia croaked out around the tears and the boulder lodged in her throat. "I'm on my way."

She hung up and ran back to Lizzy's apartment to get her stuff. She quickly looked up her flight information and changed the itinerary to catch the next earlier flight out to Palm Springs. It would cost her an additional four hundred dollars. She'd put the charge on her credit card and worry about how to pay it off later.

She needed to get home.

But Sunset Hills wasn't her home. She was just a visitor. What even made her think she was qualified to plan activities for elderly people who had limitations to actually be concerned about? She'd been reckless. Selfish. Arrogant.

This was all her fault.

Maybe it was time for her to leave Sunset Hills behind. Maybe she would grovel and ask her parents to control her life. Maybe she could take the settlement from Bakerson's Group and start over somewhere. Somewhere where she couldn't hurt anyone she loved.

But first, she had to get back and make sure Dennis was okay.

Jia grabbed her bag and called an Uber to the airport. As soon as she got into the car, she picked up her phone and called Henry. She was sure he'd likely been contacted already, but just in case . . .

"This is Henry Shin. Please leave a message." Not even one ring. His phone was turned off or out of service. Jia thought of how his message was economical and to the point. So Henry. She missed him. She wanted to talk to him and make sure he was okay. She wanted him to forgive her for putting Dennis in this position.

But would he? And even if he did, did she deserve to be forgiven?

Jia leaned back, closed her eyes, shut off her mind, and let the tears flow.

30

Henry had always hated the Palm Springs airport. It was small and dated, there were limited flights, and for some reason he'd always felt out of place once he'd arrived. But when had Henry ever felt like he belonged somewhere?

A memory of cheers encouraging him as he swayed his hips and moved his feet. Arms reaching out to grab hold of his drenched body, pulling him from the pool. Laughter around Malibu and pineapple drinks. Slaps on the back. *Well done*s and *Attaboy*s freely offered to him. Genuine thanks and gratitude as he built a number of his dog-waste grabbers. Soft skin under his fingertips, lips wrapped around his body, and the sexiest sounds coming from Jia's mouth as she came.

There. As crazy as it sounded, Henry belonged there. In Palm Springs. At Sunset Hills. Among people more than twice his age and one woman who drove him nuts in every way possible and took his breath away.

It was family. Like he'd never had before. Community. Like

he'd shunned and avoided throughout his life. And he needed to get back as fast as possible. He needed to see with his own eyes that Dennis was okay and make sure he was getting the best care.

And he needed to make sure, most of all, that his parents weren't causing havoc in Dennis's home among his friends. Henry could imagine walking in on everyone high on shrooms, sitting around in a sweat lodge, his mom leading chanting incantations for his grandfather's quick recovery while his dad went around cleaning out everyone's wallets and bank accounts.

And as luck would have it, the timing worked where he could catch the one direct flight from New York. No rental car or two-hour drive in traffic to contend with.

He was antsy the entire flight. The only thing keeping him from worrying himself to death was the audiobook he listened to. Henry put his earphones in and turned on the book. The narrator's voice, which worked well for all the different characters in the book, soothed him. He might have blushed and squirmed a little in his seat as he listened to the very spicy sex scenes, but he didn't think the person next to him noticed. He'd finished the entire book on the flight. As long as he was going to be in Palm Springs anyways, he might as well stop by the Sunset Hills Spicy Book Club meeting tomorrow night and take part in the conversation about the reading material.

Henry shook his head and laughed to himself. He knew when the book club met and now was planning on attending. He really had changed.

The hot air hit Henry the moment he deplaned. "Rookie move, Shin," he said to himself as he thought about the wool blend slacks he had on. He'd come straight from the office and in his New York uniform, a style that he'd carefully selected to convey he was a serious lawyer to be respected. But here in Palm Springs, the clothes he wore were not only impractical, they made him realize that he'd always been playing a part. And only now was he discovering who the real Henry was.

He looked down at the overnight bag in his hand. He had the urge to just chuck it in the trash and wear whatever was in Dennis's closet. Just like Jia had done at her Mimi's.

Jia.

Was she here already? She had to have heard about Dennis's accident. Would she be there when Henry walked in? Would she be talking to his parents?

Henry picked up the pace of his long strides to the taxi line.

He heard the voices as soon as he was dropped off in front of Dennis's house. Screaming?

Henry quickly unlatched the gate and ran to the front door. He'd forgotten his house key back in New York in the rush to get to the airport. But when he tried to open the door, it was unlocked and opened right up. He would have to warn Dennis about this . . . again.

When Henry stepped into the house, he froze.

The house was full of people. More than he'd ever seen in here before. He recognized most of them from the neighborhood. Some he couldn't recall meeting. Who were all of these people and why were they here?

There was a spirited card game happening at the kitchen table. And multiple pots heating on the stove with apron-clad people chatting it up. Along the hallway there was what looked to be line dancing? And a couch full of people screaming at a dog competition playing on the TV. And in the center of it all, surrounded by doting women giving him spoonfuls and forkfuls and cupfuls of food and drink, while others sat and signed the new cast around his wrist, was Henry's grandfather Dennis.

"Hank! You made it," Dennis greeted him from in his lounge chair once he noticed his presence.

"Granddad," Henry said, carefully. He wasn't sure if he was doped up on pain meds and perhaps not completely of clear mind.

Speaking of being doped up—Henry took a look around the house as much as possible for any signs of his parents. No ratty old Birkenstocks. No poorly crocheted shawls. No sand or dirt or dirty luggage anywhere to be seen. As much as he'd psyched himself up for what he'd run into, he tried not to think about how he'd feel if his parents didn't even show up at all . . . again.

"Come over here, son, and let me get a look at ya. I've missed you," his grandfather said. He pushed the leg rest down and sat upright. "Thanks, ladies, but could you give me a minute with my grandson?" All the attention quickly fizzled out to a few pats on the back for Dennis while his fan club dispersed.

Henry raised an eyebrow at his granddad.

Dennis winked back. "Amazing the attention one gets when they're gravely injured," he said, raising his wrist to show Henry his new cast.

"Gravely injured," Henry repeated.

Dennis leaned in and whispered, "Guess I got a thing for nurses, and there have been a lot of ladies more than willing to play dress-up." Dennis waggled his eyebrows.

Henry let out an exasperated laugh.

"Are you in any pain? Did anywhere else get injured?" he asked, giving his granddad the once-over.

"Welp, I hurt all over, not gonna lie. Falling and getting

back up made me use muscles I haven't in years. Hank, you gotta get me on one of your exercise plans so I can stop being such a squeaky, unused truck. If I learned one thing while lying face down on the ground trying to figure out how to get my body up, it's this: I gotta live my life like it's still got life to give. Not like I'm counting down the days till I'm done." Dennis squeezed Henry's hand with his good one. It was strong and certain.

Henry let out a deep breath. He read between the lines. The message was as much for him and his own life as it was for Dennis's.

"That's a great lesson, Granddad," he said, nodding and taking it in.

Henry thought he saw movement down by his bedroom door and leaned to take a look, in case it was his parents or . . . Jia.

"Guess they decided not to come after all," Dennis said. "Not sure I expected them to. But I was hoping it was enough to not make you get on the first flight out here to try to save the day. Seeing as you got here in less than twenty-four hours, my guess is you didn't have too much faith in them either."

Henry lifted a shoulder. "Truth is I wasn't sure what would be worse—them coming . . . or not."

"Well, one thing I know for sure, you and I are lucky we've got each other."

But what if, one day, they didn't? What would happen if Henry no longer had Dennis, the one person in his life he could count on?

Henry had trouble getting air into his lungs. He doubled over and grabbed his chest. The pain was sudden and excruciating. He reached for his bag.

"What do you need, Hank? Let me grab it. Here, come sit down." Dennis got up and pushed Henry into his chair. "Someone grab that bag by the door for me."

"Front pocket," Henry tried to say through the pain.

"Is it a heart attack? Do I call 911?" Dennis asked.

Henry shook his head. He closed his eyes and tried to focus on calming down, on taking deep breaths. Dennis put two pills into his hand and passed him a glass of water.

"Here you go, son. When you catch your breath, tell me what you need, what I need to do. Let me take care of you this one time, will ya?"

Henry looked up into his grandfather's kind, wrinkled face. "Panic attack," he said. It was time to be honest with him.

"I know. I remember you getting those as a kid. Saw the remnants of the one you had a few weeks ago too. I guess I was just hoping you weren't experiencing them as often," he said.

"If I remember the meds, I'm usually okay. Probably just need to get back into a routine and some structure, so I take them regularly."

"Oh, I know how that is. I have a great medicine dispenser and a calendar and an alarm I can recommend to you, if you want."

Henry looked up at his grandfather, who had a twinkle in his eye. "Funny."

"Well, I am sorry, though, I've added to the stress, kid. Guess I'm not helping any of that, huh?" Dennis said, a frown taking over his entire face.

Henry grabbed his good hand and held it. "You're the only thing that makes any of it worth it."

"Well, maybe me and that pretty girl across the street too?" Dennis winked at Henry.

He wondered if she was back in town yet. And if she was, what would he say when he saw her? Like he hadn't been practicing it all in his head the whole time since he'd watched her walk away yesterday.

"Son, listen to your grandpa when I say you don't have to prove to anyone, not your parents, not your job, not anyone, that you're incredible and worthy. The only person you have to prove it to is yourself. And that's by making choices that allow you to be happy. Be happy, Henry. It's the only thing I want for you."

"I don't know how to be happy, Granddad," Henry admitted.

"Well, you can start by cutting out anything in life that makes you unhappy. Get rid of everything that gets in the way. And go from there."

"Henry, honey, I brought you some tea to calm your nerves," Betty said, handing him the cup. "I've had panic attacks my whole life, so I know how it feels. This helps."

Henry smiled and thanked her as he took a sip.

"Everyone, everyone, let's get out of here and let Dennis get some rest," Gordon said.

"Henry's had a long flight too," Gladys added. "We'll pack all the food up into containers and put them in the fridge for you guys to eat later. You two watch a game or movie or something and have a quiet night."

Henry suddenly felt overcome with emotion. There was a pain in his chest. But not like the one he'd just gone through with his panic attack. No, this one felt like a stretching in his heart. It hurt, but in a way that felt freeing, good. In a way that felt loved.

"Thank you, everyone, for taking care of Dennis until I

got here. I'm so—" his voice cracked and he took a breath "—grateful."

They patted his back on the way out, and he received a couple hugs as well. These were good people. Capable people. Loving people. He was lucky to know them.

Just as the last of the neighbors left, Mimi rushed through the front door.

"Oh good, you're both here," she said. "Looks like you're having a moment?" She looked between the two of them.

Henry wiped his eyes and turned away.

"Good, it's about time. Henry you're one of us, and I'm glad you finally realized it. We love you, kiddo," she said.

Welp, there went the waterworks again. He turned to hide his face, but she walked right up to him and held him by both arms.

He turned back to her and noticed the most serious look he'd ever seen on Mimi's face.

"Now, Henry J. Shin, Esquire, I need your help."

31

Jia had told Mimi not to bother picking her up at the airport, she'd grab a taxi. What was most important was that her grandmother was there staying with Dennis until his loved ones could arrive.

Until Henry could get there.

It had been hard seeing Henry opposite her at the meeting. His cool, unflinching demeanor frightened her a little. It was opposite to the warm Henry she'd come to know . . . the man with the heart beating under that suit. Danced with grandmas, made poop sticks for ailing elders, held her tight, and overwhelmed her in every way.

But she held on to the belief that they had come to understand each other. That he knew why she had to be a part of the lawsuit. And that he knew she knew why he had to show up and fight it.

The driver dropped her off in front of Mimi's where there were more cars than usual parked on her street. As she let herself out she looked to her front door and then to Dennis's. Where should she go first? When she'd last checked in with Mimi, Dennis was sleeping comfortably, pain meds in tow and no lasting damage. Still, it would hurt for a while, and Jia hated thinking of Dennis in pain.

She'd drop off her stuff and then go visit him.

When she opened the door, she heard the voices. More than just Mimi's. And some that didn't sound familiar . . . at least not in this space.

She stopped in her tracks.

"Mom? Dad? What are you doing here?" she said as they turned to face the guest in the house.

Immediately, in the presence of her parents, Jia reduced herself to a guest here. They'd invaded this space that she'd for weeks felt safe in.

She had trouble getting a breath in. But she'd long known how to behave in front of her parents. She shrunk inside herself. Closed the windows and doors to her heart so that the emotions would be shut in. Without even having to remind herself, she put the mask on and hid behind the expressionless version of herself. She snuck a peek behind them where Mimi sat on the couch, much the same.

And for some reason, that made Jia angry more than anything.

"Jia, we could ask you the same. I think we specifically told you to head straight to Florida and not come back here." Her mother's voice had a practiced and produced lilt to it that created ambiguity around her background. Jia remembered people asking her mother where she was from. And she'd let them list their guesses—England, Singapore, Hong Kong. She would never come out and answer she was a second-generation Korean American born in New Jersey.

"I'm not going to Florida. I'm sorry, but I've been thinking about it and that's not where I want to go. I think . . ." Jia shook her head. No, those weren't the right words. "Actually, I *know* that I want to be here."

"Absolutely not. You've wasted enough time here this summer doing nothing. And that stunt you pulled with the lawsuit in New York? Jia." Her mom was exasperated, and possibly angry. Jia was used to the former. But as controlling and unforgiving as they'd been with Jia's mistakes, she'd rarely heard the latter.

"It's my fault. I called her. One of the residents took a tumble, and I was upset and needed my Jia to comfort me," Mimi explained. "She was a dear and came right away."

"Mother, Jia is your granddaughter, not your best friend. And she's hardly capable of handling issues in a crisis. Why you feel you need to turn to her is beyond me," her father said. "You're enabling her to be rudderless, ungrounded, unemployed with no prospects."

Jia thought she could handle her parents' disappointment, yet again. But for them to go hard on Mimi, it just wasn't right. This was her fault. She'd brought this on herself and her grandmother.

Jia nodded to the mug her mother held in her hand. "Mom, can I refresh your tea for you?" She walked over to them and gave her mother a kiss on the cheek and a gentle, barely there hug. She turned and hugged her dad next. His back went ramrod straight, as it always did when Jia—or maybe anyone, for that matter—initiated affection. "It's good to see you both."

She took the mug from her mother's hand and walked to the kitchen. With her back to them all, she let her head drop just an inch and tried to gather herself. She hadn't been expecting them here, that was for sure. But mixed with the stress and emotion of worrying about Dennis and how he was doing, along with wondering what shoe was going to drop next from her parents, Jia was barely hanging on.

A small hand rubbed circles on her back, and she heard the whisper of Mimi next to her. "It'll be okay."

Jia tried to regain her composure. She didn't want Mimi worried about her. "It will be."

Jia refilled her mom's tea and joined them all in the living room. She sat in the uncomfortable chair that she and Mimi had agreed they'd donate and replace. Jia just hadn't gotten around to it, along with the number of other things she was supposed to have done to help Mimi this summer.

"Um, as you know, I was just in New York—"

"Jia, how many times do I have to tell you not to start a sentence with the word *um*? It makes you sound uninformed," her mom said.

Jia had no idea how many times she'd been told this. Likely in the thousands by this point. She'd been hearing about all the words that made her sound uninformed, uneducated, unsophisticated, and just plain unworthy since she was a kid.

"What happened with your lawsuit against the Bakerson's Group?" her dad asked.

"What, a Google Alert didn't come through yet?"

"Jia." Her father's tone had an edge of warning to it, and Jia stopped herself. She wanted to ask them why they were here. She wanted to beg them to let her live her life. She wanted to ask them to leave so she could go and check in on Dennis. "We shouldn't be surprised that you're here, and yet I had hoped that maybe, for once, you would have listened to us and gone straight to Florida."

"We're actually not here to speak to you, Jia. We're here to discuss some business with your grandmother." Her mother only ever referred to her mother-in-law as Mimi or as Jia's grandmother.

"Jia is welcome to stay and listen. It affects the whole family, I'd say." Mimi's words caused a wave of fear and concern to run through Jia.

"Grandma?"

"Oh no, I'm fine, honey. Don't you worry. You know that. Strong as an ox," Mimi said, winking at Jia. Jia released all the air she held in her lungs with relief. "But your parents here thought they'd stop by, having flown all the way across the country from Florida, our *favorite* place in the whole world—" Mimi's voice was laced with the sarcasm Jia loved "—to tell me it's time to sell my house and move. And get this, darling," Mimi said, laying it on thick. She placed a hand on Jia's knee and leaned in for a dramatic effect. "They've already secured a real estate agent to help me."

"What?" Jia's parents were overprotective and overbearing, but they'd never actually overstepped. Until now. "That's not cool. Mom, Dad . . . this is Mimi's house. And you don't get to tell her what to do with it. What are you thinking? This is seriously too far."

There was a knock on the door. It wasn't the rhythmed signal of a neighbor. No, it was the knock of an outsider. All heads turned to the front entrance.

Jia got up to see who it could be. And when she opened the door, she wished she could say she was surprised.

"Hey, Jia. Good to see you. I was asked to come by."

And there, waiting to come in . . . was the snake, Matthew Singleton.

"What are you doing here?" Jia asked. "Mom, Dad, did you contact Matthew behind Mimi's back?"

"It was actually Mr. Singleton who contacted us. Apparently the market is prime right now. And since Mimi is not getting any younger, we thought it would be more comfortable for her to move to Florida with us. It will be good for you both. On top of it being a good financial decision," her mother explained.

Jia's stomach dropped. She was used to her parents trying to control her life, but they'd never really taken the choice out of her hands . . . yet. But it seemed that was exactly what they were doing with Mimi right now. "How could you do this? Absolutely not. Mimi, you don't want this, do you?"

"I do not want this, Jia, no," Mimi answered. Her voice was strong and certain.

"Oh, Jia. Don't be so dramatic. It's business, and it makes sense. You know the people here need more help than they've got. Many of them are selling their homes, making some money, and living in assisted-living facilities where they get the support they need. Where nurses can help them eat and move around and keep them occupied. It's a good decision." Her dad sounded like he was the expert of those at Sunset Hills, when he had no idea what the residents here were like, what they were capable of.

"Is that how you think of me?" Mimi asked. Jia grabbed Mimi's hand and held it tight. Her grandmother was vibrant and full of life and able to take care of herself. "Someone on the verge of death who needs some extra help just to get by each day?"

"Mother, you're eighty-five years old. You should not be driving, forced to take care of yourself, responsible for things like medication and health care. We can sell your place and move you to a group home in Florida. We'll be close and can monitor the staff taking care of you."

It was all the proof Jia needed that her mother had no idea what she was talking about. Everyone knew that among the people at The Sunset, after a certain age, you never gave the exact number. Mimi was "in her eighties," not "eight-five." Jia wouldn't allow her parents to put some judgment and an expiration date on her grandmother just based on age.

"Absolutely not," Jia said. She would not let them do this. Did they have the power to make Mimi do this against her will? How had Matthew gotten so many residents to sell their homes already? Jia didn't know the legalities of everything behind all this. And she was no match for her parents' brilliant legal minds. They'd find loopholes in everything.

She'd made a mess of everything. She couldn't protect Mimi. She'd pushed Dennis too hard, and he got hurt. And she couldn't protect the others from Matthew coming in and pushing some of the residents out of their homes.

"Okay, emotions are running high, and clearly there's more discussion to be had. Why don't you guys discuss it all as a family, and I'll come back tomorrow to talk details for putting the house on the market," Matthew said. He reached out and shook Jia's father's hand and leaned in to give his mother a kiss on the cheek. He turned his body toward Mimi and Jia on the couch, but they both dropped their heads, unwilling to even look at him.

"I can't believe you'd do this," Jia said to her parents, tears in her eyes. She'd lived her whole life feeling like she'd disappointed them. Today, her heart broke as she realized they had disappointed her.

Jia stood up from the couch and made for the door to leave. She couldn't be here even one minute longer.

"Jia, where are you going?" her mom called out.

"Let her be," Mimi said. "Let her be."

Jia rushed out the door into the pink-filled light.

"I thought I'd find you here."

Jia sat at her favorite corner where she'd watched the sunset almost every night here in Palm Springs, her safe place. After leaving Mimi's, she'd gone straight to Dennis's house to make sure he was okay. She hoped that she'd see Henry there. But he'd gone to the hospital to speak to the doctor and to the pharmacy to pick up more pain medication for his grandfather. He hadn't come back by the time she left.

The sky was showing signs of changing from day to night. She headed to her spot at her favorite time of day. It was when the pressures of everything around her went to sleep like the sun. It was when she could still her mind and trust that tomorrow would be a new day, another chance for everything to be okay. Sunset had always offered her perspective and peace. She needed both today.

And her grandmother, Mimi, was the one to give this to her.

Jia patted the seat next to her on the curb. Mimi came and slowly let herself down. Jia watched and suddenly realized how getting up and down from the ground might be difficult for Mimi. She reached over to help her, but Mimi shooed her away.

Jia felt ashamed that there were so many things she just hadn't considered about the older residents here. Hadn't she yelled at Henry for this exact thing? And here she was wondering if she'd been blind to it all. There had to be a middle ground, where people were allowed to live as they wanted, to their fullest potential, as they aged. And yet the world would consider, respect, and offer help as it was needed.

"I have creaky knees and my balance is off, Jia. But I'm neither dead nor dying. So get out of your head."

Jia smiled at her saucy grandmother.

"Are they gone?" she asked.

"Yup, left shortly after you did."

"How long had they been there?"

"A few hours. Mercilessly trying to get me to agree to sell the place. But you know me, my love. I'm made of tougher stuff than they give me credit for. I make my own decisions about my life. And, if you're willing, I'd like to sign over the power of attorney for my finances and my health to you, when the time comes," Mimi said.

"What? I'm not responsible enough. I make mistakes with the important stuff. I'm not reliable for all of that," Jia said.

"Get your mom's and dad's lies out of your head. That's not at all who you are. You are responsible. You are reliable. But most importantly, you lead with love. I trust you more than anyone in the world."

Jia couldn't stop the tears if she tried. So she let them flow down her cheeks as she leaned against her grandmother, placing her head on her shoulder like she had since she was a little girl.

"I don't know, Mimi. I feel like I've messed some shit up. I came running here to escape from my problems. I tried to hide from my life here at The Sunset, and I ended up ruining everyone else's in my wake."

"No, honey. Seems to me you came here and found yourself. And in doing so, you saved us all."

Jia let out a sob, and Mimi wrapped her arm around her, patting her shoulder. "You're doing great, Jia girl. You'll figure it out for yourself. I know you will. But you can't do it by running away from your problems. Plus, where you gonna go? Seems like you found your destination right here. So plant those feet and face life head-on."

Her words rung in Jia's ears. She knew Mimi was right. She just wasn't sure how.

The sun continued its journey down to the horizon, the sky having almost completed the cycle of the colors it rotated through every night. The process was beautiful, no doubt. But Jia came out here for more. She came out here for the promise that there would always be another day.

What would Jia do with her next day?

And as the day turned into night, tomorrow's plan began to take shape.

32

Jia had walked past the unassuming office space multiple times as it sat next to the gelato place she and Mimi often went to downtown. There wasn't any signage. Just a frosted-glass door. She had no idea that this was where Matthew Singleton had been conducting business for months now.

She looked twice at the address before opening the door and entering.

"Hello. Can I help you?" said a younger woman sitting at the reception desk. The space was small with just the lobby and three other doors. One led to a larger conference room, the others to individual offices. It was furnished in more modern office pieces, unlike the wood and muted tones of the Bakerson's Group offices Jia had experienced in the past.

Here the desks were made of glass and the chairs black leather, and vibrant modern art hung on the walls. There was nothing that made it clear this was a real estate office. And honestly, Jia wondered if that was the only business being conducted here.

She didn't want to believe the worst of Matthew Singleton, or her parents, for that matter. But she'd made all kinds of scenarios up in her head that ranged from fraud to kidnapping to mob-boss shit. Okay, so she had an active imagination and had read a number of highly entertaining romance novels by the pool this summer.

"My name is Jia Chung. I'm here for a meeting with Matthew Singleton," she answered.

"Yes, he's expecting you. Let me take you to the conference room. And can I get you anything to drink? Sparkling water, Poppi, iced vanilla latte?"

Those felt like very specific offerings to Jia, but she declined nonetheless. A part of her wanted to warn the young woman that over-the-top acts of service didn't always cut it in the corporate world. She was evidence of that. But all goodwill left Jia's mind the moment she walked into the room and saw her parents sitting at the conference table next to Matthew.

Jia did not have a contentious relationship with her parents. She loved them, actually. But she had determined that she would do everything in her power to fight them on behalf of Mimi. Maybe she'd never really been able to stand up to them for herself and her own needs and wants for her life, but she would do it for her grandmother.

She walked around the table and bent down to give her father a back hug and her mother a kiss on the cheek. Despite this awkward and frustrating situation, as their only child she would not let them dismiss her.

What she did not do, however, was even acknowledge Matthew. Petty, maybe. But Jia was pissed. She couldn't believe she had gone out on a date and wasted flirting energy on this guy. Nope, any and all pleasant thoughts had burned to dust the moment she realized what a snake he was. Even before all romantic thoughts had been taken over by one Henry Shin.

It hurt to think of him now. She missed him. She was certain he'd want nothing to do with her. First because of the lawsuit. Second because of Dennis's accident. And that was clear because she hadn't heard from him since she'd left the offices of the Bakerson's Group for the last time.

"You didn't come with your grandmother?" Jia's dad asked.

"No, she said she'd meet me here. She had something she needed to do beforehand," Jia answered. She, too, thought it odd that Mimi would want to come to the meeting separately. But she trusted her and knew she'd get there in time.

Just as she finished that thought, she heard the voices out at reception. Voices? More than just Mimi's?

Jia turned around and being directed by the receptionist into the conference room was a woman she'd never seen before, Mimi right behind her, followed by the most gorgeous person Jia had ever laid her eyes on, Henry.

"Mother, what are you doing bringing a bunch of strangers into our business?" Jia's father asked.

"Seems you were the first to bring a stranger into family stuff, no?" Mimi answered, nodding her head in Matthew's direction. Point, Mimi.

"What are you doing here?" Jia whispered to Henry.

He lifted the side of his mouth into a small smile, gently touched her elbow as he passed, and went to introduce himself to her parents.

Her parents!

"Hello, I'm Henry Shin." He reached out his hand and shook her father's. And then her mother's. He offered his hand to Matthew as well. Henry was much more generous than Jia could ever be.

"What are you doing here, Shin?" Matthew asked.

"I'm serving pro hac vice for Hadley Bellinger." Henry turned to the woman Jia didn't recognize.

"Mimi," Jia leaned over and whispered to her grandmother, who had taken the seat next to her, "who is Hadley Bellinger? And what is Henry doing here? What the heck is *pro hac vice*?"

"Okay, so it's like this. I needed Henry's help, but he can't practice law in California . . . yet. So he called a law school friend, Hadley, and she agreed to take my case, and he gets to help her due to some California law that allows it. Isn't it great?" Mimi's voice was filled with excitement.

Jia looked at Hadley Bellinger. She was in a perfectly tailored shift dress with an unbuttoned double-breasted blazer over it. She was pretty. But moreover, she just had the air of a badass. Jia liked her for Mimi.

But she took one more look between Hadley and Henry. Stern, serious expressions, the both of them. No spark or chemistry that she could detect. She felt better. Henry might not want Jia. But she could tell he didn't want this Hadley person either. Jia knew what it looked like when Henry Shin was attracted to someone. She'd seen it firsthand. It had taken her breath away.

Okay, nothing to be jealous about here. Now they could all get to work.

"Hi, Jia," Hadley said. "Nice to meet you. You ready to kick some ass?" Oh yes, Jia liked her a lot.

"You know it," Jia said.

She turned to Henry and gave him a nod. She trusted him.

And she trusted his recommendation of his colleague Hadley to fight for Mimi. That was all that mattered right now.

"Okay, Mimi, do you want to explain what this is all about?" Jia's mother asked, waving her hand over the table as if everyone there wasn't present because of her parents' doing.

"You wanted to play hardball, so I brought in the big guns," Mimi said. "Certainly as lawyers yourselves, you didn't expect me to make any decisions without legal counsel."

"You want this to be between lawyers? This should simply be a conversation between family. Reasonable," Jia's dad added.

"You're the ones who made this a fight," Jia noted. "You brought in this—" she waved her hand in Matthew's general direction "—shark. A soulless man targeting the elderly residents of Sunset Hills—a community with good people who've worked their whole lives to be able to retire and live their later years the way they choose—to try to take their homes away from them. And now, as if all of that weren't bad enough—" Jia's voice cracked, and she took a breath before going on "—you're joining him in doing it to your own mother. My grandmother. You're treating her like she doesn't have a choice, and that's unforgivable. If you do this, I will never forgive you."

"Jia, stop being so dramatic. It's embarrassing," her mother responded.

"I think what's embarrassing is that you aren't listening to what your daughter is trying to say to you." Henry's low, steady voice had a tone of reprimand, and it silenced the room immediately. Jia didn't know if anyone had ever spoken to her mother that way.

Jia watched as her mother's back straightened and she placed both hands on the table, rising to stand and leaning in to make herself heard. Jia held her breath. She couldn't watch her mom unleash on Henry. She hadn't prepared him for her lawyer mode.

But Henry seemed unfazed. In fact, his back also straightened. He placed his elbows on the table, tenting his hands in front of his mouth. And he leaned in to meet her.

"Mimi is, at this point in her life, not entirely capable of making her own decisions," her mother said. Jia grabbed Mimi's hand under the table and squeezed. Mimi squeezed back.

She huffed out loud but didn't say a word. It was all so ridiculous.

"Mimi Chung is willing to undergo all physical and mental testing required to deem herself competent," Henry said. "Furthermore . . ."

Oh shit, he pulled out a *furthermore*. Jia had only ever heard that word in courtroom dramas on TV. To be followed with the knockout blow.

She squeezed her legs together and waited. First because Henry was fucking hot like this, all scary and official and badass-lawyerlike. And second because she knew he only played to win. And he knew all the rules of engagement. What bomb would he drop on them next?

"Mimi Chung has also filed all the paperwork to appoint her granddaughter, Jia Chung, as the executor of her trust and has given her the power of attorney for decisions for her life if she ever is incapable of making them on her own."

"That's ridiculous. Jia isn't competent to oversee her own life, let alone her aging grandmother's. She can't even keep a job." Jia's father said the words she always knew they believed. And he said them like accusations, not just disappointments, in front of others.

Jia felt the wind knocked out of her, and she deflated in her chair. She lowered her head and wanted to crawl under the table.

"Don't you ever speak to my granddaughter that way. I raised you better than that," Mimi said to Jia's dad.

"What were you thinking giving her power of attorney—"

"Why would you do something so drastic—"

"The paperwork has all been drawn up—"

"So does Jia have to sign off on the sale of the house—"

Everyone was talking at once. Jia's mind swirled in the cacophony of voices, dizzy with all the finger-pointing (her parents), the defending (Mimi and Henry . . . awww), and the legal jargon (Hadley), and some other gibberish (Matthew, the snake).

"Stop," she said. The voices continued.

"Stop!" she screamed. Everyone shut their mouths immediately, all eyes turning to her. Jia was tempted to rise to her feet to be on the same level as everyone else. But she didn't. She could say what she needed to say sitting down, calmly, powerfully.

"Mom, Dad, you have made it clear my entire life that I have been a disappointment to you, that I have only brought hardship and heartache along with me. I have tried to overcome this sense of not being good enough, trying to mold myself into some shape of a person you could be proud of. But I didn't fit. Because it wasn't who I was meant to be. I'm sorry that I love freely. I'm sorry that I lead with joy. I'm sorry that I live life looking at possibilities and not worried about mistakes. No—" she stopped and thought about what she was saying "—actually, I'm not sorry. I'm proud of who I am. I'm just sorry that you can't accept that person. But at the end of the day, this isn't about me. This is about Mimi. And I swear both in my heart and now on any legal documents I need to sign that I will take care of her her entire life. Because she's the one person who believes in me. Who cheers for me. Who sees me as someone remarkable."

"Jia, honey, you are remarkable," Mimi said, sitting down and grabbing Jia's hand.

"Thanks, Mimi. And thank you for giving me a chance here this summer. To land somewhere safe and to find my own way and figure it out myself."

"It's been a gift."

"Jia, you can't live life just to be happy. You have to be stable. You have to be successful. You have to invest in the future. You can't putz around in your grandmother's retirement community like you have no responsibilities." Jia's mom let out a deep, frustrated sigh as she, too, collapsed into her chair.

"I feel I need to clarify what it is your daughter does at Sunset Hills and the impact she makes on the residents. Because, listening to you, I'm quite certain that you have no idea." Henry looked first to Jia's mom, then her dad, and then turned his face to hers.

"Jia is, indeed, remarkable. She has a zest for life that is contagious. She takes the darkest of places, lost in shadows, and she shines light. She convinces people that life is worth living and then shows them how to do so. She's kind and funny and affirming. And she sees people for who they are and not what they bring to the table. In fact, she sees people more clearly when they have nothing to offer her. She's the most incredible person I've ever met, and I feel sorry for you—" his eyes turned back to Jia's parents "—for never having known your daughter at all."

Tears ran down Jia's cheeks. She looked to the surprised expression on her mother's face and the bowed head of her father.

"Wow," Mimi whispered in awe. "Our Hank is well and truly in love with you."

Henry turned back to Jia. "Yes, I am."

"What?" Jia couldn't believe her ears. Henry was in love with her. "You're in love with me?"

Henry tucked his lips under his teeth, hiding his smile. "Is that so hard to believe?"

"But I make your life a pain. I exasperate you. I argue with you about everything. I . . . I pushed Dennis too hard, and he got hurt."

"No, don't you dare take that on yourself. Dennis's accident was just that. And he's fine. He'll be fine. That was not your fault, and I won't let you blame the woman I love for something she had nothing to do with," Henry said.

"You love me," she said. This time no longer a question. "And I love you," she added.

"Look, this is all really touching and all. But what about the deal? Mimi's house? Hello?" Matthew waved his hand trying to get everyone's attention.

"There won't be a deal," Jia's father said.

"In fact, we may be opening an investigation into some of your real estate handlings in the recent history here in Palm Springs. Something doesn't seem right about it all, and we'll need to check it out, just in case," Hadley said.

Matthew turned white as a ghost. "Everyone, out! Out of my office. Take your crazy family and leave me alone."

"With pleasure," Mimi said, standing up and gathering her purse.

Jia's father and mother walked over to her, faces grim. "Jia," her mom started.

"It's okay, Mom."

"But it's not, Jia. We're worried, we've only ever just been worried about you," her dad added.

"Well, I guess this is something we're all gonna have to work on. Communicating honestly. And maybe accepting each other as we are," Jia said.

"C'mon, everyone. Let's go back to my place and hash it out. I've got a good mind to ice you guys out of my life for the next year or so just to make you see what life without me and Jia would be like. But I'm not that cruel," Mimi said. She turned to the woman beside her. "Hadley, thank you," she added. "And you." Mimi placed both hands on Henry's cheeks. "You're a good boy. Don't mess this up." She patted him gently and let go. "Love you, Jia girl." Mimi wrapped Jia in a hug.

"Love you too, Mimi."

"Now, take my granddaughter out to dinner, have some drinks, and get a hotel for the night. I don't want to see either of you for at least twenty-four hours, maybe forty-eight if the gettin's good."

"Mimi!" Jia cried, cheeks blushing.

"Look, everyone at The Sunset has a vested interest in you two getting together. We've worked hard for this. Give us a reason to celebrate, would you? We don't get enough of those at our old age."

"I'm on it, Mimi," Henry said. Standing next to Jia, wrapping an arm around her shoulders, he looked down into her eyes and smiled. "You heard the woman. Let's get out of here."

"Why do I get the feeling everyone else was in cahoots trying to push this agenda?" Jia said, pointing between the two of them.

"Don't give them all the credit. I was pushing pretty hard myself," he admitted.

Jia smiled.

She looked over her shoulder one last time and said, "See ya later, snake." And walked out of the office into the Palm Springs heat with the man she loved.

33

They were quiet in the car. Like they hadn't just gone through a battle together. Or maybe because they had.

Jia didn't know where Henry was taking her. He drove straight down Indian Canyon Road. There were only two main streets downtown. This one led toward Sunset Hills. But she had a feeling they weren't going there.

When he got almost to the north end of the city, he turned and headed up a small hill. He pulled into the parking lot and turned off the car. It was quiet here, it being off-season and all. Henry turned to look at her with a small smile.

"Come with me?" he asked.

Jia nodded, and they both got out of the car.

It was late afternoon, and the heat was at its highest. Jia closed her eyes for one brief moment and took a deep breath. After the chaos of the day, the quiet of the desert hit her, and she felt fortified by it.

Henry walked around to her side and stood in front of her,

blocking her from the blinding sun. With it hiding behind his tall frame, illuminating him from behind, he looked like an angel. She smiled at him, and he grabbed her hand, and they walked into the visitors center.

Henry got them two tickets for the Aerial Tramway. Jia remembered riding this as a kid, but it had been years since she'd been to the top of the mountain. The ticket counter was busier than she expected, and the small number of cars in the parking lot didn't reflect all the people inside. She looked down at her watch and then out the window and realized it.

Henry and Jia and all these other people would make it to the top close to sunset.

"I promise I'll feed you after," Henry said.

Jia leaned into him and put her head on his shoulder. "Always coming to my rescue," she said.

"And you mine," he replied.

She didn't know what that meant. Jia hadn't rescued Henry, not like he had her. Twice now, he'd put on his lawyer hat and saved Jia from her enemies, from her own peril.

They boarded the tram and started the slow journey up into the sky. Jia stood near the window in the back of the car, watching the city move farther and farther away as they made the climb. Henry stood behind her, her back against his chest, his hand steadying her on her hip.

Their tram car had a family and two other couples aboard, so Jia remained quiet despite all the questions she wanted to ask Henry. It could wait.

When they got to the top, Henry got off and offered Jia his hand to help her step out. Most people went inside the visitor area in the air conditioning, but Henry and Jia walked to the outdoor observation deck and stood side by side, taking in the view.

"Thank you, Henry," Jia started, "for coming today. For helping Mimi. For helping me."

"Jia," Henry said.

"And thank you, for saving the day in New York too, at the Bakerson's Group. I know that couldn't have been easy," she said before he could brush off what he'd done for her.

"I quit," he said, like it was no big deal.

She whipped her head around to face him. "What? You loved that job. It wasn't because of me, was it?"

"I didn't love that job. In fact, I hated it. And I hated who I was doing it. And quitting was most certainly because of you. I couldn't stand how they treated you and the other women. They might have been able to find a loophole with the law, but it didn't negate the fact that they mistreated you. I just didn't want to do it anymore. In fact, I don't want to do New York anymore." He let out a sigh like he'd just admitted a truth he'd been hiding for a long time.

Jia wrapped her hand around his. She didn't want to assume what this could mean for them. She wouldn't get her hopes up.

She asked what had been on her mind since the moment he walked into the office today. "How did you end up working with Mimi? Last time I asked you to help with this issue, you said you weren't able to."

She hadn't meant to sound hurt, but she was a little. She'd asked, and he'd said no. So what had changed?

"I was scared of getting involved . . . emotionally," he said.

"With the residents? Or with me?" Jia asked.

He looked down at her, and the side of his mouth lifted. God she loved that small smile of his.

"Both."

"And you're not anymore?" Jia pressed.

"Scared shitless," he admitted. "But unwilling to walk away from them. From you."

He turned his body to face hers, and she met him there. He wrapped his arms around her waist and pulled her closer. He smelled woody and fresh. Jia wanted to bury her nose in his neck.

"I agreed to help Mimi because I had something worth fighting for. Something I cared enough to risk it all for. That's you. And her. And Dennis. And the people at The Sunset. All of it."

"That's amazing, Henry. But I don't want you to give up your whole life for this. I don't even know if I'm staying here, to be honest. I still have to find a job and—"

"You have a job. If you want it, that is. When Mimi came and asked me for help at first, it wasn't about your parents and Matthew. It was about working with the board at Sunset Hills to secure a new community manager position. One that will oversee the property and the residents. One that they want to offer to you," he explained.

"What? Are you serious?" Jia couldn't believe it. It had become her dream job, something she'd secretly hoped could form in reality. One she was going to suggest to them once she got up the nerve to do so. She wanted to stay at The Sunset and continue to help the residents, and she hoped that there could be a way to make it her life's career, her calling.

"Yup. I have the offer letter with me in the car. It's a small but livable salary. And there's housing included. So you still get to be the youngest resident of Sunset Hills. A badge of honor you relish, I know." He laughed. And she laughed with him.

She couldn't believe it. She could stay.

She'd have to deal with her parents and the aftermath of the day. And she'd have to tie up all the loose ends back in New York. But she could stay.

"Henry," she squealed, "I can stay!" She jumped at him and wrapped her arms around his neck, squeezing him into a hug. His arms embraced her back and held her tight. Jia pulled back, brimming with energy. "I have so many ideas about how to better everyone's quality of life here. Not just fun events. But I was thinking about how we could incorporate things like health screenings and palliative care when it becomes necessary. And after today, I'm certain that some of the residents could use legal advice and counsel to know their rights as elders. And maybe even, I don't know, have a small vintage clothing and wares shop on the grounds that could be open to the public and help make some extra cash for the residents." She still couldn't believe she was being offered a job and could get paid to do it all.

She let out a deep breath and closed her eyes. "I'm so happy."

"I'm happy for you," Henry said. Jia opened her eyes to find him looking at her, a wide smile on his face.

"And you? What's next for you?"

He placed his hands on her hips and touched his forehead to hers. "Well, I'm going to stick around here for a while. I figured, if you can find yourself at Sunset Hills, maybe I can get a little of that magic and find myself too."

"There are so many people that could use your guidance and expertise," Jia added. "Lots of chances to pull that hero shit you've been doing so well lately," she teased. "Trading in your bespoke suit for a cape."

"I draw the line at wearing tights, though," he said.

"We'll see," she said. "Bet I could convince you to wear some superhero tights."

"You are so very convincing," he said.

He leaned down and whispered against her lips, "Secret is I'd do anything for you." And he kissed her.

It was warm and tasted slightly salty, and she wanted to crawl into his mouth and just let his tongue do its magic. God, she loved this man. "I love you." She decided to be brave and say it aloud.

"Love you too, sweet Jia." He kissed her again. "Gorgeous Jia" and again. "Vibrant Jia" and again.

This man was very good with words.

Jia noticed the sky had started its show, pink when they arrived, darkening into the hues of orange now.

"It's sunset," she said, turning in Henry's arms to face the horizon.

He wrapped himself around her from behind, bending to rest his chin on her shoulder. "Best time of the day. Living in New York, I never even thought about sunset. It was just day and then suddenly night. How had I missed the magic of the transition, the in-between time?"

"It's different out here in the desert. I never noticed it in New York either. But here? I try to never miss it."

"Let's try to catch it as often as we can together," Henry said.

It was the most romantic proposition she'd ever received.

"Absolutely," Jia said back.

It was a promise. Between two people in love.

And it was everything Jia had ever dreamed of and more.

EPILOGUE

"You sure you wanna do this?" Henry asked.

He didn't want to pressure Jia. But it had been a long time coming. Months, actually. It never seemed to bother her, except that it remained a loose end she wanted to tie up.

"Yeah, let's get it over with. I don't know why I didn't deal with it sooner," Jia said.

Henry grabbed her hand, and they walked together into the airport.

When Jia had first come to stay with her grandmother in Palm Springs, the airline had lost her luggage. It had arrived shortly after, but she just never wanted to go and pick it up.

Henry was secretly happy she hadn't. Because there was something about the way Jia described herself and her life when they'd both lived in New York that kind of broke his heart. She'd struggled financially, and she'd struggled finding herself. A woman without an identity. Her clothes became a way to pretend she had it all together, despite not being able to afford that life.

Coming to the desert, she'd shed all of that. She'd found herself. She didn't need to play dress-up anymore. Henry always found Jia sexy and adorable and put-together in her own way. He loved her bright colors and vibrant patterns. But he loved her freedom and confidence even more. She didn't need to hide, so she didn't.

"There are some really great pieces in there that I think would sell quickly in the vintage shop. It would be nice to make some extra money to put toward the graduation gifts," Jia said.

Sunset Hills was having its first graduation class for the eight residents who had gone through and passed their inaugural CPR/First Aid course. It was an exciting time.

"Hi there. I'm here to pick up my luggage," Jia said to the older man working the customer service desk. "For Jia Chung? It's a big yellow suitcase."

"Well, goddamn. You actually showed. I woulda won the entire pool if you'd have come just two days later. Horace," he yelled at someone in the office behind him, "looks like you're taking home the pot, you lucky motherfucker."

"What is happening?" Jia leaned in and whispered to Henry.

"Looks like there might have been a betting pool on when you would come to get your bag."

"Huh. Wonder how much Horace won," she said.

Henry kissed Jia on the top of her head. He, like Horace, knew what it felt like to be lucky.

"Jia, babe, we gotta go. We're gonna be late," Henry called from the front door of his condo downtown. He hadn't been sure where he wanted to end up, exactly. But he liked this particular block, with his favorite coffee shop and a really good workout gym. And it was walking distance, two blocks, from his office where he read up on cases and had already been studying diligently for the California Bar Exam.

Plus, it was less than five minutes to Sunset Hills, and that was an easy-enough drive to visit the people he loved the most.

"Coming. I can't find my shoes," Jia called out from the bedroom.

"Which ones?" Jia only had three pairs: sneakers, sandals, and flip-flops. Two were sitting right there at the doorway. "Your sneakers and flip-flops are here."

"Wait," she said and popped her head out, "did I wear my flip-flops here? I think I did. So my sandals must be at my place. Ooops." She smiled and came out to meet him, wrapping her arms around his neck. "I'd lose my own head if it wasn't attached to my body. I swear, when I downsized moving out here, I feel like it got harder to keep track of stuff."

Henry gave her a quick kiss and pushed her out the door. They had exactly seven minutes to get there, which, if they caught every red light along the way, would make them late.

"Did you finish?" she asked as she strapped into his car.

"Yup, last night."

"Why didn't you wake me up, then?" She pouted. "You promised."

"But you were completely out, snoring and everything," he said.

"I don't snore," she said.

"If you say so," he teased.

"You were supposed to try that thing once you were done," she whined.

"I'll try it when we get home later."

"Which home are we at tonight?" she asked.

"Yours. It's closer, and I'm not sure I trust myself driving home after."

Jia's face broke into a smile, with a bit of an edge. She was excited.

Frankly, so was he. He could not wait.

"God, you were so sexy talking about the themes of the book tonight. I wanted to crawl into your lap right then and there," Jia said, pulling Henry into the house. His mouth was already on hers.

He slammed the door shut, kicked off his shoes, and lifted her up. "Wrap your legs around me, baby," he commanded.

She did as she was told.

As the new community manager at The Sunset, Jia got to live in the manager's cottage behind the office. It was a cute two-bedroom home, small but tidy. She'd gotten the approval to do some renovations from the board, and she couldn't wait to get started.

Jia and Henry split time between her onsite home and his condo downtown. She loved both places for different reasons. It didn't matter where they stayed, frankly. She just loved being with him.

A few months ago, she wouldn't have dreamed that the two of them could end up together, in Palm Springs no less. Near their favorite people, doing fun activities like Book Club, where they had just come from.

Tonight's romance novel was a spicy romantasy that Jia had

devoured. Henry took longer to finish it, taking in every detail of the world-building and dissecting the themes. Jia flew through the dialogue and the sex scenes. They were chef's kiss. It was a great recommendation from her favorite online book reviewer, @irene.loves.love.books.

The reviews were mixed among the Sunset Hills Spicy Book Club, however. It was a spirited discussion. But Jia could barely focus, what with Henry's flirtatious glances and smiles.

What they hadn't discussed, thankfully, was a specific scene in which the male main character did some unspeakably dirty things with his tongue to the love interest. Henry was supposed to try those same things on Jia last night.

Except her snoring had scared him away.

But she was ready for him now. God, was she ready.

Her man was, she had come to find over and over again, incredibly talented with his tongue.

Looking down at the gorgeous woman underneath him, Henry was reminded how lucky he really was. Just a few months ago, he had been in a thankless job, living a joyless life, and resigned to a loveless existence.

And then came Jia . . . with her zest for life. And her huge heart. And her knack for pushing all of Henry's buttons in the best way. He was a goner.

Jia helped him see that life was worth living in community. Who knew that the community he'd be surrounding himself with would be a bunch of senior citizens?

He was happy.

And he loved seeing Jia come into her own. Find herself. Thrive.

Henry lowered his body down onto hers. Her legs were open and waiting. He greedily lined himself up and slowly pushed his way inside her.

He'd never get used to how good it felt being connected to Jia this way. It was like he was made for her and she was made to receive him. He pushed all the way in, and the moan it elicited made him even harder, if that were possible.

"Henry," she whispered, "I love you."

It made him emotional every time she said it, and she said it often.

"I love you too, Jia," he said. And he began to move, slow thrusts at first. But when she wrapped her legs around his and pushed her feet into his ass, the message was loud and clear. *Faster, harder.* She lifted herself slightly, meeting him with each pump.

Jia dug her fingers into Henry's hair, and Henry knew she was close . . . again. He'd made her come already with his mouth, tonguing both the front and the back just like they'd read about in the book. She giggled when he explored the back side but let herself relax into it when she realized how committed he was to keep going, how much he loved eating her out.

Henry pounded a little harder, and the sound of their bodies slapping together was like the sexiest beat he'd ever heard. The weather had cooled down by winter. But it was still warm compared to what it was like in New York. And without the ceiling fan on, Henry's and Jia's bodies were slick with sweat. He'd wash her off in the shower later.

Henry felt Jia stiffen underneath him as she squeezed her cunt around his cock. "I'm coming," she yelled. Thank god her cottage was set off the main road without any neighbors on either side of her. His girl was a screamer.

"Come for me, baby," he said.

"You come too," she insisted.

"I'm almost there," he said as he pushed himself inside her warmth.

She let out a scream as her pussy began pulsating. He pushed in once, twice more before the wave of his own pleasure took over. He rode her through it until it became too sensitive for her.

When Henry gently pulled himself out, Jia felt like a boneless blob. He'd marked every inch inside of her. She sighed, completely satisfied. God, she loved this man.

Henry wrapped his entire body around her from behind, and they held each other. It was warm and they wouldn't stay in this position long. But she savored it for now.

Jia couldn't believe this was her life.

She'd been fired from a thankless job just a few months ago. She'd felt rudderless and uncertain of the future. Now she had a job she loved, in a neighborhood she felt safe and secure in, with a man that made her feel like she could conquer the world.

Life was funny. And no longer felt overwhelming.

Because even on days when it was hard, Jia knew that, like clockwork, there would always be the sunset.

And after sunset, always, the promise of a new day to come.

ACKNOWLEDGMENTS

I am deeply grateful for the ability and opportunity to write love stories. I don't think I realized how it would come to save me time and again—writing books about the power of love.

Thank you to those who helped make this book come to life: my ever-patient and encouraging editor, Michele Bidelspach; the entire team at MIRA/Harlequin/HarperCollins, who have tirelessly worked behind the scenes to get my stories told; my superhero agent, Taylor Haggerty; the incredible team at Root Literary; and librarians, booksellers, readers, reviewers, and everyone who takes a chance on me and my words.

I have a very bad habit of being a bit of a recluse. So I need to thank my friends in this industry who pull me out of my black hole time and again and make me see light and touch grass, give me much-needed perspective, and surround me with love, especially in this past season: Christina (&) Lauren, Ali Hazelwood, Julie Soto, Kate Goldbeck, Lindsey Kelk, Alexis Daria, Adriana Herrera, Nisha Sharma, Nikki Payne, BK Borison, Lyla Sage,

Jessica Joyce, Priscilla Oliveras, Ali Rosen, Sasha Peyton Smith, Brian Kennedy, Axie Oh, Jessica Kim, Sarah Suk, Graci Kim, Grace Shim . . . I love you.

To the seven who feed my spirit: Namjoon, Jin, Yoongi, Hobi, Jimin, Tae, and JK . . . welcome home. Thank you for *Arirang* and the reminder to be resilient and transformative and to love where we come from.

Mom, Sunny, Caleb, Wayne, Butter, and Karou . . . I love you.

It never bothered Julia Song that she was thirty and single with a terrible track record at dating . . . until her beloved grandmother drops the bomb that she is sick and her dying wish is for Julia to get married. So Julia reluctantly asks her family for help: set her up on three dates to help her find The One.

But it will never work—Julia is undateable. If only there was a coach for that . . .

Please turn the page for an excerpt from Susan Lee's Julia Song Is Undateable, *available now!*

1
BRIBE BAGS
Julia

JULIA SONG HATED being the center of attention.

So standing here at the head of the conference table, expectant eyes of Very Important People all on her, was pretty much torture.

But Julia was the CEO of Starlight Cosmetics, this company was her baby, these VIPs the executives she hired to help grow the business. And the news she had to share with them was monumental.

She scanned her memory for the advice from her executive coach for this kind of situation. The only thing she could remember was, contrary to everything she'd ever been told before in her life, *never* try to picture your audience naked. It would make the nerves even worse.

And, of course, now that's all Julia could think of.

She closed her eyes for a moment to clear her mind of all the unfortunate images fighting to run through her head.

What was that *one thing* her coach told her?

Squeeze your butt cheeks to hold the plank. Wait, no, that was her abs coach.

If the recipe calls for garlic, double it. Wrong again. That was her cooking coach.

Oh, screw it. What was the use of having all these people to help Julia better herself when she couldn't call upon the advice when needed?

She cleared her throat and decided to wing it.

"I know you're all busy, so I'll make this quick. Look, it's not how I wanted to do this . . ."

Her dream, rather, was to one day point at each of them and tell them an exorbitant dollar amount for a bonus. Enough money for them to buy new homes in the hills or on the beach, whichever they preferred.

"Wait—are you firing us?" someone cried out from the other end of the table.

Julia's eyebrows shot up to her hairline. "What? No, of course not. Don't be ridiculous."

Always start with something personal and positive to get people excited about what you're going to say. Oh yeah, *that's* the brilliant advice her coach had mentioned.

"Oh gosh, I'm so sorry. I didn't mean to sound so ominous." Julia quickly backtracked. "It's just that, well, at the risk of getting too squishy in a work meeting, I really wanted to thank you all for taking a chance on me way back when all of this was just an idea in my head."

Julia swallowed the emotion building in her throat as she looked around at the team she'd put together to lead this company. They were the ones who took her idea to merge the best in the Korean skincare market with the high demands of the US consumer and built what was now one of the fastest-growing organic, clean K-beauty brands in America.

"I just want to tell you how much I appreciate your hard work and loyalty. I don't know that any of us anticipated this kind of success. But honestly, none of it would have happened without each and every one of you and your contribution. And now I have some really great news. As you know, Starlight's Lotus Bamboo Essence was selected for *Allure*'s Best of Beauty awards. Which was a dream come true for us. But it doesn't end there."

Julia inserted the dramatic pause her public speaking coach had encouraged her to use. The looks of anticipation around the room fueled her excitement.

"I'm thrilled to share that the same Lotus Bamboo Essence has also been selected as one of this year's Oprah's Favorite Things!"

There was a silent pause of shock, followed by an eruption of applause and cheers, high fives, and hugs shared around the table.

"We'll need to reforecast sales projections. We're gonna blow up with the exposure . . ."

"We're gonna have to update a comms plan . . ."

"We have to think of how we add this to the packaging design . . ."

"We need to make sure the supply chain can handle the increased distribution . . ."

"Oprah still has major influence on Gen X consumer spending. It's a big win for a product . . ."

Yup, that was her team . . . no-nonsense, capable, loyal, honest . . . and the hardest-working, most talented people in the industry. And they were all business, just like her.

Her chest swelled as she watched them leave to get back to work, patting each other on the back as they walked out, taking the noise with them.

Julia started this company at only twenty-six years old. She'd disappointed her parents by changing her major from pre-med to business administration. She lived off ramen and PB&J sandwiches for a good year just to scrape by as she worked tirelessly to research the industry, to find the holes, the opportunities. She fought pushback from the Korean beauty companies who hadn't exactly welcomed her with open arms. And she stomached the start-up community's boys' club as she tried to secure funding for the company.

And four short years later, they were on the verge of something huge. Hard work and dedication had brought them to this level of success. So yeah, she was proud of them, proud of herself. And at only thirty, she was finally in a position financially to take care of her family without worry.

When the last person left her office, Julia turned to look out the windows, the hustle and bustle of Santa Monica ten floors below. She took a deep breath.

"That's right, motherfuckers," she screamed, while pumping her fist. She shook her hips back and forth, adding in some aggressive hair throws and, why the heck not, followed it with a body roll. "Oh yeah, uh-huh . . ."

"Oh dear, that's something I'm not likely going to forget seeing."

Record scratch.

Julia halted her celebratory dance and quickly patted down her hair, trying to tuck her I-knew-I'd-regret-these bangs behind her ear as her assistant, Annette, entered the office.

"Unlike what your schedule says on paper, you've only

actually attended that hot yoga class once. Should you really be trying to move your body like that?" Annette asked. "I wouldn't want you to hurt yourself."

"You're fired."

Annette passed her the cup of black coffee in the *Morning Person* mug that she knew was a lie, along with a multivitamin and a probiotic. Breakfast of champions.

"Just remember that I know where the bodies are hidden. Oh, and I have those pictures of you from that one holiday party . . ."

"Okay, fine, you can stay," Julia conceded.

"Is it a good time to ask for a raise?"

Julia tried to shoot Annette a glare but couldn't keep back the smile. It was a secret to no one that Annette was invaluable to the Starlight team, and most days she was the one bossing Julia around. Julia shook her head and took a seat at her desk. "Can you forward the *O* magazine email to the team so they know all the details?"

"You betcha," Annette said. "Have you told your folks yet?"

"No, not yet. I don't think they'd even understand what a big deal this is."

"Make sure to tell them." Annette wasn't only her assistant, she was also her work-mother as well. "Oh, and here is the updated short list of investors we might want to approach for global expansion. One bad meeting doesn't have to halt progress."

One bad meeting was an understatement. The last time Julia had met with an investment firm for an informational meeting, they kept asking about her significant other, driving home that they were a family-run business built on traditional values. They looked at her as young and inexperienced not because of her age—she knew plenty of male CEOs who were thirty—but because she wasn't married with children. In their eyes, Julia wasn't reliable because she wasn't settled . . . settled *down*, that is.

Her accomplishments, alone, weren't enough.

I'll show them, she thought to herself as she gritted her teeth.

Julia grabbed the list from Annette with a little bit more force than necessary and nodded. "Thanks."

"Hey." Annette softened her voice like she so rarely ever did. The one word in that tone made Julia surprisingly emotional. "It's a good day, boss lady. You should be proud." She patted Julia on the shoulder before walking back to her desk just outside Julia's office.

"It really is a good day," said a bright and familiar voice from the doorway.

Julia pulled back as she saw her best friend, Sonia Oh, there with a bottle of champagne in one hand and a . . . saber? . . . in the other.

"They let you through building security with that?" Julia lifted her chin toward the very dangerous-looking knife.

"It was in my bag," Sonia said, as if it was the most normal thing to be carrying around in one's tote. Julia's eyebrows shot up as she slowly leaned back away from the saber's sharp point. "Don't give me that look. Sabering champagne bottles is a lost art. Don't worry, I know what I'm doing."

Sonia lined the blade up to the top of the champagne bottle, and with a dramatic flick, the cork went flying.

Impressive.

Julia grabbed the plastic cup of champagne and tapped it to Sonia's.

"To being selected as one of Oprah's Favorite Things. The accolades keep coming!"

Julia still couldn't believe it. If all went as expected, her small but growing company would solidify its status as a real success in the States.

But Julia's big dream was to go global, especially to be taken seriously in the South Korean market. Without that, Julia felt a bit like a fraud. She would have to look deeper into the daunting hurdle of Korean distribution and marketing sooner than later. She just wasn't sure they could tackle something so huge on their own. Funding—investors—would be a safer route for a move that big.

She looked back at the list on her desk. Someone on it could be the right fit for Starlight. And they'd do it for the company's merits and *not* based on Julia's marital status.

"Did I hear the celebratory sound of plastic cups clonking in here? Classy. I want in on this action."

"Why do I feel like plans were made without me?" Julia asked as her other best friend, Rachel Park, sauntered into the office.

As practical as Julia was in her signature monochrome tailored black slacks, silk blouse and her singular focus on business, and as quirky as Sonia was in her flowing skirt, off-the-shoulder sweater and champagne saber in hand, Rachel was the glamour girl of the trio, with the latest fashion trends, magazine-cover-worthy style, and always the perfect red lip.

Julia, Sonia, and Rachel had shared a dorm their freshman year in college and had been best friends ever since, despite, or maybe because of, being so different. Their one thing in common was what strengthened their bond: they shared the same joys and pains of growing up Korean American.

"You didn't think we'd let you not celebrate this, did you?" Rachel said as she placed a pastry box in front of Julia. "Mochi doughnuts, your favorite."

"Way to come prepared," Sonia said.

"Knowing you," Rachel said, pointing at Julia as she walked over to the credenza to grab plates and napkins from the cabinet, "you were probably planning on going home, ordering a pizza, and catching up on *The Challenge* to celebrate."

Honestly, all of that sounded like a perfect celebratory plan in Julia's mind.

"Whoa, you're really spoiling your halmoni for her eightieth birthday," Rachel said, motioning with her head to the four very large, very full gift bags on Julia's conference table in the corner.

"Um, none of those are for Halmoni," Julia said. "They're for my mom and aunties. Starlight's new ginseng line of skincare. Gucci scarves. Prada sunglasses. Bottega leather key rings. My plan is to woo them with goodies to distract them so they won't focus on my hair, my weight, my dating life, why I'm not married . . . the usual. It cost me a pretty penny, but it'll be worth it."

"Korean families can be so rough. I thought I was past it once James and I got married. But now we're on to the *When are you having babies?* part. It's relentless," Sonia said.

"And just another reason I'm glad I don't have any family," Rachel added. "No one around to give me shit for never wanting to get married."

Rachel had lost her family at a young age. And though she didn't mention them often, when she did, it was usually with a flippancy that made Julia worried she might be dealing with something. She made a mental note to check in with her best friend later to make sure she was okay. Rachel would hate it if they forced her to talk right now.

Julia threw a quick look toward Sonia, who met her with a tiny head nod. She'd noticed too.

Sonia got up and walked over to the table, subtly giving Rachel's shoulder a gentle squeeze.

"How do I get my hands on one of these bribe bags?" Sonia asked, peeking inside. "Nice."

"They were a last-minute splurge, technically a backup plan. Originally, I was going to play sick and maybe get out of going home for Halmoni's birthday weekend altogether."

"Well, you're too chicken to pull that off. Your halmoni might be the only person in the world you're scared of saying *no* to. You'd never disappoint her," Rachel said. "Plus, anytime you try to play sick, it ends up sounding like a lifelong smoker."

"Huh, I always thought she sounded like a phone sex operator," Sonia added.

"Those aren't a thing anymore. You need video now and an OnlyFans account," Rachel added matter-of-factly.

Sonia nodded. "Wow, I didn't realize you needed technology for cheap thrills now too."

"Hello, vibrators?"

"Can we not talk about vibrators at my workplace please?" Julia chimed in, not able to hide the smile on her face. It felt like they were back in their first off-campus apartment, laughing, drinking Mike's Hard Lemonade, and sharing notes on their sex lives.

"I have an idea. Just tell your family you've had a longstanding relationship with a guy you've been hiding. His name is Bob," Sonia suggested.

"You know I'm a terrible liar."

"It's not a lie," Sonia insisted. "You *have* had a long-term relationship with Bob, your Battery Operated Boyfriend. Get it?"

"So we're sexualizing dad jokes now. Is that what we've

become?" Rachel's voice was laced with mockery, but her smile gave her away. She'd be the first to laugh at all of Sonia's dad jokes.

"I'm not faking a boyfriend," Julia said. "I'm knee-deep in this next wave for Starlight. I have no time for any boyfriends, fake or real. Plus, I shouldn't have to fake it. What's the big deal? I'm single at thirty. You'd think, the way some people see it, I've committed a crime against humanity or something."

"We're supposed to *have it all* by now," Rachel said, dramatic air quotes punctuating her eye roll.

"According to whose standards? It's such an antiquated notion that having it all looks the same for everyone and means the same thing as it has for generations," Julia responded.

"Fair point," Sonia said. "But what's with the sudden existential crisis?"

Julia shrugged. "I've just given up on dating."

"Uh-oh. Who was it this time, and what happened?" Rachel asked.

Julia let out the deepest breath. This was supposed to be an impromptu celebration of her accomplishments with friends. She downed the dregs of her champagne from the plastic cup, swallowed her pride along with it, and let it out.

"I finally gave in and went out with that commercial real estate guy from Malibu."

"The one who was on the reality TV show?" Sonia asked.

Julia held back the groan.

"And?" Rachel nudged.

"You both know how it is. I'm awkward with people. I have no social skills, which translates badly to any dating situation." She shrugged. "I told him he looked different in person than on TV."

The pained expression on her friends' faces confirmed what Julia suspected: It had been the wrong thing to say.

"Which led him to feel the need to share his entire history of body dysmorphia and then ended with him telling me I'm undateable."

Silence.

Rachel elbowed Sonia.

"Well, that's just nonsense," Sonia sputtered. "You're not undateable. You're perfect,"

"Let's not lie to the girl. Undateable, no. But, there is no denying you're awful at the art of dating." Rachel, ever the realist. "Remember that time you told the guy who showed up in a bowling shirt that Charlie Sheen wanted his wardrobe back?"

"He was doused in Drakkar Noir like he'd just walked out of the nineties. He was asking for it." The three of them met each other with matching eye rolls.

"And remember how she made *The New York Times* bestselling author cry when she admitted she couldn't get past the second chapter—"

"And when that founder got all defensive because she called his Patagonia vest and Allbirds sneakers *start-up chic*—"

"Okay, so not my finest moments, I'll admit," Julia said. "Men are so sensitive these days."

"But in your defense, some of these guys were turkeys. The hedge-fund guy who came back from Burning Man and decided to give up showering?" A shudder ran through Rachel's body, her face scrunched up as if she smelled something bad. And she wasn't even *at* that date.

"Well, as fun as this trip down memory lane has been, I don't have the time or energy right now to worry about fragile feelings or inflated egos. So I'm a lot to handle, too much for most people. I've accepted that. My coach told me I should be honest with myself about my strengths and weaknesses. Strength: I am kick-ass at business. Weakness: I'm terrible at small talk, fake niceties, and awkward social interactions—basically dating, in a nutshell."

"Wait, your *Pilates* coach told you that?" Sonia asked.

Julia stared at the absurdity of the question. Granted, she did have a lot of coaches in her life. So many that even *she* got them mixed up sometimes.

"Plus, I'm trying to get my parents set up financially so I can talk them into finally retiring. I'm looking to hire a driver for my grandma so she'll stop trying to do it herself. I have a family that I need to take care of. And a business that requires all my time and focus. Not a lot of guys out there find my kind of baggage sexy."

She thought about her halmoni, once owner of the largest apothecary back in Korea before marrying her grandfather and becoming a farmer's wife. And Julia's mom, a successful engineer, married her dad and now worked at their dry cleaners. She wasn't judging their choices. In fact, it was, in part, because of their sacrifices that Julia was the successful woman she was today. She was doing all of this as much for them as she was because of them.

But she was not going to follow in their footsteps and give anything up for someone else.

And based on her tragic dating history, she just wasn't going to find a man who could handle her as she was and the level of success that came with it.

When being too much was the reason you weren't enough—a memoir.

"So I'm done even trying. For the time being, I'm off

the market. Mr. Malibu called it. I am, officially, undateable." Family-values investors and Korean aunties be damned.

"Anyways, I'm not opposed to buying my aunties' silence about it for a few hours if I can," she said, eyeing the large gift bags.

"Well, I think it's a solid plan. You always take such good care of your family." Sonia walked over to the glass product cases that lined one side of Julia's office. She grabbed a small container and lifted it up to Julia, an eyebrow raised in question.

"Our new shea butter hand cream in primrose. Try it. If you like it, ask Annette to grab you a couple on your way out," Julia offered.

"Hey, what about me?" Rachel asked.

"You won't like the scent. A little too sweet for you. You should try the body scrub in sandalwood," Julia said.

"God, you're sexy when you talk free products," Rachel said.

"Anyways," Sonia cut in, still rubbing the hand cream in her palms, "you are the CEO of one of the hottest new cosmetics brands. You're featured in *Forbes* '30 Under 30.' You're a guest lecturer at Stern and Wharton business schools. You've been *busy*."

"Thanks, Sonia. Can you come with me to Halmoni's birthday party and read my list of achievements to my family? Maybe they'll believe you. As it stands, as far as they're concerned, they won't be impressed until I have a fat diamond engagement ring or get a shameless product placement in a new K-drama."

"It's our fate. It's the Korean han, our cultural burden. All Koreans always carry around the shame of somehow not feeling good enough and then putting it onto the generations after them. Stuff your face with birthday cake and tteok and just nod when they start asking questions. You'll get past it."

"Plus, you've got Oprah now. If anyone can help turn the tide during your dinner, it's Oprah," Rachel added.

The three of them raised their glasses for another toast.

"To Oprah," Julia offered. "May the news magically render my family silent from their nagging."

"To Oprah," her friends answered.

"And if that doesn't work, here's hoping those will," Rachel added, looking over her shoulder, lifting her chin. "To bribe bags."

Julia took a deep breath. She lifted her glass with her last bit of strength, hoping that this plan would, indeed, end up working. Julia was the CEO of a multimillion-dollar company. She had handled the choppy, aggressive, unforgiving waters of the business world. She could handle one night with her family, right?

"To bribe bags," she said, downing the rest of her champagne.

Don't miss Susan Lee's Julia Song Is Undateable,
available now!